Wicked In His Arms

Wedded by Scandal Series

Wicked In His Arms

Wedded by Scandal Series

STACY REID

Entangled Publishing, LLC
2614 South Timberline Road
Suite 109
Fort Collins, CO 80525
Visit our website at www.entangledpublishing.com.

Scandalous is an imprint of Entangled Publishing, LLC.

Edited by Alycia Tornetta
Cover design by Erin Dameron-Hill
Cover art from Period Images

Manufactured in the United States of America

First Edition January 2017

SCANDALOUS

For Dusean: Without your love and support I am incomplete; I love you.

Chapter One

The worst had passed.

A wracking cough jerked Viscount Bathhurst's frame from the bed, and Lady Olivia Henrietta Sherwood—Livvie to her friends and family—reached for a washcloth and dabbed the spittle from the corner of his lips. It brought tears to her eyes to see her stepfather like this, when up until only a few months ago, he had been hale and hearty. A fall from his horse, then an attack of the heart, had rendered him thin and frail.

Livvie had worked diligently to hide her terror when she thought he'd been dying. She'd already lost one father, and she had yet to recover from the devastation. Everyone, including the servants, had anticipated the passing of the viscount with grim visages. However, he had rallied and now seemed to be on the mend.

He struggled to sit, a grimace settling on his weary but handsome face. "My dear Livvie," he said, "we must discuss your future."

"Please, Father, conserve your strength. I am certain now is not the time for such conversations."

He smiled. "Nonsense, the doctors have given me a good report. I shall be well, my dear, very well indeed."

Renewed hope blasted through her heart at his wonderful optimism. "I prayed and lit a candle for you every night for the last few weeks."

His face softened with tenderness. "I daresay God heard your prayers, Livvie, for I can assure you my mending started several weeks ago. What shall I do without you?"

Oh no. She knew where he was going with this…

After successfully settling against the mound of pillows, he reached for her hand and clasped it gently in his. "I have written to ask my cousin, the Countess of Blade, to sponsor you into society," he said, diving straight to the heart of her fear.

"Father, you are mending. Surely there is no haste?" She had hoped there would be no more talk of her facing the cruelty of London's society again. After her dismal and harsh reception three years ago, she had made a vow to be true to her own heart, and she would follow it. And her heart was not intent on wading through the fierce and delicate waters of high society to find a husband, at least not until she had her own money. She would not be persuaded to select a gentleman simply because he had over ten thousand a year.

"You are twenty-two, my dear, and close to becoming on the shelf."

"Twenty-two isn't decrepit," she said softly.

He shook his head, sympathy lighting his eyes. "Because of your ghastly experience of losing your papa and then facing the vileness of society's expectations, your mother and

I have been too indulgent. We understood your aversion to another Season and the possibility of facing rumors about your father's...unfortunate demise again. But you must learn to move past it, Livvie."

Unfortunate demise. Such an understatement of the heartbreak she and her mother had been made to suffer. Familiar grief twisted through her.

"And I thank you for sparing me such pain, but I am not hiding from the *ton*, I am living a life I am truly happy with."

His fingers stroked over her knuckles in a soothing caress, but his lips remained firm. "Though we had the best intentions, we did you a disservice having you here at Riverhills running wild, fishing, swimming in the lake at all odd hours, selling your paintings when you should have been in Town, attaining enough social polish to land yourself a well-heeled gentleman."

A well-heeled gentleman? "Father—"

"Come, Livvie, surely you expect to be married someday?" He said it gently, but there was steel underlying his tone.

"Eventually...if I develop an attachment to someone."

"Many people have formed comfortable and lasting attachments without the finer sentiments guiding them. I wish I could grant you your desire to remain unmarried. I dearly wish I could leave more for my daughters if I should perish." His eyes darkened. "I wish for many things, my dear."

She knew for what he wished. That the law made it fit for him to leave more than five hundred pounds per year to his wife, Lady Helena, and one hundred pounds to Livvie and her younger sister, Ophelia. They were not to benefit from or partake in any of the houses and monies the viscount owned, for everything was entailed and belonged to William—her stepfather's son and heir.

There was a modest cottage in Derbyshire, which was not entailed, and she, her mother, and her sister were to move there when Father died. With the income they had, and if they practiced economy, her family should have a comfortable life, though not a wealthy one. "Father, please, I do not need a husband. I—"

He patted her hand. "Hush, now. Do not let this old man worry about you, Livvie. You've been independent for far too long and it's time for you to have another Season to secure a husband."

Her stomach knotted. The idea of wading through the painful gossips again was unbearable. Worse, there was a dreadful scandal in her past. The stain of her real father, Lord Harcourt, killing himself was never to be overcome, even if years had passed since the tragedy.

Her papa's cowardly actions had sullied Livvie's character, as surely as if she had been the one with the gambling debts and a mistress he had found impossible to live without. It indicated a weakness of character that she might pass on to her sons.

"Once a woman marries, she is at the mercy of her husband. She has no rights of her own. I…I…will have no rights. Everything I love to do will be curtailed. I would very much appreciate a gentleman who would let me be, but I do not think there is such a man."

Her father grimaced. "I never thought you a romantic, my dear."

"I simply do not want to make myself dependent on a man unless I would derive some benefit."

Her mother had faced the mountain of debts her first husband had incurred. The creditors had taken everything that was not entailed or entrusted, and almost all the fixtures and fittings in their home had been sold to pay bills. If not for the benevolence of the viscount, Livvie was unsure how her mother would have fared.

The hardships and endurances of those months after

Papa's death had been unpleasant. After being turned out of their home within weeks, as Papa's heir claimed his inheritance, they had lived in a small well-kept house at the generosity of Cousin Iphigenia. And while they had been able to retain a cook and a housekeeper, they had to make do with no other servants. There had been days when food had been hard to procure, and even their housekeeper had eventually departed because Mother had been unable to pay her wages. That winter had been the coldest Livvie had ever experienced, and she had learned then to hate weeping...for it was all her mother had done for months.

A few weeks ago, Livvie had been appalled to see her mother planning for the viscount's death by simply trying to prepare her to find a husband. It infuriated Livvie that her mother had never considered they could manage themselves.

"Livvie, are houses, carriages, servants, and money not beneficial comforts?" her stepfather demanded, pulling her from the dark memories.

"Those are the things I can buy with my own money, which I am determined to earn. I have sold seven paintings, and I have put aside a tidy sum. The only things I want from a husband are the things I cannot get with money—acceptance and love," she said frankly. She accepted that might never happen because of her supposedly wild, independent ways, including the stain of a weak nature. She would not pine away hoping for some gentleman to find her virtuous and honorable when there was nothing wrong with her.

"*You are a smart and beautiful young girl. Don't you ever change, Livvie,*" her papa had told her several times, when she'd lamented she was not the daughter her mother desired. She'd loved him dearly and had been broken when he took his life. She had held on to the lessons he'd taught her in life, but his final lesson, the one he taught her in death, was the most profound.

"I want to concentrate on being the best painter I can be. I'll choose a husband when I am ready."

"You are naive, my dear. I do not criticize you harshly for it, but it will not serve you well in the world you were born to." A deep sigh issued from the viscount. "You will go to my cousin and she will help launch you into society."

"Father—"

"No, my dear, Livvie. Heed me in this, for I shall accept no compromise. You *will* be married within the year. Do not force me to make a choice for you."

She swallowed her protest. The last thing she wanted to do was upset him when he was finally on the mend. The entire bed jerked then as he was consumed by a fit of coughing. She murmured soothing nonsense, stroking his knuckles, watching keenly as he rallied.

"Forgive me, my dear," he said hoarsely.

She offered him a smile. "There is nothing to forgive."

"I've already spoken with William. If I do not recover as is hoped, you are to receive a Season and a dowry."

She squeezed his hand, unable to speak past the lump growing in her throat.

Her stepfather nodded, relief settling on his face, before allowing his eyes to drift shut. She stood and drew the drapes open, allowing a measure of light to fill the room. She hurried into her room and collected the book she had been reading earlier. Then she went back to her stepfather's chamber and sat in the chair closest to him. Livvie hoped the somewhat gothic and mysterious stories of *In the Service of the Crown* by Theodore Aikens would be soothing.

She skipped to her last read page and leaned closer to her father. She started to read. "*Danger rode the air, the hum of it sliding across his skin like a sharp cutting blade. Wrotham slowly lowered the hidden floor panel into its proper place and rose with fluid grace to face the man who had discovered him.*

A low vibration of warning thrummed through his veins. He recognized Jasper, one of the deadliest assassins of the sixth order. A surge went through Wrotham, and he realized it was the thrill of the hunt, the inherent danger in facing off with a man that might even be more merciless than he. He slid a dagger from the cuff of his sleeve and slipped into the shadows, allowing icy resolve to flow into his veins. Only one of them would make it out of this encounter alive..." Livvie paused from reading to glance at the peaceful look on her father's face.

"Father, are you sleeping?" she whispered.

A smile tugged at his lips. "How can I when I must discover how Wrotham will fare against an assassin from the fearsome sixth order?"

With a chuckle, she continued reading. For now, her father seemed as if he was on the mend, and she quieted the fear in her heart. She would immerse them into the exotic cloak-and-dagger world of danger and espionage the author had created, leaving their fear behind...even if only for a few hours.

An hour later, Livvie strolled with her mother, Lady Helena, Viscountess Bathhurst, down the winding staircase of the elegant manor that had been their main residence for the last eleven years. Her mother had once been an extremely beautiful woman, and in middle age retained traces of the fragile flower she had once been. Even now, she walked gracefully and was dressed elegantly.

"How was your visit with your father?" her mother asked, her voice cracking with grief.

"Father won't die," Livvie said firmly. "Dr. Greaves has said he is on the mend, and we must do all what we can to improve his spirits."

"Your optimism is wonderful, my dear, but my husband has summoned his heir from Town." Her throat worked. "To do that, he must believe there is a chance of relapse."

A loud crash sounded from the parlor and they faltered. Her stepbrother's wife, Lady Louisa's, voice filtered through the heavy oak door of the drawing room. "You would deprive your family for…for that—"

Livvie winced. "Come, Mother, we can take a turn in the gardens and have tea later."

"No, we must hear what is being said."

"Mother, please—"

"Upon my honor my father asked me to provide a dowry and Season for Livvie if he dies," William snapped. "It is a sickbed wish, how do I ignore it with good conscience?"

"She is not your real sister! Why should we deprive our son and daughters of a sum of two thousand pounds, for people who are not real family? I have never heard a more ridiculous notion. The only person we have some obligation to is dear Ophelia and she has years before she will be out of the schoolroom. When the time comes, you can sponsor her Season."

A heavy sigh sounded. "Louisa—"

"No, William, a dowry and a Season would be wasted on Livvie. Some may call her beautiful, to be certain, but are you forgetting the stain on her name? Her father *killed* himself," Louisa said furiously. "For years we have had to suffer such an undesirable connection because your father took it upon himself to wed Lady Helena and her…her improper and soiled daughter came with her. Our name was brought into disrepute, and surely, *surely*, my darling, you cannot think to continue with such ill connections after your father passes. I assure you, he will not know if his wife and stepdaughter are in Derbyshire, where they belong, or in Town."

Her mother swayed.

Improper and soiled? Anger burned through Livvie, and she took a step toward the drawing room only to be halted by her mother's hand on her arm. The torment on her lovely features had fury beating in Livvie's breastbone. She wanted to storm the drawing room and provide Lady Louisa with the tongue-lashing she richly deserved. To be so heartless!

"Mother, let me speak with Lady Louisa. I will be mindful with my tongue—"

"No. What she says is true," her mother said through bloodless lips. "It is painful to acknowledge, but William does not need to honor his father's wishes."

"He most assuredly does. We are—"

"I have been married to his father for years, and you have tried to be a good sister to him, but we have never truly belonged."

Livvie clasped her hands, hating to acknowledge the truth of her mother's words. Her stomach dipped at the idea of their future becoming so uncertain again, but she would ensure they weathered this as a family. "Father is mending, our worries are for naught," she said, hating the doubt snaking through her.

Her mother's eyes were dark with sorrow. "And if he does not?"

It was such an unbearable thought, but she had to be strong for her mother. "Then we will mourn as a family, and then do what is needed. I am most content to retire to Derbyshire with you and Ophelia. I am fluent in three languages, and as you know, I paint rather well. I will seek jobs—"

"Hush, Livvie! There shall be no talk of you working. You are a gentleman's daughter, a lady, and I will hear no talk of you acting beneath your station. We will find you a husband."

"Mamma, I am truly not averse to working."

Her mother's golden eyes flashed with determination. "I

will hear no word of you working. You are the daughter of a baron, and you shall act like it until the day you die. Your sister will need to form a suitable connection."

Exasperation rushed through Livvie. "Ophelia is eight, Mamma."

"Be that as it may, we will need to lay the groundwork for her, and that will not be done by living in a cottage with a widow's portion of five hundred pounds yearly," she said, strolling toward the side doors leading to the gardens.

"We must make our own future and not rely on the goodwill of others. In Derbyshire we—"

"I will not consent for us to live in such squalor, Livvie. You need a husband."

"I do not need a man to live comfortably," she snapped, then regretted her harsh tone. "Forgive me, Mamma, but if I marry a man and he passes, then we will be right back where we started."

"No, if you marry a rich and titled gentleman, when he dies you will be left with a good widow's portion that will see us comfortable."

"Mother…"

"It is your duty to this family to marry, and marry well. I will hear no more talk of being independent. It is just not done. Now, let's say a prayer for your father together and then prepare for dinner."

When her mother spoke in that tone, there was no point in arguing with her. But Livvie had to find a way to make her mother and stepfather understand. She could not relinquish her freedom to any man and then be made to suffer how her mother had suffered when Papa had left them. The lines of grief and worry now lining her mother's features indicated how much she had fretted about the death of her second husband and facing the harsh reality of genteel poverty once more. Livvie would much prefer to concentrate on building a comfortable life without depending on the wealth and security of being any gentleman's wife.

She gritted her teeth and said nothing more. She would not come of age until her twenty-fifth birthday. By then she will have been married off, if her parents had their wish.

How was she to escape this mess?

Several hours later, Livvie was snuggled beneath the warm coverlets, reading the latest volume of Theodore Aikens's novel of espionage. His stories were powerful, evocative, and usually scintillating. For the past four years, society had clamored to discover the identity of Aikens. Some had speculated that Theodore Aikens was a pseudonym for Lord Byron because of the dark passionate flair he wrote with. The poet, however, had said much to his regret that he could not claim the credit.

Aikens's hero, Wrotham, bordered on the brink of disreputable indecency with his lewd cutting tongue, and his dangerous patriotic services for the crown made him dashing and admirable. Livvie's mother had scolded her several times for reading the scandalous books, but she was too enthralled by the stories to pay her any heed.

There was a sharp rap on her door, and before she answered, the handle turned and in walked her brother. Alarm had her closing the small leather volume, dropping it on the sheets, and stumbling from the bed. "Is it Father?" she demanded, tugging her robe from the peg and slipping it on. "Has he taken a worse turn?"

William frowned, then gently closed the door. "No, he is recovering well."

She rested a palm against her heart, taking even breaths to still its furious pounding. "Then why are you in my chamber?"

"I've come to discuss your future."

Of course, his wife had made her ultimatums, but Livvie did not desire to hear it tonight. She wanted the ability to have a proper night's rest before facing the uncertainties of tomorrow.

"Can this wait until in the morning, William? It is a bit... unsettling having you in my chamber." Her brother had never visited her in her sanctuary before. His rooms were, in fact, on the opposite side of the manor.

He lifted the candle high, and for a moment the shadows painted his face in a sinister mold. Her heart lurched, and she silently scolded her imagination for running wild.

"No, it cannot wait. I find I am eager to start...our relationship."

She blinked. "Is this about Father's request?"

"It most assuredly is," he said, walking even farther into her chamber. "Despite our low coffers a few years ago, Father provided money for a Season for you. It was wasted. There should be no expectations now, with you being buried in the country for three years after your spectacular failure, that society will receive you favorably and an offer will come your way."

She flinched at his blunt assessment. There was greed in his eyes as he gazed at her with shocking boldness. Her heart lurched in acute discomfort. She found it prudent to move away from the bed and toward the door. "William, I—"

"I've thought long and hard on this, and I have decided to have you as my mistress."

She faltered. *Mistress?* "I beg your pardon?"

He nodded firmly. "Let's be honest, my dear. Settling a dowry on you will be a waste. No man will have you after your father's cowardly action and you have no polish. But you are delectable, and after deep consideration, I find the best place for you will be in my bed, where I've long wanted you to be," he ended thickly. "I will settle the same two thousand pounds, and I will let a house for you. You will have servants and carriages and a few pieces of jewelry now and then."

Her palms grew suddenly damp as alarm shivered through her. They had not been as close as brothers and sisters ought to be, and his regard of late had been somewhat unsettling, but she had simply thought it an aberration.

"How charitable of you," she said faintly, her heart beating an erratic cadenza in her chest.

He narrowed his eyes. "I could see you turned out without a farthing when Father passes. It is tempting to take you now, but I do not want Louisa to know about us, or your mother." He walked closer to grasp a loose tendril of her hair. "I will be generous with you, Livvie, and I will take care not to foist any bastards on you."

Bastards? She recoiled, disgust roiling though her. "I am your sister!"

"Wrong," he snapped. "We have no blood ties."

"What you are suggesting is reprehensible." Her father had put a gun to his head and pulled the trigger without hesitation, leaving her and her mother to face debt and society's derision alone, because of a *mistress*, and William would dare to suggest she assume such a position? "I have lost all good opinion and respect I once had for you," she whispered furiously, hating the burn of tears filling her eyes.

He had the temerity to appear puzzled at her rejection. "You will never get a better offer, surely you must see this?"

"You seek to dishonor me after years of friendship."

"I offer you a life of wealth and leisure."

Dread swirled like acid through her veins. "How can you so calmly abandon all the wishes of our father?"

"*My* father, Olivia, my house, my wealth…and the only way I shall part with it to you, is if you are in my bed."

"Leave my chambers at once," she growled. "Or I shall

scream and bring the household down on us."

William tugged her to him and slammed his lips against hers with a speed that shocked and terrified her. His breath smelled of liquor, and the fumes almost made her gag. His larger frame dwarfed her, and she struggled to be released from his crushing embrace. Disgust and shock tried to steal her thoughts and when he tried to insert his tongue into her mouth, she bit down hard.

He pushed her away, and she stumbled. Rage contorted his features. "You damnable bitch!"

"Get out," she shouted, trembling, fear twisting through her.

"Think on my offer, *sister*. I assure you it is the only one you will be receiving. I shall anticipate your answer by the end of the week." With rapid strides, he left her room.

As if she would ever countenance such a despicable and unfavorable proposition. She staggered to the chair by the window on shaky legs. She sank into its depth and curled her feet underneath her. What was he thinking?

A mistress.

Humiliation burned through her. William was much changed from the boy she had grown up with over the years. He was still as handsome as ever, with his dark brown hair and light blue eyes, but beneath the veneer of affection lurked something more lustful that she had been ignoring, believing it to be her overactive imagination. How wrong she had been.

He had conducted himself most dishonorably and she was at loss about what to do. To burden her father now, on his sick bed, would be cruel, and her mother did not have the constitution to handle such dreadful news. Livvie sighed. She would have to take care of the matter herself, and if he were to ever accost her person again, she would execute one of the lessons Papa had taught her before he died.

She would use her knee against William's most private

parts.

Still trembling, Livvie climbed into the bed and pulled the coverlets to her chin. Dear Lord, now that she had to deal with William's disgusting advances, staying at Riverhill was no longer an option. The blackguard would remain underfoot until their father recovered and that could take several weeks. She would have to stay with the Countess of Blade to acquire the polish to enable her to land herself a well-heeled gentleman.

Botheration!

Chapter Two

The earth shook with the power of the stallion's hooves. Tobias Theodore Walcott, the Earl of Blade, urged his steed even faster, cutting the corner at a breakneck speed. The wind whipped along his face, stinging him, but he relished the freedom of racing along the lanes of his home. Thunder rumbled and small drops of icy rain wetted his skin.

He inhaled the cold fresh air into his lungs, most content to be away from the pollution, noise, and grime of Town. He was also relieved to be far from the rest of the hardheaded lords he had been painstakingly trying to woo to his side. England had been suffering since the war, and much needed to be done to help the widows and orphans left bereaved and the thousands of veterans starving and struggling to find work with livable wages.

The Prince Regent had been too busy holding lavish parties and balls to be concerned with their plight, and the rest of society seemed content to follow in his footsteps. Tobias encouraged his horse to more speed as he put the thoughts of the political fight he would tackle on their behalf aside. He cleared the corner, and his heart suddenly jerked in his chest. The oncoming horse reared, and the rider struggled to stay seated. Tobias drew on his reins, twisting his horse to the left and by a mere hair's breadth avoided a collision that would have been disastrous.

Even so, the rider slipped from the horse and landed in an undignified heap on the muddy earth. Curses spilled from the rider, the soft, sensual tones at odds with the vernacular words pouring from her throat.

"Reckless idiotic buffoon," she muttered, trying to stand and sliding along the muddy path once more.

Good God.

She surged to her feet and managed to find purchase. "You could have gotten us both killed!" she yelled, fisting her hands at her side. "What kind of madman clears the corner at such speed? What if I had been closer or going faster? What were you thinking?"

Tobias was rendered speechless. "Christ." He scrubbed a hand over his face. "What are you?"

The most enchanting pair of light green eyes he had ever beheld flashed in outrage. "I beg your pardon?"

"I did not misspeak," he said drily. "What are you?" He knew he was being insulting, but in this moment, he did not care. While the fresh air had helped, he still felt impatient, out of sorts, and his fingers were itching to grab a pen and write away his frustration.

At times like these, when society was just bloody infuriating, he lost himself for a few hours in the fictitious world of danger, lust, and secrets he had created. Whenever he wrote he felt peace, a tranquility he'd never experienced elsewhere. It had been that way ever since he was a boy and he'd used his imagination and the written words to escape the dark days of his childhood.

She stiffened. "You insufferable lout!"

He arched a brow. Her speech indicated she was educated, but she certainly could not be a lady. Though she was dressed in a simple dark-blue riding habit, its hems were soaked in mud, and dark red hair spilled across her shoulders in riotous waves, the ribbon that had held it together dangling over her forehead. There was mud splattered everywhere on her, even on her chin and cheek. And if he was not mistaken, she was wearing breeches underneath her riding gown.

With a soft growl, she marched toward a horse he recognized from his stables, grabbed the reins, and with an efficiency and skill he found surprising, mounted the horse… astride. Her posture was one of confidence and refined elegance.

Tobias's mouth went dry. The skirt of her riding habit crept up, revealing the naked skin of a pair of luscious calves above her mud-splattered half boots. She made to ride off, so he turned his horse across the path.

"Who are you?"

She narrowed her eyes. "That, sir, is no concern of yours. If you will let me pass, I will be on my way."

It suddenly occurred to him she was beautiful. The notion so startled him he blinked, wondering what about her outrageous appearance could be considered even passably pretty. But in truth, he need not wonder, for it was so devastatingly evident. Such a delicate, heart-shaped face she had, with a pert nose, elegant cheekbones, and very soft and sensual lips. Thick lashes framed her extraordinary eyes, which had an exotic slant.

She was breathtaking.

But he despised those who ignored propriety and courted scandal, and if he was not mistaken, she belonged to the class that must not think about such things or face the consequences of their folly. "I think not."

"You cannot detain me, sir."

"The sky has darkened and rain is on the air. It is best you return to the main house."

Her eyes flashed. *Magnificent.*

"What I do with my time is not your concern."

"I am the lord of this estate and owner of the horse upon which you sit; I daresay everything you do must be of concern to me."

She stiffened, drawing his eyes to the manner in which the jacket stretched across her chest. What the hell was wrong with him? The very idea he could be attracted to such a hoyden filled him with distaste.

Her eyes widened and a flush climbed her cheeks. "I…I… Lord Blade?"

"In the flesh."

"Oh! I…was told you were in Town or I would never have dreamed of borrowing your horse without your permission," she said, blushing furiously. "Please, forgive me."

"Liar," he drawled, instinctively recognizing her nature. She was the type of woman he had shied away from for years. The reckless, improper, and scandalous sort.

"It is very unkind and not the mark of a gentleman to so baldly call a lady a liar," she said frostily.

"Perhaps, but you are no lady."

Her eyes flashed with anger, then cooled to chilling civility. "How arrogant and obnoxious of you to equate being different with unladylike qualities."

"How ridiculous of you to believe your reckless and wanton behavior is simply being different. Your very wild appearance invites scandal," he said cuttingly.

Hurt and some indecipherable emotion flared in her eyes before she lowered her lashes. Then she jutted her chin. "Of course. I recall the rumors that speak to the Earl of

Blade as being uncommonly cold and proper. I can see how a small thing as a lady riding astride in the country with an expectation of privacy would be shocking. How trite your life must be," she said. Then her eyes widened in distress.

It became apparent then to Tobias that she had not meant to let loose her tongue. Instead of being insulted and angry, he was intrigued.

He frowned. Why did she seem so enticing? He had the sudden urge to take her into his arms and kiss the outrage that he could see simmering in her catlike eyes. The thought was so unlike him he was rendered speechless for precious moments. "I assume you are Lady Olivia?" he asked, hiding his unwelcomed reaction to her.

She frowned, wariness settling on her face. "Yes. I was not aware you were interested in my presence at Grangeville Park, my lord."

"My mother wrote to me weeks ago informing me of your stay in my home. From our encounter here, it is quite easy to surmise you are the young lady in *dire* need of social polish."

Her glare almost skewered him. Then with a tight smile, she said, "I wish I could say it has been a pleasure, my lord. If you will excuse me, I must freshen before your mother returns from calling on the Duchess of Wolverton."

She spun the horse around and nudged the side of his massive stallion, then rode away with such beauty and grace, the little hoyden actually held him spellbound.

Good God.

• • •

Hooves thundered behind her, but Livvie refused to glance back. Embarrassment burned through her limbs. The wretched, wretched man. Why did he have to arrive a day early? As the Earl of Blade, the beautiful and well-situated estate of Grangeville Park was his, but the dratted man could have alerted the household of when he would travel down from London.

Had she known, she never would have acted with such wanton disregard and dared to take out one of his most powerful and graceful stallions for a run. But she had needed those few hours of freedom after weeks of being indoors, taking deportment lessons that had made her eyes cross. There were so many rules to remember, so many mistakes she could commit. A lady must learn how to cultivate the art of conversation, walk with refined elegance, take tea with decorum. Even smiling was an art she must relearn. On more than one occasion, the countess had remarked with disdain that Livvie should not show all her teeth when she smiled. It was just not done.

The dowager countess was a once-beautiful woman who had not aged well. Her naturally slim figure had become angular rather than rounding as she got older. Her iron-gray hair drained what color remained in her face and she refused to use rouge to replace what years had taken away, and the deep lines that had engraved themselves upon her face revealed an unhappy and querulous disposition.

Livvie had been fretting constantly whether she would ever live up to the expectations her mother and stepfather had for her. Livvie was not even sure she wanted to meet their lofty goals. Surely most men, if not all in the *ton,* would hold similar opinions to Lord Blade. He had been outrageously insolent and she had done nothing to warrant such a reproach.

Would he inform his mother of their encounter? The countess would provide her with a tongue lashing should she learn Livvie had ridden astride. The first day, she had gone fishing by the lake and his mother had fainted when she had discovered her audacity. Livvie had been at loss what to do, and she had quickly realized that she needed to conform to the expected social behavior to avoid repeated swooning fits and hysterics from the countess. It was exhausting, and she was finally looking forward to her time in Town, if only to escape the lessons and endless restrictions she was enduring.

"Don't you ever change, Livvie."

"I won't, Papa," she whispered in the wind, urging the stallion to greater speed.

The earl overtook her, and she admired the easy way he rode and the restrained power in his movements. He turned his horse across the lanes, forcing her to come to a halt.

"Yes?" she demanded, a bit too tremulously. He mustn't see that he had rattled her.

A smile tugged at his lips, and she forced her gaze away. The earl was dressed in dark breeches with knee-high riding boots. His white shirt was shockingly without a cravat and it was parted enough so she could see the strong column of his throat. She had to own he was a very handsome man. He was in possession of the brilliant emerald eyes that appeared to be a trademark of the Blade men. All of the men's eyes in the paintings lining the picture gallery inside the house boasted the exact same shade of green. A shock of black hair, which he wore in the fashionable *Coup de vent*, was topped by his beaver. He had high-sculpted cheekbones and a strong patrician nose and a full, sensual mouth. She blushed at noticing these details.

The earl was obviously tall and muscular, yet so graceful in his movements…and so arrogant. It was a pity he wasn't more affable. Outrage still burned through her regarding his rude demand as to *what* she was.

"I will ride back with you."

She blinked. "I appreciate the courtesy, but I am not in need of a chaperone." Surely it would not be wise for her to be seen with him alone.

His cold eyes swept over her. "Yet you shall have my

company."

His presence was almost intimidating. She'd only met a few men like the earl, where their aristocratic razor-edged elegance cloaked immense personal power.

"I borrowed your horse because I wanted to be alone with my thoughts for a few moments. Your presence…would be unsettling to the peace I desire."

The fierce intensity with which those brilliant green eyes ensnared her had her pulse leaping.

"Ah, your recklessness is explained," he murmured caustically.

Profoundly disturbed by the earl's intense stare, Livvie glanced away. She had never been so uncomfortable in her life. "I suppose you wouldn't consider my reason an acceptable excuse."

"You supposed correctly."

Mindful of her deportment, she said evenly, "I had intended to go around the lanes once more before I returned to the main house."

He grunted and kneed his horse to move up beside hers. They trotted together in silence, and Livvie wondered if she should make an attempt at conversation. She desperately wished her hair had not tumbled during her ride and that she had not fallen into the mud. How terribly unladylike and unkempt she must appear.

"In her letter, my mother beseeched me to travel home and assist with your dancing lessons."

"I beg your pardon?"

"It seems at least two dancing tutors have abandoned you on account of your terrible form."

She gasped. "I…I do not have a terrible form," she muttered, acutely embarrassed. "It was unkind of the countess to say so." It infuriated her to feel tears burning her throat. What else had the countess complained of? Livvie thought she had been doing so well. She'd never had a dance tutor before, nor had she attended finishing school, so she was not as graceful on the dance floor as she ought to be. The only time she ever felt elegant and had good form was when she rode or fenced.

The earl blinked. His only reaction. "Did I bruise your feelings?"

"Of course not."

"I am relieved to hear it. Your eyes do appear a bit red, and I would not be able to abide your tears," he said icily.

She set her teeth, dearly wishing she had not felt the sharp pinprick of hurt at his callous recital of her faults.

"You insult me by suggesting I would dissolve into hysterics simply because you know I am a clumsy dancer," Livvie said lightly, burying all traces of earlier discomfort. The vile whispers about her father had created within her a thick hide. She'd not let a man whom she just met pierce her shield.

He made a gruff noise in his throat. "How unusual, a lady who controls her emotions. Never before have I met the like."

He is insufferable.

"Insufferable, am I?" he mused softly, and it was then that she realized she had spoken aloud.

Her cheeks heated. "I shall not apologize when you are acting so odiously."

A surprising smile tugged at his lips. "Are we to take another turn around the lanes?" he asked, ignoring her outburst.

Her stomach tightened. "Are you suggesting you will ride with me, my lord?"

"Yes."

He reached up and his thumb brushed against her cheek in a featherlight caress.

She jerked away, shocked. "My lord! You...are being improper."

He seemed equally surprised at his actions, before his countenance became remote. "There is a smudge on your cheek…and chin, blue in color."

Oh! How embarrassing. "It's paint. And please refrain from touching me."

A fleeting smile touched is lips. "Of course. Forgive my lapse, Lady Olivia, it most assuredly will not happen again."

His thigh brushed against hers as their horses walked beside each other. A tingle of awareness spread, becoming a rush of heat that made her breasts tingle. Her reaction was mortifying, unusual, and so shocking. Never had she reacted so to a man, and she was at a loss as to what was happening.

The sense of tranquility that usually enveloped her when she rode vanished. She tightened her fingers on the reins, wanting to be out of his presence. Without thinking, she urged the horse forward, and Lord Blade leaned in and tugged on her reins, forcing her to a halt once more. Somehow his thumb slid over the sensitive skin of her inner wrist. A single bold and improper stroke, and her stomach did a frightening little flip.

He released her as if he had been burned. Then his face shuttered. He stared at her, and the icy distance she spied in his expression had her mouth drying. He barely tipped his hat. "Good day to you, Lady Olivia. I will let you enjoy your ride alone."

She nodded and he spun his horse around. "Lord Blade?"

He tensed. "Yes?" He answered without looking back.

"Will you keep this encounter between us? Your mother would be most displeased if she knew I took Arius from the stables." His mother was a woman of uncertain temper and Livvie found it best not to prick her moods.

"A secret," he drawled.

She frowned. "Well…yes, a secret if you will."

He glanced over his shoulders and considered her. A

barely there smile touched his lips, then he urged his horse forward in a powerful surge without answering. Livvie felt bereft and surprisingly fascinated by the man. A foolish thing to feel for a gentleman like him, who would never be interested in a lady like her, and she would certainly not want favors from a man who thought her ridiculous for simply indulging in a ride.

Since her travel to Grangeville Park, her aversion to marriage had slowly been eroding. She recognized her fear was that no man would truly desire her for *her*...and she would be trapped into a life where she was unable to express herself for fear of condemnation. Though she envisioned another life for herself, she knew she could not support her family on her paintings alone. Not in the comfort they had long been accustomed to.

The freedom she had now was a wonderful thing, and she could not imagine it permanently being curtailed. But she truly was unsure whether a husband would want to force restrictions on her person. If she must marry, and she feared deep in her heart she would have to, it needed to be to a man of affable charm, one who would appreciate everything about her, and one who most preferably have at least ten thousand pounds a year. That would satisfy her mamma.

The hope that had been on her mother's face and the excitement in her eyes swam in Livvie's vision. She had to give this...whatever *this* was, a fair chance. Livvie had to do everything in her power to ensure her mother never suffered such loss of hope again. While she had not minded the genteel poverty they had weathered, her mother was too delicate in her sensibilities to endure such a state again.

With a grimace, Livvie conceded that she truly had to secure a good match. But she wished the very notion of marrying did not make her stomach feel so hollow.

Chapter Three

Lady Olivia really was the loveliest creature Tobias had ever laid eyes on, and also the most disagreeable in her temperament. It was a pity she wasn't more...gently bred. Lord and Lady Bathhurst, her parents, had been disingenuous in describing their daughter as demure and respectful in her ways. While she might hold the courtesy title, her behavior was the furthest thing from ladylike.

In fact, Tobias would say she was a hoyden. She was very unsuitable to be the friend of Lady Francie, his mild-mannered sister. He had seen a rapid deterioration in his sister's behavior since Lady Olivia had descended on their household six weeks prior. Her stepfather, the Viscount Bathhurst, was Tobias's mother's cousin, and the man had sent her to the dowager countess of Blade, his mother, for social polish, so the chit could land herself a wealthy, well-connected husband.

Tobias shook his head, mystified that they thought it was even remotely possible. In the two weeks since he had first been in her presence, she had only proven more completely how *inappropriate* her behavior was. He watched as the beautiful hoyden tried to convince his sister to take a dip in the lake. Well, he assumed that was what she was trying to do, from the pantomime happening below. From where he sat mounted on his massive gray steed, he could not hear their conversation. But he could only imagine Lady Olivia was trying to convince his sister to behave in a manner as foolhardy as she did herself. Lady Olivia gesticulated, pointing toward the main house in the far distance and then back at the lake. His sister shook her head, then folded her arms, her lips setting into stiff lines of what he knew was disapproval.

Lady Olivia threw back her head and laughed. It was husky, sensual, and unfettered. Nothing like the sweet, simpering, elegant chuckling the ladies he knew displayed. With a casual shrug, she undressed.

Sweet Christ.

Was the lady completely without propriety?

Look away.

The gentlemanly thing would be to ignore her actions. Instead, he was rooted to the spot, his mouth drying as she slipped out of her simple high-waisted day gown. She wore no stays, a shocking thing for sure. Tobias knew no lady who would behave in a manner so scandalously. Lady Caroline Lamb had been rumored to be just as wicked with her inappropriate mode of dressing and her affairs, notably with Lord Byron. But what would a sheltered country miss like Lady Olivia know about behaving badly?

Against his own volition, his interest multiplied, and an idea to shape his current heroine in a similar manner took root. *Absurd…but so damned fascinating.* She stood in her chemise, and with a toss of her hair, ran down the gentle slope and executed one of the most elegant dives he'd ever witnessed into the lake.

He was reluctantly impressed.

She continually thumbed her nose at the normal expectations of ladylike behavior. Young ladies did not cavort in their undergarments in the middle of the day, where anyone could see them. No…they should be inside, designing meals, reading, practicing their instruments, planning their wardrobes for the Season, or even bloody sewing.

The only thing she did that seemed normal was paint, and even in that he had been erroneously wrong. He'd spied a painting of his estate that she'd left unattended in the parlor and Tobias had been riveted, unable to credit that a young lady of only twenty-two years had produced with such skill, precision, attention to detail, and mastery. The painting had made him observe Grangeville Park through fresh eyes. Everything had seemed more vivid, more beautiful, more peaceful and serene. On an impulse, he had offered to purchase it, and had been pleased and baffled when she'd offered it instead as a gift, for his generosity in having her in his home.

Lady Olivia jangled at nerves he had kept detached and unemotional since he had been a boy of twelve years. He'd learned early to master the Blade's volatile temper and emotional vulnerability, tempering his emotions with logical thinking and carefully guarded responses. Yet how easily her mere presence irked and fascinated him in equal measure. He found her decidedly strange…and dangerous.

His sister shouted something and pointed toward the main house. Olivia nodded, and Francie fairly skipped away, leaving her alone. Tobias would need to have a talk with her. One did not leave a friend to fend for themselves when they indulged in reckless endeavors. Someone needed to ensure their hides were safe. The thud of hooves stirring the earth had him momentarily shifting his gaze from the very beguiling and vexing woman.

Grayson, his younger half brother, rode up. His mother

would be furious that he had invited his father's by-blow, as she referred to Grayson, for a spot of fishing. But Tobias had never been one to let someone else's anger determine the path he would choose for himself. The minute he had discovered his brother, he had reached out to him, for it mattered not to Tobias if Grayson was a bastard. He was his brother. He was deeply regretful, however, that his mother had to endure the pain of her husband's betrayal.

"What has drawn you over here? We were having the most invigorating race and then you simply headed off without a word," Grayson said. He was six years younger than Tobias, but there was no doubt they were brothers. They were the spitting image of their late father, with their dark green eyes, black hair, and physiques that might have better suited the hardworking class than fashionable men of leisure.

"I cannot account for your inability to keep up with the power of my stallion."

Grayson grinned. "You would like to—" He froze and then a long, low whistle of male appreciation slipped from him.

Tobias followed his brother's gaze, and his mouth dried. Lady Olivia was climbing from the lake, her thoroughly soaked underclothes plastered to her body. Though her chest was only modest, her bottom was delightfully curved. Well-rounded, it looked like they would fill a man's palm and then some. A breath hissed from his teeth. He was annoyed she could tempt him to desire. He was used to women more beautiful and more scantily clad than her.

Devil take it! He had a lover who was more provocative, and she had never made his cock so achingly hard so quickly, even when dressed in her most daring peignoir.

"Turn away," he commanded flatly.

Grayson jerked, curiosity shifting in the depth of his eyes. "Is she yours?"

Tobias smoothed his features into a cold mask of disinterest. "What she is supposed to be is a lady, though she is not acting like it. I will join you at the main house shortly."

Grayson arched a brow and then, instead of arguing, nudged the side of his horse and left for the main house.

Someone needed to take a switch to the hoyden's backside. The damnable chit stretched before lowering her arms, leaning left so her mass of wet hair tumbled down. She gripped a fistful and wrung it. The chill in the air was evident, yet she stood there as if the biting cold was not affecting her.

Before he could talk himself from it, he eased his horse forward and rode down the incline. Her head snapped up at the sound, and she gasped when she spied him. She scrambled for her discarded gown and held it to her front.

"It is a bit late to be thinking of modesty, don't you agree, Lady Olivia?"

She chewed on her lower lip, before lifting her chin defiantly.

"Have you truly lost all sense of propriety?" he inquired in a steely voice.

Her face flushed a becoming pink. "It was but a swim," she said through obviously gritted teeth. "A pleasure I've seen you indulge in several times at this very lake."

"I'm a man," he drawled, deliberately provoking her.

"Of all the ridiculous notions," she spluttered. Accusation and ire shot from her eyes. "You delight in vexing me, my lord. It's very ungentlemanly, if I may say so."

No…he delighted in seeing her face flushed and her eyes darkened with fury. She was so transparent in her feelings. He stiffened at the unwanted thought, and anger snapped through him. He ruthlessly buried it, calming the sudden unwanted spike in his heart.

"I thought you were away on business, and none of the countess's guests have yet descended on us for the house party. I thought it safe to indulge," she offered by way of explanation, a soft blush dusking her cheeks.

"I left London at first light." He would not admit that the thought of how she fared had been tugging at him to return to the estate after only a few days.

"But you were not to return until tomorrow," she pointed out, no doubt to be contrary. "It's also ill-mannered to creep up on a guest."

"Ill-mannered?"

She nodded empathically. "Most assuredly. Nor are you acting in a gentlemanlike manner now by remaining when I…I…am not decent."

Tobias allowed his gaze to run insolently over her wet form. *God's blood.* She was delectable. An unwelcome rush of desire went through him, and his body reacted with painful immediacy to her state of deshabille. He restrained the response. It made no sense for him to even dwell on his lustful urges. Lady Olivia was looking for marriage, and she was the last woman he would offer for. The lady was simply not the type of woman he would make his countess. His wife would be respectable and of sound character, with no hint of scandal surrounding her.

He had a family history to defy, and his sons and their children would not be associated with the reputations of the past Blades. He would ensure it. At the moment, Tobias did not possess the pressing urge to wade through the marriage mart, despite his mother's urgings. He was only twenty-eight years old and quite content with directing his energies to restoring his estates, which his father had brought to the brink of ruin with his excesses.

When he selected his bride, he would marry a woman incapable of stirring too much passion in his blood. He'd been unfortunate enough to inherit the famous Blade men's temperament, which had been a curse on their marriages for more than two hundred years. Hell, his great grandmother had shot her husband because he had turned his terrifying anger on her and she had been insensible with fright. The stain on his family name from the many scandals had been called legendary by some.

It was not only their tempers the Blade men had in excess. It was all emotions—jealousy, love, grief, and it had led them to do terrible things. Tobias buried the memory of his father's rages, his mother's crying, her holding her bruised cheek as she dealt with another of his father's jealous fits. No... Tobias certainly did not want a woman to inspire him to act with such reckless emotions, without regard for others. He'd fooled himself for years that he was different from his father, his uncles, his grandfather, but then...he had discovered what a fool he had been. Even now, at times he could still see the blood on his hands and feel the crunch of bones under his fist as he succumbed to rage.

He shook his head roughly, trying to clear away the haunting memories.

"You are...staring, my lord."

"Am I?"

She swallowed. "Yes," she said softly and shivered.

"You are chilled," he observed.

"I am. Francie had intended to return with a blanket. I am not sure what has waylaid her."

Lady Olivia deserved to be chilled. Maybe then she would act with some decorum.

"Are you to offer me your coat?" she asked with a disarming smile.

He met her eyes and what he spied strangled his breath. Without a doubt she was attracted to him. Her cat eyes glowed with wariness, but beyond the fear was desire. He had been politely distant to her since she had been in his household. It seemed he would have to be curter to ensure she would direct her tempting interest elsewhere. "No, I will not."

"How disagreeable of you." She sounded as if she had her teeth clenched.

"You were foolish enough to dip in the lake without thought. I trust you will be able to figure out how to enter the house without my mother seeing you or trailing water over the floor." He tipped his hat. "Good day to you, Lady Olivia."

Her eyes widened. He spun his horse around and cantered off. It made no sense to indulge in the desire surging through him. Despite the fact that she roused his lust, she also roused his ire, and that, he well knew, was a most dangerous combination.

• • •

Her heart pounding, Livvie watched the earl urge his horse into a flat run and disappear over the incline. Lord Blade already disapproved of her, and it infuriated Livvie that she *wanted* his approval after going her whole life without ever wanting such a reaction from a man. The least he could have done was offer his coat. Instead, he'd only stared at her in that bold, piercing way of his.

"Wretched man," she muttered, hurriedly slipping into her dress. The only thing currently wonderful about the earl was that he had the most beautifully stocked stable of thoroughbreds.

If only he wasn't so infuriating, so cold toward her, so sinfully handsome. Whenever he was near, she felt different, more alive, and more aware of herself. There were days she ogled the man, even though she had no idea why, for she did not like him, and he certainly held no affections for her. Her very existence seemed to vex the earl and the continued disapproval on Tobias's face stung. But despite that, there was *something*. She had always been drawn to the forbidden.

Everything the earl represented.

Her papa, despite everything else, had treated her like the son he'd never had. He had taught her how to ride, shoot, hunt, and fence.

At the age of eight, she had been determined to learn to swim so she could join her papa on his morning rituals by the pond instead of her mother in the drawing room. She had snuck out and had almost drowned, but within a few days she was floundering on her own and in a few weeks was a proficient swimmer.

Another of her forbidden misadventures had been when the boys in their village had climbed the large oak tree by the local inn and carved their initials. She had followed and marked her own initials. And on the way down had fallen and dislocated a shoulder. But she had done it and Papa had been very proud of her bravery.

At eleven, after she had moved to live with her mother's new husband, she came across a dog that had seemed like a wild, starved wolf. Determined to save it, she endured many scratches and even a bite in the process. They were the best of friends even today.

Every time she had gone after something she desired, she had been hurt.

What price would she pay if she danced too close to the earl's icy flames? For she admitted, finally, that she wanted to feel the press of his lips against hers and the sensation of being wrapped in his strong arms. If only once.

"Good heavens, what is wrong with me?" she muttered.

Livvie pinched the bridge of her nose, clutched her unruly thoughts, and then pushed them firmly aside. She moved briskly across the lawn, chafing her palms against her arms to generate heat. She would not waste another second thinking about the infuriating man. Worse, she believed he recognized her attraction to him and was appalled. Humiliation burned through her at the very notion. She vowed to do all in her power to ensure she appeared immune to his charms.

It would not do to be obvious in her admiration for a man who clearly disliked her.

Chapter Four

Three days later, one perfectly elegant and well-mannered Lady Wilhelmina, who insisted on being called Willa, descended on Grangeville Park with her parents, the Baron and Baroness Ranford, at Tobias's mother's invitation. Lady Willa was poised, very demur in her mannerism, and uncommonly beautiful, with her light blond hair and azure eyes. It soon became clear to Livvie that the countess intended Lady Willa as a suitable bride for the earl.

The countess's report of Lady Willa was highly favorable and she did everything in her power to see them thrown together, from suggesting they drive along the lanes in a landau to experience the beauty of the estate to most ardently encouraging them to take several turns in the gardens alone, and even now, tonight, seating them beside each other at dinner.

It might not have been by design on her part, but Lady Willa's pale blue high-waisted gown somehow picked out the dainty flowers in the drapery covering the windows of the main dining hall. The dining room had been recently decorated by the dowager in hand-painted wallpaper in tones of blues and creams. The blues also echoed the dinner service in Wedgwood jasperware, which the dowager had also chosen. Livvie personally disliked the large pieces that decorated the mantelpiece and the large silver epergne that acted as the centerpiece for the huge mahogany table.

"You look lovely, Willa, dear," the dowager countess murmured once everyone was seated. Lord and Lady Ranford quickly echoed the sentiment, ladling lavish compliments upon their daughter.

Willa, of course, basked in the attention, and made it evident she had set her cap at Lord Blade, with her parents' beaming approval. Livvie considered the dowager's seating plan to be quite incorrect, particularly as Willa's rank was no higher than her own and the Earl and Countess of Hempton had also been seated farther down the table. The dowager had argued she was aiming for informality to justify her seating arrangements. Livvie had been seated down the table between an unctuously prosing vicar who was balding prematurely and an extremely deaf retired army Colonel. The Colonel luckily had a string of fairly amusing anecdotes to tell about his time in the army, with which he continued to regale her, loudly, drowning out most of the vicar's pious utterances.

Lady Willa giggled quite often, batting her long lashes at the earl and finding several reasons to touch his arms or shoulders fleetingly. Yesterday on their walk in the garden, she had even caused her ankle to twist so that Lord Blade had to lift her in his arms and carry her back into the parlor. That contrived "accident" had caused an uproar. Livvie watched it all with some amusement. Willa's parents were clearly excited and pleased with their daughter's progress and the countess beamed whenever she spied her son with Lady Willa. The countess had even complimented her several times on her graceful deportment, with pointed glares at Livvie.

But Tobias's reaction fascinated Livvie. His eyes were devoid of everything but boredom. Nothing the young lady did enticed him, and in fact, it seemed his thoughts were miles away. Even now, he had an air of cold insouciance about him, as he scanned his guests from the head of the table, but she sensed the powerful, clever personality reined in below the surface.

His disinterest was perplexing and strangely filled her with relief. Of course, she would prefer to spend the afternoon sewing before she'd ever admit she might have been a tiny bit jealous of such blonde, ladylike perfection.

Footmen came out with platters of cream of parsnip soup, grass lamb served with an onion sauce, baked trout, asparagus in butter sauce, venison in a raised pie, and the eating and conversation began. Livvie dearly wished she were alone, comfortable in her bed with *In the Service of the Crown*. The various guests she had dined with since her stay at Grangeville Park had either ignored her or treated her with veiled disdain, which the countess had pretended not to notice.

"Will you be present for the duration of the house party, Lord Blade?" the baroness queried with a smile. "My daughter is looking forward to partnering with you in the croquet match to be held on Friday."

Tobias's gaze settled on the baroness. "I had not thought to stay. I have business in Town."

"My lord, surely you will be here for the weekend, at least," Willa gasped, looking genuinely appalled at the notion her quarry would be out of reach.

"Tobias," his mother said, quickly dabbing at her lips with the napkin. "Do not be so rude. Lord Ranford, his wife, and daughter have traveled here especially to get to know you better. It would be such an acute disappointment for me if you were to leave."

"Rude? You are mistaken, madam, I am being excessively

polite," he said drily. "I will think on it."

His mother gave him a pleased smile, and conversation once more flowed around the table.

"Are you very excited about your debut into society, Lady Olivia?" Willa asked.

Livvie took a sip of her wine, ordering her thoughts as she became the focus of several pair of eyes…including Tobias's.

"I—"

"This is not Olivia's first outing, my dear," the dowager countess said with a tight smile. "She debuted a few years ago and society found her wanting."

"Mother!" Francie glared at her.

Francie looked very pretty tonight in a high-waisted lavender silk gown, her dark hair piled atop her head with three strings of pearls around her neck. Her dark green eyes glowed with secrets, mischief, and a good deal of ire. She'd always rushed to Livvie's defense whenever the countess issued one of her not-too-subtle insults. She loved Francie for her unfailing support.

"I have not misspoken. But I will admit that is what we are doing now, affixing the Blade stamp of approval on Lady Olivia in the hopes she will make a good match."

Willa's blue eyes collided with hers. "Is that the truth of it, Livvie? May I call you Livvie? I've heard Lady Francie refer to you as such and it is such a darling way to shorten your name."

Livvie emptied her wineglass, then gently placed it on the table. "I would be pleased to have you call me Livvie… Willa. And I think the truth of it is more that I found society wanting. Or perhaps society and I were of a like mind."

The countess's face pinched in disapproval, and she directed the conversation where she wanted, launching into a rousing debate with the baroness on the latest fashions.

"Did you?" Tobias asked.

She glanced at him, very aware of the keen attention Willa and Francie were paying to them. "Did I what, my lord?"

His stare was unnervingly direct. "Find society lacking."

"Yes."

His eyes became guarded and she wondered what he was thinking behind his bland facade.

"Are you not going to ask me in what manner I found the *ton* wanting?" Not that she would ever reveal how devastated she had been when the whispers about her father had started circulating, and the cruel way society had judged her for his actions. But she was very curious as to what the earl was thinking.

"No," he finally answered. "I would not want you to let loose your wayward and uncontrolled tongue at this moment. I find I am not in the mood to cross swords with you."

Lady Willa tittered delicately behind her napkin.

"You are being rude, my lord," Livvie said quietly, very aware of suddenly being the focus of everyone at the table.

"Surely not, merely honest."

"How like a gentleman to claim his *inappropriate* speech as blunt honesty, but in a lady it is seen as brash and scandalous behavior. I would have only been honest as you are, my lord."

"Are you attempting to match wits with me, Lady Olivia?"

"I believe I succeeded."

A deceptively wicked smile played about his mouth.

"You are quite decisive with your tongue, young lady," the baroness said with a frown.

Before she could retort, Lady Willa interjected sweetly and softly, "Dear Livvie, a young lady must never be seen as vulgar in her comportment."

The baroness harrumphed her approval.

"I daresay she should not be a docile doormat, either," Livvie said with a small smile, and then deliberately stuffed her mouth with a piece of lamb to prevent herself from saying anything further. She would wait five more minutes and then excuse herself. Five minutes. She could do this, she assured herself.

"Upon my word," Francie said. "Forgive my brother, Willa, I daresay there are days he and Livvie bicker as if they are an old married couple. It's quite fascinating really."

"Good God," Tobias snapped low and hard into the silence that fell at the table. "I've never heard a more appalling jest from you, Fran."

She smiled widely, a glint in her eyes that made Livvie distinctly uncomfortable.

"I rather think you and Livvie would make a riveting couple, don't you agree, Mother?" Francie asked sweetly. "They are positively charming together."

The dowager countess glared at her daughter, and Willa flushed, narrowing her eyes at Francie.

Then Tobias spoke. "I'd rather be drawn and quartered."

The cold rejection pierced Livvie's heart. That he would so baldly say that he found her unsuitable in front of company stung, deeply. Her hands trembled and she lowered her knife and fork, unable to glance in his direction. It angered her, that he could have provoked such an emotion in her heart. What she hated even more was the sudden silence at the table. The meal was almost over, she only had to survive a few minutes longer and then she could plead a headache and retire.

"Well," Lady Blade said, "I understand that lovely Lady Willa has been practicing a delightful new piece for the pianoforte. Shall we withdraw to the drawing room so she can play for us?"

After a few seconds of no reply, Livvie looked at Tobias. Her breath strangled in her throat. She was the sole recipient of his piercing and unflinching regard. Would he apologize? Not that it would improve her reputation in the eyes of his guests after his cutting words, but it would soothe the unrelenting sting in her heart. She held his eyes for precious seconds, then his cold magnetic gaze lowered and dismissed her. There was a soft gasp from Francie, as humiliation and anger burned through Livvie in equal measure.

"I would be most pleased to hear Lady Willa play," he said, his face impassive. "After the gentlemen have drunk their port."

His calm indifference was beyond rude and it did not improve Livvie's temper. Her chest hurt with the effort to remain apparently unaffected. With as much comportment as she could muster, she placed her napkin on the table, and stood. "If you will excuse me, I have a headache and wish to retire to my room." After a slight curtsy to the general assembly, she walked quietly from the large dining hall.

Instead of heading to her room, she rushed through the hallway and went to the side entrance out into the gardens. She took a deep breath. Then another. It did not help. Anger still coursed through her veins. How could he be so boorish and uncivil? She rushed down the path, breathing the cold air into her lungs, remembering her lessons. A young lady must never openly display her anger or emotions. Her lower lip trembled and she bit into it to make it stop. After staring at flowers unseen, a smile touched her lips.

She knew exactly what she needed to do to feel better… It was highly unladylike and improper, and in this moment she did not care one bit.

Several hours later, Livvie waited stealthily beside the stairs of the east wing. It was talked of by the servants in whispers as Lord Blade's wing. He was the only person at Grangeville Park to reside in this section of the house. All the current guests, his sister, mother, and her rooms were in the west wing.

She had spent hours immersed in painting, waiting for when he would retire. She had barely escaped his rooms, and had even passed his valet at the top of the stairs with the bucket in her hand. Mr. Ackers had seemed flummoxed, and she had given him a wide smile and continued on her merry way, praying he would not turn down the sheets for the earl.

After Lord Blade finally left the library and climbed the stairs, she waited a few minutes before following. Now she was sitting on top of the stairs in her very ugly, bulky, and favorite nightgown feeling decidedly foolish. Oh, what had she been thinking? What if he was so outraged at her ill-conceived prank that he had her kicked out?

Jumping to her feet, Livvie rushed toward the earl's chamber. She needed to find a way to distract him and remove the slugs. A loud, surprised bellow echoed in the hallway. She faltered.

Too late.

A crash was heard and what sounded suspiciously like an enraged snarl echoed through the door before a chilling silence. Instead of great satisfaction, she felt distressingly small. The door was wrenched open and the earl framed the doorway. She swallowed, her eyes glued to a powerful male chest. He was only clothed in a purple banyan…which was so loosely tied, it bordered on indecent. "I…my lord…I…" What could she say? What defense did she have?

"It speaks," he said dangerously soft, and all the contrition she had been feeling melted away.

It?

"I beg your pardon?"

"You are clothed in the drabbest God awful sack, your hair…your hair appears to be a bird's nest— Can you not tame those maddening curls?"

Before she could retort he continued, "With only one candle in the hallway, I thought you a frightful apparition until you opened your mouth. I must assume your presence here in my wing is the reason I have a dozen or so slugs in my bed? I swear I can still feel one in an area no unmarried young lady should know about."

His mien was so icily polite his indifference intimidated her, and she resented it most heartily. "You insulted me most grievously earlier and I have settled the account."

His dark eyes were intent on her. She could have imagined it, but she thought his lips twitched. "I see," he murmured.

"Yes, you were rude…and hurtful."

He was irritably silent and the tension made it hard for her to swallow. "Now if you will excuse me, my lord…I bid you good night," she said in a voice of careful nonchalance.

His gorgeous lips curled into a cruel smile and a warning danced down her spine. Then she glanced up. *Oh dear.* "It seems one of the slugs has a particular partiality to your hair."

"Hmm," he said noncommittally, then his hands darted like a striking adder and grabbed her. Before she could protest, he dragged her into his chamber, lifted her into his arms, and dumped her onto the bed of slugs. *Good heavens!* A cold, wet sliminess slithered down her neck. She shrieked and scrambled from the bed, tumbling to her knees on the lush green Persian carpets.

Livvie surged to her feet, gripped the slug attached to her cheek, and threw it at him.

The dratted man chuckled, provoking amusement dancing in his eyes.

He is the devil.

Within two strides he was in front of her, pulling her to him so she was flush to his chest. "My lord!"

Her heart clambered up to her throat, and she fought to gather her composure at their close proximity. She became very aware that she was alone in his chamber at such an indecent hour. Not that any time of the day would have rendered her visit respectable. But somehow, knowing it was dark outside, and the household slept, and that they were *alone* in an entire wing had nervous energy coursing through her veins.

"Release me at once," she said, and to her acute annoyance and embarrassment, she sounded breathless.

Dark green eyes roamed over her face. "No."

She floundered. "No?"

"You invited yourself to my chamber, and you chose to come when all servants are abed, now… Do you truly wish for me to release you, Lady Olivia?"

She almost fainted. Was she imagining the menace in his tone? The earl was a tall man with very wide shoulders, so she had to tilt her head at an odd angle to meet his eyes. He was so still…and watchful.

"I did not invite myself to your rooms! I was at a perfectly safe and respectable distance in the hallway."

Once again, he remained maddeningly silent.

"I am sure you know the consequences of keeping me here."

The dratted man smiled. "If this is a ploy of yours to be caught with me, know that I will never marry you," he said drily.

She stared at him, dumfounded. "You are the one who pulled *me* into your chamber," she whispered furiously. "And I assure you, my lord, there is nothing on this earth that could induce me to marry such an arrogant—"

She spluttered as he plucked the slug that had finally slid from his hair to his forehead and held it close to her face. She prevented herself from twitching.

"Are you ready to place them back in their home?"

"Their home?"

"I assume you went by the lake?"

"Yes," she admitted softly.

He nodded and released her, suddenly looking brisk and business-like. "I have a long day ahead of me, Lady Olivia, I suggest you get to work."

"Me?"

"This was your handiwork, was it not?"

She drew a deep, steadying breath. "I'm deeply sorry," she said abruptly.

His eyebrow arched in evident surprise. "An apology?"

She looked at him helplessly. "It was childish of me to place slugs in your bed. I felt no satisfaction from it."

"You had one or two snails in there as well."

Her gaze sought the massive bed in the center of the room and the gray mass situated comfortably in the middle between silken sheets. There were indeed a few snails. "Do you accept my apology?"

His face shuttered. "If you would be gracious enough to accept mine."

"I…what?"

"I insulted you. There was no cause for it, nor did I make amends when it was evident you were grievously injured," he said gruffly. "Forgive me."

Her mouth opened, but no words came forth. He'd rendered her speechless. Never had she expected him to offer any apology.

She smiled tentatively. "Thank you. So are we to be friends?"

"Good God, no. I am sure we will be back to crossing swords tomorrow. The sooner the better."

A pang went through her heart. "I will fetch the pail."

He frowned, taking a few steps away from her. "It's best you return to your chambers. The servants will sort it out in the morning."

"Are you certain, my lord?"

"Yes."

"But where will you sleep?"

"The bed is big enough for me and my slimy friends."

It certainly was. The large four-poster bed dominated the earl's chamber. But what if they migrated onto him through the night? "My lord, I—"

"Go! Before…" He lowered his lids and hissed between his teeth.

Before what? "My lord, I—"

"Go," he snapped again, low and dangerous, and once more awareness of their seclusion slithered through her.

"Of course," she muttered hastily, and hurried from the room. Livvie all but ran down the hallway and the winding staircase, feeling her way in the dark, confident of her steps after memorizing all the fine details of the house before she painted its interiors.

Her heart was a beating mess inside her chest. She had been childish enough to place slugs into the earl's bed and he had apologized.

For a few moments no animosity had existed…and… and…it had been *wonderful*.

Chapter Five

Tobias jogged toward the cliff's edge abutting his estate, his three great boarhounds rollicking along at his side. They bounded up the hill, and he laughed, enjoying the invigorating run. They crested the peak, and he slowed to a walk, picking up a few twigs and sticks and throwing them. His dogs ignored his antics and instead bounced against his side, urging him to play. Sinking to his knees he tousled with the massive animals, laughing as they slobbered over his face, one even going as far as to nip him on the collarbone.

"You were always the rebel weren't you, Hera," he murmured, gripping her by the scruff and rolling with her. He hated that he had to return to London soon. The peace and tranquility he felt at Grangeville Park, he'd never found elsewhere. But there were problems to solve, meetings to be had, influential lords to convince to his way of thinking, or to blackmail if his gentler methods of persuasion failed. There was so much to do to alleviate the poverty he found in the city.

There was another reason he needed to depart for Town with haste.

Lady Olivia Sherwood.

Hot, urgent desire stirred inside at the mere thought of her and the realization touched a raw nerve. Surging to his feet, ignoring his dogs' howls for him to continue playing with them, he walked to the edge of the incline overlooking the rolling hills and ravine of his lands. There he stood, the wind at his back, tugging at the simple white shirt he had donned with his breeches and top boots this morning.

He tilted his head to the heavens, breathing in the crisp fresh air, trying to clear the vexing woman from his thoughts. Then he felt it. Eyes were on him, piercing and intent. He held himself still, absorbing the sensation of being watched and instinctively knowing such a bold regard belonged to Lady Olivia. Without glancing about, Tobias could tell she was studying him…avidly. Her stare strolled and kissed over his skin like a silken caress. A grim smile curled Tobias's lips. The knowledge that she was just as attracted to him was unaccountably appealing. *Why?*

He turned his head left and spied her sitting under his favorite cypress tree, her light pink dress billowing across her ankles. She had a sketchpad gripped in her hands, her cheeks and chin were smudged with paint, and her glorious hair tumbled in loose waves around her shoulders. He suddenly wished his hands were buried in her tangled, silken mess. At that realization, he returned her regard, causing her eyes to widen and a flush to work its way up to her cheeks. There was something charming about her when she was flustered.

Temptation tugged at him with relentless force. Clenching his teeth until they ached, he urged himself to look away without acknowledging her presence. He'd left their guests playing charades in the parlor; he should have known Lady Olivia would flee such merriment to bury herself deeper in the countryside. His mother complained incessantly that Lady Olivia was fast and scandalous, despite possessing a comely figure and keen intellect. It was a great pity, according to his mother, that she was not more docile. An assessment he had instinctively rejected. This morning, Lady Olivia had fenced and had soundly thrashed Lord Muir, who had not realized his opponent was a woman until she tugged off the mask. The gasps and outraged whispers were multiple—they had spread through the house at alarming speed. Yet instead of being annoyed...Tobias had been amused at her mettle and had admired her skill, perhaps he had even felt some admiration for the lady herself.

Anger snapped though him at that very unwelcome thought. It was only last week that she had been outrageous enough to dare place slugs between his sheets. Since then, every damn night he had dreamed about drawing the minx underneath him, parting her legs and feasting on her wetness, then sinking his cock deep and thrusting into her repeatedly for hours on end.

He needed to escape the estate and her tempting presence. *God's blood*, he didn't even like her. His desire for her had made him curt to the point of shocking churlishness. Olivia, instead of quivering like many who had experienced a whiff of his displeasure, had traded with him blow for blow. It was unusual for him to appreciate her fieriness. Though it could have been because Lady Willa was underfoot, since that young lady seemed to agree with everything he said. It was as if she had no original thoughts of her own, despite the keen, devious intelligence he could see in her gaze at times.

He had to leave before he did something stupid like stroll over to Olivia now and sit beside her. Then take her lips between his teeth, letting his tongue tease her into opening her mouth. She had the most intriguing mouth he'd ever seen and never had he wanted to kiss a lady as much as he did Olivia. With a soft growl under his breath, and with a sharp command to his dogs, he spun and retreated in desperation back to the main house.

He would leave tonight. There was not a moment to delay. He must go before he went insane.

* * *

Tobias recognized it was time to admit defeat. Lady Arabella's inviting stares held no appeal. His thoughts were miles away. She had been trying to entice him upstairs to her bed for the past few hours to no avail. They had been lovers for almost two years, and his desire for her had been waning for some time now.

No....it had been waning since I first met Lady Olivia.

He had ridden from Grangeville Park and headed straight to Arabella...and even at such a distance, the infuriating female was preventing him from indulging in his pleasures. He'd truly believed a night with his mistress would cure him of this unrelenting ache he had for the hoyden. How woefully wrong he had been. He'd been unable to even kiss Arabella.

He swallowed the last of his brandy and placed the glass on the center table in the parlor and stood. "I am leaving."

His lover pouted, her calculating eyes tracked his movements. "Have you found someone else?" she asked from her reclining position on the chaise lounge.

"No."

"You seem a touch restless, Tobias." Arabella shifted, and draped herself on the cushions so she was provocatively posed, the silk peignoir cut low where her breasts were displayed to their best advantage.

She meant to beguile him, but he felt nothing. It was alarming the degree to which Lady Olivia entranced him, which had him so on edge. "I intend to return to Derbyshire."

Arabella stiffened. "So soon, darling? You've only just arrived in town."

"Duty calls," he said, shrugging into his superfine coat without assistance.

For a brief instance, anger flashed across her face, before she buried it underneath false charm. "I so miss you when you leave." She cleared her throat delicately. "My good friend, Lady Bartley, received an invitation to your mother's very exclusive and much sought after house party."

He glanced at her. "And?"

A flush climbed her face. "I...I would like an invitation, if you would be so kind."

"No," he said bluntly. His mother had already cornered him and asked if there was any truth to the rumor he and the widow of the late Viscount Trotman were lovers. Tobias had been disgusted with the ease at which the rumor mongrels thought to discuss his private life with his mother. She, of course, had been warning him to stay away from Arabella's bed, for all of London knew she was seeking her third husband to support her own extravagant lifestyle. Tobias had shook his head and simply changed the topic, much to his mother's frustration. She had then attempted to throw one of her fits, even crying a few tears, to which he had been coldly immune. Then she had taken to her rooms for the rest of the afternoon. Nothing unusual—he was familiar with such pathetic attempts at manipulation. Tobias acknowledged, however, how important society's views and expectations were to her, so he would not invite his mistress to his estate while his mother, sister, and the scheming Lady Willa were in residence.

"Why, my darling?" she asked, pouting.

"I am quite certain we had this conversation last week, and we will not have it again," Tobias said flatly. Arabella was a good sport, and he enjoyed their talks of politics as much as when he conversed with any man. She was learned, witty, and beautiful, but he would not allow her to manipulate him.

"Why not?" Pique filled her tone. "I shall write to your mother and introduce myself as your dearest friend and—"

Icy displeasure filled him, and he did nothing to suppress the emotions surging through his veins. He met her eyes and she faltered. Arabella suddenly found uncommon interest in the armrest of the chaise lounge, and Tobias sighed. He did not like the idea of any woman being wary of him. "There is no need to shy from me, Arabella."

She glanced up. "Your anger is…very alarming, Tobias."

"I am not angry."

Skepticism flashed across her features before a polite smile tipped her lips. Her reaction annoyed him. From the moment he'd inherited the earldom, every waking breath had been spent trying to restore the honor of the Blade name. Society had waited eagerly for him to follow in the step of his ancestors. They had wagered among themselves when he would soon start the whoring, gambling, and brawling with cuckolded husbands over their wives. They expected him to keep numerous mistresses and to indulge generally in wild debauchery. What young man of twenty would behave differently when they came into their inheritance at so young an age, and with his family's reputation? Tobias had. He'd had a lifetime of such indignities and he had ruthlessly worked to achieve another reputation for his line, one his future sons and daughters would be proud to inherit and be a part of.

He'd achieved it through a rigid adherence to his own strict rule of conduct, which he'd crafted as early as his eighteenth year. He'd never been drunk and never would be, and he would not duel or fight with another man over a woman, nor would he *ever* allow his temper or passions to be compromised to recklessness. He had done nothing to warrant the unease Arabella showed. He strolled over to her and brushed a kiss against her cheek. "I shall see you when I am next in town."

"And when will that be, Tobias? I've hardly seen you since the opening of Parliament and you avoid the social whirl. I am sure I shan't see you for the rest of the year."

"Perhaps," he said noncommittally, retrieving his topcoat and cane, which housed a hidden foil. Whenever he visited his friend, the Marquess of Westfall, as Tobias planned to do this evening, he walked with a weapon. The marquess favored the seedier and more dangerous parts of the city and seemed to be more comfortable among the depraved and villainous.

After spending a few more minutes reassuring Arabella that he would visit soon, Tobias departed the town house. He jumped into his waiting carriage and tapped the roof. His driver knew his next destination and they rumbled into swift motion. He had been funding several ventures with Westfall, all aimed at helping the poor and unfortunate who dwelled in the slums of London. They were building homes, a school, and even a hospital to ensure affordable care to those less fortunate. The land was on the edge of town, out toward the countryside where the air was fresher but where they could still reach their employment.

The carriage slowed and then halted. Tobias stepped down into a dirty, narrow, and very smelly alley only a few minutes from Smithfield, where the meat market was. He glanced at his driver. "My company will see me home, you may go." It made no sense to leave the man out for pickpockets and other nefarious elements to fall upon him.

"Very well, my lord," the driver said and tipped his hat.

Tobias waited until he was gone before strolling inside the tavern. It was mostly empty, and at a glance, he saw Westfall in the far corner, nursing a mug. Westfall had made no concessions to his surroundings and had dressed as fashionably as ever. Tobias was flabbergasted that his fastidious friend would consume anything from this place. He made his way over and sank into the chair opposite the marquess. "You are aware we could have met at White's or Brooks? Or better, in your town house?"

"I am aware," the marquess said blandly, flicking a fly away with his long, tapered fingers.

"Then why in damnation are we *here*?" Tobias growled.

Westfall smiled, the scars roping the left side of his face twisting. "I'm a bit partial to Jenny's Inn. The people here are more trustworthy than those at White's. Here, I know they all want to fleece me, stick a knife between my ribs, and take my boots, watch, and anything else of value. I am comfortable because I know what to expect. There is no hypocrisy in the slums."

Hell.

"I heard tell that you are soon to be engaged."

"For a man disinclined to scandal and gossip, you are well-informed."

Tobias smiled. "My mother delights in gossiping, especially when the subjects concerned are my friends."

Westfall grunted.

"Are you intending to marry a society miss?"

"Perhaps."

Tobias was stunned. Westfall despised society and those who belonged to it, and he made no effort to conceal his distaste to the *ton*. He refused to conform and they labeled him a degenerate for it. His exploits were bandied about Town with relish and Westfall only associated with ladies of questionable morals, which was why Tobias was surprised to hear he'd formed an attachment with a young society miss, one Lady Honoria. He remembered her as being very excitable and had personally seen the young lady faint at least three times. What was Westfall thinking?

"I can see you are itching to dissuade me from the idea of matrimony. I've decided, so it makes no sense to waste your energy on arguments, Blade."

Tobias had nothing to say to that. "Are those the plans?" he asked, jutting his chin toward the rolls of papers.

"Yes. There are hundreds of children that need me…us. Many lost their fathers in the war. Some are abandoned in poor houses and baby farms."

He nodded and dived into the detailed building plans, discussing monies required to be invested and the time scale each would take to construct, the difficulties they might face to wheedle further funds from wealthy patrons, and what they were willing to do themselves. Hours passed, and the entire time he conversed with Westfall, in the back of Tobias's mind, his thoughts were filled with Olivia.

After she had placed the slugs between his sheets, he had spent the rest of the night in the library, writing, trying to drain the lust pounding through his veins with words. He'd been surprised when he'd returned to his chamber in the morning, after a hard ride across the lanes, to find her bent over his bed, her delicious posterior in the air, gently collecting her slimy conspirators and putting them in a bucket. She had actually helped clean up her mess. He had been eternally grateful that a chambermaid had been present or he was sure he would have done something like push her gown up and bite her on her delightfully shaped behind.

He chuckled darkly. Westfall glanced up from the architectural drawings.

"Do you care to share what has you amused?"

"It's not amusement, it's anticipation," he said, shocking himself.

The marquess arched a brow and slouched more insolently than before. "*Ah*…you are hunting a particular woman. Another Cyprian? Rumors report that your current *chère amie* has been complaining to her bosom friends. She feared you were getting restless."

Tobias froze, then scrubbed a hand over his face. What

the hell was he even talking about? "I misspoke. I do not want her…yet she intrigues me. A decidedly complicated situation, for I have no intention of ever acting on my desires."

Westfall considered him, then a smile twisted his lips. "If she is a doxy, bed her, pleasure her well, and move on. If she is a lady of quality, do the same. Both types of women are not to be trusted and your instincts are already warning you. Heed them." After administering his cynical sage advice, he went back to studying the plans and making notes in exquisite flowing script.

Tobias leaned back in his chair. What was he to do about Lady Olivia? He desired her. It was now an inescapable fact. She was a damn distraction, and though she was everything he did not desire in a woman to be his wife, he was drawn to the breathtaking hoyden.

Since he did not want to take her to be his wife…*his mistress?* God's blood. She was the daughter of a baron. She was a lady and he was coldly plotting to debauch her when it was possible she might secure a suitor and a life of respectability. Tobias stared off vacantly into the distance, trying to settle the thorny problem of his lust for Lady Olivia. The best thing to do was to stay away from his country estate until she traveled to Town for the Season. But tomorrow was the ball in which his mother would formally introduce her to their neighbors and the select few she had invited down to stay for her house party. He wanted to be there, if only to provide a distraction and allow Olivia to turn her wayward tongue his way. That was all he would provide, a buffer, and as soon as she was received by the guests reasonably well, he could hide himself off in Scotland until she was wed. Maybe then he would be able to banish her alluring face and far-too-tempting body.

If only he believed such a thing possible…

Chapter Six

The laughter and hum of conversation faded into a distant buzz. Tobias had known Olivia was beautiful, but watching her descend the stairs drove the air from his lungs. She was exquisite, bewitching, and also a complete sham. She looked nothing like the hellion who had ridden Arius across muddy lanes or the scandalizing minx who had swam in his lake.

The young lady before him now was composed, elegant, and ravishing in a high-waisted, white-spangled gauze overdress with the palest green satin underskirt. Her silver satin dancing slippers sparkled under the candlelight. Her dark red locks were wrapped around her head in a plaited coronet, with a few artful tendrils caressing her shoulders. Tobias allowed his eyes to dwell on every swell and dip of her body, and he gritted his teeth when his body stirred. Only a dead man wouldn't react to such mouthwateringly succulent sensuality.

"Good God, man," a voice whispered to his left. "Have you ever seen a young lady so becoming?"

Never. But to admit it to Grayson was akin to speaking

blasphemy.

"I wonder who she is?" his brother asked, moving to stand beside him. Grayson was a man of fashion and he was dressed in crème-colored breeches with a matching waistcoat and a dark blue jacket.

"You saw her a few weeks ago at the lake," Tobias said drily.

"You jest. Lady Olivia? I would not have recognized her had you not named her."

Tobias had nothing to say to that announcement. They watched in silence as his mother introduced her to several well-connected ladies, smoothly steering her charge to the few women of power who were present. Olivia smiled, nodded, and performed to the best of her abilities, but even from where he stood, Tobias could see the strain in her smile. A languid feeling coursed through his veins. He *liked* watching her. Unusual indeed.

"She's a stunning creature, isn't she?" Grayson murmured, sipping from a glass of champagne.

"I don't find her all that admirable," Tobias said icily. "She is too…" What the hell was she? Too desirable? Too decisive? Too opinionated? He was disturbed to find that he was not as disinclined to her character as he had been.

In fact, he had been modeling a character in his book after the vexing beauty and had written several pages last night. With her fieriness and vivacity, she would fit easily into his world of danger and espionage where the women were bold, daring, and even at times lethal assassins themselves. Oh yes, a woman like her would make a perfect mistress for his hero, Wrotham. He'd named his hero's lover *Lady O*. His new diabolical villainess, a perfect match for Wrotham's cunning. Who would credit he found such inspiration from Olivia?

"Are you aware you cannot remove your eyes from her?" Amusement colored his brother's tone.

"I am but observing her reception."

Grayson's chuckle was suggestive, and Tobias stiffened.

"Lady Olivia is my guest and tonight is her first ball in years. Mother asked me to be in attendance tonight and, of course, I must dance with the hoyden," he remarked ruefully.

"You…dance?"

Tobias grunted.

"All of London will be atwitter with such news. The Earl of Blade deigning to lower himself to dance with mere mortals."

"You are being insufferable. And we are in the country…I doubt me dancing with Lady Olivia will cause such a stir."

Except it just might. Tobias gritted his teeth in annoyance. He did not have time to suffer the fickleness of society. He had estates to repair and a well-protected safe house to build for desperate women and children. The last place he truly wanted to be was here…staring at a woman he would never allow himself to have. One he was undeniably lusting after and whom he must dance with, though he had not taken such a pleasure with any lady of society for about three years. He had grown weary of the theatrics of the Season and the overly dramatic nature of each crop of debutantes. The tears, the swooning fits, the plots to trap him into marriage.

The gossipers of society attending this country ball at his estate would indeed start wagging their tongues at his unprecedented interest. Though they were in Derbyshire, the scandal sheets would report he had only danced with Lady Olivia and then the speculations, the unceasing watching and reporting of his every move would begin again.

God's Blood.

He would have to swallow his tongue and ire and dance with at least one other young lady before taking into his arms the woman he truly wanted to avoid more than anything else. Then Tobias would have to ensure he stayed away from her, once and for all.

· · ·

Her first ball in nearly four years and Livvie was not huddling in a corner, bleeding from a multitude of cuts as she had always imagined. The countess of Blade was very popular, and invitations to her country parties, which were held before the opening of the little Season, were well sought after. Tonight's ball was a crush. The gentlemen and ladies were dressed in the height of fashion, and the ballroom buzzed with laughter and inconsequential conversation.

Livvie's mouth ached from keeping her smile bright. Everyone was pleasant, but she could see the questions and the recognition in their eyes. She was the girl whose father had killed himself. No lips uttered the damning truth but it was glaring that almost an hour had passed and no gentleman had asked for her hand to dance. The disgrace was never to be forgotten.

The countess had melted away with a *shoo* for Livvie to mingle, and she had found herself lingering on the edge of the ballroom with a glass of champagne in her hand, dearly wishing she was snuggled in her bed, reading *In the Service of the Crown*. She had left it at a particular rousing chapter, where Wrotham was seducing the Princess of France for highly classified secrets. Livvie had never read a seduction before and her nerves were quite titillated by the pages.

"The Duke and Duchess of Wolverton!" the butler's booming voice announced.

There was a ripple of excitement from the throng as the duke entered with his beautiful duchess. They mingled and smiled, and Livvie wondered if she had ever seen a more beautiful and well-matched couple. The duke looked besotted, and he and his duchess fairly glowed.

"It's the mad duke," Francie whispered behind her.

"Francie!" Olivia smiled, relieved to see a familiar face.

"Where were you?"

A blush heated her friend's face, and Olivia noted her lips were a bit swollen. "Francie?"

She looped her hands through Livvie's. "It's the truth. That is what the *ton* calls him, you know."

"You are disassembling. I have it on the highest authority that well-kissed lips do appear a bit swollen, as yours are at this moment." Of course she would not admit the authority on kisses she referred to came from a fictional character in a book. "Unless a bee stung you?"

Francie's cheeks bloomed pink. "We will certainly not talk about kisses here," she said with a surreptitious glance across the ballroom. "However, we can discuss the mad duke, for everyone else is certainly doing so."

"He looks quite sane to me."

"And so very handsome. I've heard many young ladies cried when he was taken from the marriage mart."

A very unlikely notion, but Livvie held her tongue. "If he was so desirable, why was he called the mad duke?"

"I have no notion," her friend said with a giggle.

"Oh, Francie, you are hopeless, listening to such gossips."

She arched a brow. "Does this mean you are not interested in a very juicy tidbit about the duke and his duchess?"

"No, I am not," Livvie said firmly.

"Have I found something you insist on being *proper* about? Be still, my heart."

She grinned. "Very well. You may tell me, but I shall not repeat a word of it."

"They married a few months ago because she trapped him by climbing into his bed!"

She gasped. "Scandalous...and wonderful!"

"Indeed," Francie said smugly.

Livvie watched the couple, admiring the duchess's daring. Tobias approached, and from the fleeting grin and nod he bestowed on the duke, it was evident they were friends. "She is very beautiful…and from the way the duke touches her, I do not think he minded terribly that she compromised him," she said softly.

"Oh no, from all accounts, he is love-struck with her, and she with him. Mamma says it is a good match."

A good match. The very thing her mother and stepfather were depending on her to make, but Livvie was painfully aware no one had asked her to dance, even though she had been presented as the guest of honor. It would crush her mother to realize no gentleman would truly want her with the stain of her father's weaknesses and her lack of fortune.

"Oh! Tobias is dancing," Francie said, rousing Livvie from her musings.

She was about to query why such a thing would be unusual when she became aware of how many people were staring at him and his partner and whispering. The young lady fairly glowed, and Livvie could pick out which of the matrons was her mother from the sheer smugness on her features. "Who is his partner?"

"That is Lady Phoebe, the Marquess of Westfall's sister."

Livvie frowned. "I am not familiar with him."

"I should hope not! He is a disgraced lord"—Francie leaned in close—"who has publicly claimed his bastard to the distress of his father, the Duke of Salop."

Livvie gasped. "Francie! That is a horrible thing to repeat, and how have you become aware of it?"

She sighed. "Mamma is a notorious gossip. She and her friends tend to speak a lot when we make the rounds."

Livvie nodded, unable to remove her eyes from Tobias and Lady Phoebe. "They are very charming and beautiful together." And she was the daughter of a duke, well-connected and without blemish. No doubt the type of young lady Lord Blade would take to be his wife.

"They surely are, but do you see the way she is glowing and giggling? If he had any interest in her, he has already lost it."

Livvie would analyze later why the notion filled her with relief. "He has?"

"Yes, my brother does not appreciate a too-obvious public display of emotion. He has already suffered one broken engagement because of it."

Livvie's heart jolted. "Tobias was engaged?"

"Yes, to Lady Sophie, now Viscountess Wimple. Rumor has it, he missed an outing without notifying her. He had been called away on an emergency and was hard-pressed for time to send a note," she whispered.

Livvie frowned, unwilling to engage in gossiping but wanting to know more about the coldly intriguing earl. "And then?" She contained a wince at her own whisper.

"Lady Sophie threw a tantrum. No doubt she never imagined he would break the engagement. It was the scandal of the Season that year."

Livvie shook her head in disbelief. "He ruined her reputation because she was *angry*?"

Francie hesitated. "When Mother asked him to reconsider, Tobias said he'd had enough tantrums and hysterics to last him several lifetimes and he would not be persuaded to reconsider Lady Sophie. My brother values modesty, grace, and good sense in a young lady. His words."

Livvie understood a bit more about Tobias, and she was startled at the ache blooming in her heart. It was not that she wanted the man for herself, but it was finally clear why he did not like her.

"There she is," Francie whispered. "It was perverse of Mother to send an invitation to her family."

Livvie glanced in the direction Francie indicated to see a very beautiful young lady staring intently at Tobias. A man stood at her side chattering, gazing at her with something akin to adoration, but her eyes remained firmly on the earl.

A young man walked over then, a smile planted on his face, his eyes glued to Francie's loveliness. He bowed. "Lady Francie."

Livvie dipped into a curtsy after swift introductions had been made. The gentleman was revealed to be young Lord Andrew, heir to a viscountcy.

"May I have you as a partner for the next set, Lady Francie?" he asked, all affable charm.

With a quick smile, she agreed, and he flushed, bowed, then scampered away.

"Oh, Livvie, no one has asked you to dance."

She ignored the pinch in her heart. "Think nothing of it, for I shall not."

"I shall importune upon Lord Andrew to ask you—"

"Francie, I would never forgive you! I do not require his or your pity."

"It is not pity. You are more beautiful than most of the young ladies here, and he is the kind of man your mother would want for you to attract. His family connections are considerable."

"No."

"Come on, Livvie, there must be someone you find agreeable. Remember you are here to find a husband."

Her traitorous eyes sought out the Earl of Blade. Just looking at him made her body feel incredibly alive, every sensation felt keener...sharper. Surely she must be afflicted to even be attracted to the wretched man.

"I want whatever attentions I garner to be from my own efforts, Francie, and if you insist on traversing such paths, I will ask questions as to where you were earlier that has left your lips looking as if they have been thoroughly ravished."

Francie froze, her fingers fluttering to her lips. "You

mustn't breathe a word, Livvie. But it is the most glorious thing…he has asked me to marry him, and I am desperately in love."

"You are engaged? To whom? Oh, that is wonderful. Will an announcement be made tonight?"

She gripped Livvie's arm with strength. "You must not say a word, it's a secret. I cannot tell you his name as yet, but I will soon, I promise you."

Livvie tugged her closer to the potted palm away from the crush. "Why is it a secret?"

Her friend's eyes glowed with happiness. "Tobias may not approve…but I am in love, Livvie. I never thought I would be so fortuitous to be given the chance to marry the man I have the utmost respect and love for."

Love.

Her heart clenched in acute yearning and the realization jolted her. As if they had a will of their own, her eyes sought Lord Blade's powerful dancing frame. Her stomach twisted itself into a knot and her breath hitched at the weak feelings that assailed her. Livvie's breathing went from uneven to erratic at the awareness that she was rather taken with London's coldest earl.

Chapter Seven

Tobias released a giggling Lady Phoebe. Without giving him time to recall his breath, her mother descended on them, glowing.

"My lord, what a fine form you were in after not having danced for so long," the Duchess of Salop said loudly. "Of course, you and my daughter looked wonderful together. So elegant and full of charm."

The young lady released a squeal of high-pitched giggles and blinked her eyes at him so rapidly, for a moment he wondered if she was trying to dislodge an object stinging them. "It was a pleasure, Lady Phoebe," he murmured, bowing over her raised hand. Her eyes widened in delight, while cunning glowed in the duchess's gaze.

He bowed again. "If you will excuse me, ladies, duty calls."

"Of course."

They reluctantly shifted and he made his way over to his sister and Olivia. He tried to reassure himself that as the unofficial host of the ball, it was his duty to lead her to her first dance. But in truth, he wanted to be closer to the vexing beauty and there was a need in him to dance with her even once, before relinquishing her to the bevy of suitors that would soon be flocking to her side for the rest of the Season. Many watched her with uncertainty, no doubt remembering who her father was and commenting on her lack of dowry. According to his mother and sister, if he were to be seen dancing with Olivia, her chances for a good catch would drastically improve.

As he drew closer to his sister, her voice filtered to him.

"Oh, Livvie, I love him so much. I am so frightened to tell Tobias. What if he does not approve?"

My sister is in love? With whom? He had not taken notice of any particular gentleman paying his addresses. Certainly his mother would have informed him. This was her first Season, and she had yet to be presented to Queen Charlotte, or even to attend Almacks and be launched into the *ton*.

"In love, Francie? What have I warned you about such sentiments?"

She gasped and twirled around, her hand fluttering to her chest. "Tobias!"

But it was Olivia he watched. For a second, pleasure lightened her features before she smoothed her face into a blank mask. Surely she had not been happy to see him?

"Lord Blade," she greeted coolly. "Why am I not surprised you do not believe in love?"

"Love is a ridiculous notion that only inspires the foolhardy."

Francie looked crestfallen, and Olivia narrowed her eyes. "So what do you believe in?"

"Power, tangibility, and logical reasoning."

"Oh, you poor man," she gasped a bit dramatically, her eyes crinkling at the corner. "No wonder you are so wooden when you dance."

He arched a brow. "Wooden?"

She gave a tiny sniff of scorn. "Yes, I observed you with Lady Phoebe earlier and you were so...so...bland and uninspiring. Though you commanded her movements through the waltz, you exuded icy restraint and none of the flare and passion that comes with such a thrilling and provocative dance."

His sister groaned lowly. "I can see you both are about to start and my nerves do not have the willpower to deal with it tonight. I daresay old married couples bicker less."

"Good God, Francie, strike the notion from your thought. This is the second time you have made such an utterance and I assure you it is in poor form," Tobias said.

"I am off to procure some refreshment," his sister said, flouncing away.

Tobias suppressed his smile at Olivia's affronted expression. He moved closer to her. "So you were watching me earlier."

"I was observing Lady Phoebe," Olivia said frostily.

"Were you now?"

Her eyes flashed a warning, and he knew she would not hesitate to administer a scathing set down.

A smile curved his lips. "You look very beautiful, your mother and father would be proud at your transformation."

She blinked, and then blinked some more. He waited for a scathing retort to fall from her lips, something along the lines of the miraculous nature of him paying her a compliment. But...she only blinked once more. Was he really so harsh in his dealing with her that a simple compliment would render her speechless?

"Have I truly rendered your waspish tongue speechless, Lady Olivia?"

Her lips curved into a wide smile. "I will pretend you did not nullify your compliment just now and offer my thank you very graciously, my lord."

Tobias dragged his gaze from her mouth. *Sweet Christ.* Her lips were wide and full, shaped sensually, as if they were made to be debauched. They begged to be kissed, thoroughly.

She touched his arm lightly. "Ask me to dance."

Her slight caress sent his heart pounding against his ribs, and he wanted to roar at the unexpectedness of his reaction. "You had to ruin it," he said drily, striving to appear unaffected by her closeness.

She gazed at him with intense curiosity in her green eyes. "I did nothing of the sort."

"You were well comported and glowing with reserved beauty, and you had to ruin it by asking me to dance. Ladies do not ask gentlemen to dance. You had best remember, or you will soon have your name on the lips of every gossipmonger from the *ton*."

Her nose wrinkled. "I certainly did no such thing. I told *you* to ask me to dance. Vastly different," she muttered, but a flush had bloomed on her cheeks, and if he was not mistaken, that may have been contrition in her eyes. "I'm sorry, my lord. I knew better, your mother gave me a most severe lecture before we came down and it seems I forgot one of the most important of her lessons."

"Which was?"

"I must not be bold at all, nor shall I speak of the fact that I paint, swim, and fence. I think I am not to speak of my interests at all."

Tobias was nonplussed. "Then what are you to converse about?"

She frowned, as if trying to recall the lessons. "Whatever the gentleman I am with wants to speak of."

He froze, remembering the myriad of women—from the more seasoned to the young debutantes he'd held discourse with in the past. They had always appeared vapid, with no original thoughts, only listening to anything he uttered, while

giggling and batting their lashes. Many young ladies had tried
to charm him by acting featherbrained.

"Good God," he muttered. "Are you saying that is a tactic
young ladies use to make themselves more appealing?"

"Yes." She laughed lightly. "I must perfect the art of
nonsensical conversation and ensure I am not deemed to be
too intelligent. I must never prattle on about the things I like."
Her lips turned up in the familiar mocking smile. "I wonder,
what shall I do with a suitor who has no interest in me?"

"Run from him or your life will be painfully boring."

She sobered, staring at him with an intensity that was
unnerving. "Thank you. I never expected you to say that."

"Then I have been more of an *insufferable buffoon* than
I realized."

Her eyes widened and then she laughed, a full, rich sound
that made his heartbeat accelerate. "Will you ever forgive my
unruly tongue, my lord? It was beyond the pale for me to hurl
such insults at you."

"Forgiven."

Her pouting lips stretched in a sweet smile. "How
charmingly generous."

Her mouth should be outlawed. *Damnation*. What right
did she have to be in possession of such tempting lips and to
intrigue him so effortlessly?

"My lord?"

Tobias frowned. "Yes?"

"I…I had asked a question."

He was having difficulty following the conversation. His
concentration was centered on her mouth. "A question?"

"Are you well, Tobias?"

Pleasure punched through him. He liked the sound of
his name on her tongue. He would not mention her slip in
referring to him with such intimate familiarity. "Will you
honor me with the next dance, Lady Olivia?"

She favored him with her brilliant smile. "I…yes, thank you, my lord."

The strains of another waltz commenced; he led her onto the dance floor and swept her into the rousing dance. She moved with energy and a hint of recklessness in her movements. It brought to mind the energy and passion she would bring to bed play.

Good God. He almost stumbled at the unwanted thought.

Not quite trusting himself to speak, Tobias made no effort to converse as he moved her around the floor. As he twirled her, he didn't feel wooden or uninterested, like he had with Westfall's sister. Olivia swayed in his arms, sensuous, yet innocent in her movements, a most appealing combination.

"So, my lord, what are your interests? I've been at Grangeville Park for almost eight weeks and I daresay the only thing I know about you is that you enjoy swimming and riding. You disturb the fishes every morning at seven…I have a clear view of the lake from my chamber," she admitted with a rueful half smile.

It was Tobias's turn to blink. When had a young lady ever asked him about his interests and seemed so genuine? He sent his mind into his past with alacrity and was flummoxed to find the answer to be never. And she watched him as he took his morning swim. The knowledge had a disturbing effect on his heart. It sent it racing in the most unwelcome and frustrating manner. "Must we converse, Lady Olivia?"

She flushed. "Why yes, it is polite and expected that when one is dancing, some polite discourse should take place."

His lips twitched. "I see."

"And it's quite wonderful we are not…sniping at each other, isn't it?" she asked tentatively.

It was. Although, Tobias did not think it was prudent to admit to such a notion. If they were pleasant to each other, might it not lead to other things? Because even now, the interest that glowed in her eyes as she stared at him was not innocent, and it stirred a primal desire in him to see her stripped and laid bare before him. "It is quite refreshing."

She beamed at him approvingly, then the audacious lady winked. *Winked.* He suppressed the smile, for the last thing he wanted her to believe was that he approved of her audacious behavior. They spun in silence for the remainder of the waltz and he was grateful for it. The dance came to an end, and he bowed. "Thank you, my lady. Please enjoy the rest of the ball."

Disappointment crossed her face before she attempted a smile. "And I thank you, Lord Blade." Her curtsy was elegant and unfortunately gave him a peek into her décolletage. The soft expanse of thin flesh stretched over her chest and collarbones begged to be kissed. It was disquieting to know it was his lips Tobias imagined pressed there, inhaling her scent and introducing her to pleasure.

With a tight smile—and tightening front trousers— he walked away. As he turned, he spied a shock of almost- white blonde hair that belonged to only one woman of his acquaintance. His mistress. Tobias froze, scanning the graceful lines of her neck and shoulders. He moved through the crowd intent on reaching Lady Arabella.

The lady turned and their eyes met across the span of the ballroom.

God's blood.

"Lord Blade, I have been seeking an opportunity to speak to you about the housing project you are working on with Lord Westfall and my husband. I am keen to hear of the progress of its development and what precipitated the idea," the Duchess of Wolverton murmured at his side.

Impatience bit through Tobias, and he strangled the useless emotion instantly. "Are you interested in contributing?"

"I am. I think it is wonderful you and Westfall have taken such a keen interest in championing the poor and suffering children of London. I understand the marquess has a vested interest, but what is your motivation?"

The duchess was daring to so boldly hint at Westfall's bastard daughter, whom he had rescued recently. She completely distracted Tobias from his intention to pursue his mistress and demand an explanation.

"Shall we take a stroll on the terrace and discuss your charity work, Lord Blade? I'm sure Wolverton will join us," the duchess said with a smile.

"It's best if we retire to the library."

With a nod, she acquiesced and they departed the ballroom. Tobias signaled to the duke, and he made his way toward them. Half an hour later, Tobias had secured the added patronage of the Duchess of Wolverton, and she assured him she would bring more support from other members of the *ton* as a fundraiser. Westfall would be pleased to know she was interested in building a school for the orphans, and she was bold enough to want them to receive a tailored education that would allow them to obtain respectable positions and advance their prospects.

Tobias reentered the ballroom and scanned the occupants. Though he searched for his mistress, his eyes found Olivia first. She was dancing a quadrille, and she was smiling. Satisfied she seemed contented for the moment, he did a quick search for Arabella. Through the crush he spied a flash of white blonde hair. He was wading through the crowd toward his mistress when a footman intercepted him and handed him a piece of paper. Tobias flicked it open.

My Darling Tobias. I am sick to heart at the displeasure I saw on your face earlier. I had to come, to see you. I've missed your lips, your touch, and your pleasures. I secured an invitation through my good friend, and I have been most discreet. Do you remember our scintillating adventures at Lady Beechman's house party? I would have you in a similar manner tonight. I will either be in your bed, the linen closet on the second floor of the west wing, or the gazebo. Please let me make it up to you. I am your willing prey…hunt me, my darling, and claim your reward.

Your lady A

The footman who had delivered it stared straight ahead.

The anger snapping through his veins was unnerving in its intensity. Tobias had no mood for one of Arabella's sexual escapades tonight. Damn her stubborn hide. What game was she now playing? To think she would flagrantly disregard his position on the matter. The fact that his mother was not wailing and demanding an explanation from him meant she must not yet be aware his mistress was currently under the same roof as her.

Knowing Arabella, she would truly remain hidden until he came or a servant discovered her and some nonsensical commotion would ensue. He should grab hold of her and throw her out on her damn backside. He had no time for deceptive and manipulative games. He would end their liaison. Tonight.

Chapter Eight

Livvie slipped up the stairs, relieved to escape the crush of the ball and even more excited to return to her book. Though it was after one in the morning, she would read at least a chapter or two before retiring for the night. With a soft sigh, she reached the landing and paused as she swore she saw Tobias strolling down the hallway. Her heart leaped. His chamber was on the other side of the manor. What was he doing in the west wing? Should she engage him in conversation?

Dancing with him had been so thrilling. Disappointment had pierced her when the waltz had ended and he had drifted away in the crowd. Stupidly, she'd wanted to remain in his arms and enjoy at least another dance. Several times, his mouth had curved into a smile that made her want to lean in and lick his lips. No doubt if she acted on the desire in private it would confirm all the unladylike ideas he had about her.

Livvie hurried along the corridor to catch up to him, and slowed her steps when she saw him pause at the door of a linen closet. Instinctively, she flushed herself against the wall and stepped into a pocket of shadows. She frowned when he looked left, then right, before opening the door and slipping inside. What was he doing? Livvie was intrigued.

Maybe she had been mistaken that it was Tobias. She hurried to the door and lifted a hand to knock. She bit her lip, feeling silly. So what if the earl wanted to hide himself away in a linen closet? It was his house. What was worse was the desire she had to enquire if he was well…or if he wanted company. Not to be in the closet but company to talk. Making a decisive decision, she knocked once on the door. "Tobias?"

Then she held her breath.

There was no answer. Feeling ridiculous, she turned to leave. The door was wrenched open and an arm circled her waist and pulled her into the darkened room. Before she could squeak, a hand clamped over her lips.

"What are you doing here and why would you send me such a note?" It was the rough annoyed voice of the earl that prevented Livvie from turning and raising her knees to his man parts. It was truly *Tobias*. In a linen closet? No doubt he had intended an assignation. A shocking thing for sure. He was so coldly arrogant and proper she had not expected that. She bit down hard against his palm and felt gratified to hear his pained curse. His hand lifted from her mouth.

"Why did you draw me in here…and who did you think I was?" she snapped, painfully aware of how close they stood, of his heat against her body. It took all of her willpower to not melt into his firm body.

"*Lady Olivia*?" The shock in his voice was profound.

"Yes," she answered a bit smugly, pleased to have rattled his constitution, albeit unintentionally.

Her pleasure was swiftly stifled under the virulent curses that sprang from his lips. Her cheeks burned and unwanted tears pricked behind her lids. She knew he did not like her, but not *that* much.

"Let's go," he muttered roughly and opened the door.

He stepped into the hallway, dragging her behind him, and then froze. Loud voices carried from the corridor, and with another harsh curse he pushed her back in the closet and closed the door.

"Release me," she muttered, thoroughly vexed with his reaction. He had planned to meet someone else in the closet. So it wasn't the situation he was averse to…but *her*! The swift pain that pinched her heart, angered her even more. She made to leave, but strong arms gripped her hips, effectively halting her.

"What are you doing?" he growled.

"I am leaving. I certainly do not wish to pain you further with my unwanted presence. Not that I invited myself to this…this…tryst!"

He stiffened, and Livvie wished she were able to make out his features. She could only smell his warm masculine fragrance, feel his vitality, and she resented the curious hunger it roused.

"I did *not* plan a tryst," he said stiffly.

As if she would believe such an assertion. "Then why are you skulking inside the closet?"

"In the event it had escaped your notice, I am in my home."

"And?"

"One cannot skulk in their own house." His voice was exasperated.

"If you are hiding in the closet, and not partaking in a tryst, you are indeed skulking."

She narrowed her eyes at the soft amused laugh that puffed from him. First she had horrified him and now she was the butt of his amusement? "Unhand me, Lord Blade."

"You cannot leave, there are guests in the corridor."

"And I suppose the worst thing that could happen would be for you to be caught with me?" she enquired scathingly.

"Hell's teeth, most assuredly."

The icy disdain in his tone made her want to lash out and kick his shin. *The insufferable man.* It was not as if she were ill formed. Many had remarked upon her pleasing features, especially her light green eyes. She would not remain inside with him a moment longer. "I am sure they are gone by now."

A loud laughter pulsed, mocking her assertions, and they both froze.

"Be damned quiet," he snapped.

The soft growl that slipped from her throat surprised her with its ferocity. "You, my lord, have no gentlemanly qualities."

"Are *you* scolding me for bad behavior?" he clipped quite icily.

It seemed as if the tentative peace they'd formed in the ballroom had dissolved. "Yes!"

"You wouldn't know refined sensibilities if they bit you in the posterior."

"Oh! You…you…"

"Christ, will you lower your voice?"

She gritted her teeth until her jaw ached.

"What are you doing here?"

She ignored him.

"I will not ask again," he said in a dangerously soft tone.

Livvie swallowed, heat burning her cheeks. "I saw you, and I only meant to enquire whether you were well. Very silly of me and now I am exceedingly embarrassed I acted on the thought."

"Ah…once again you were acting recklessly."

"Of course not. I had no notion you would drag me in here." She took a calming breath. "Why *are* you here?"

"That is none of your business," he said cuttingly.

"I take it back," she whispered. "I do not want to be forgiven, you are an—"

"Good God, have we reverted to the insufferable

buffoon? And here I thought I had detected some growth."

Before she could whisper a furious rebuttal, warm lips pressed on her, silencing her and alarming her, sending a shock of desire to her system, and stripping her of her defenses. She went absolutely still, her heart a pounding roar in her ears. Tobias was kissing her! Livvie dimly realized he was just as frozen, and she could feel the thud of his heart. She raised her hand and pressed it against his chest.

Thud.

He shuddered. Then he parted his lips and rimmed his tongue against the seam of her mouth. Her knees buckled and his arms came around her and hauled her even closer to him. His hand moved in a slow soothing stroke over her back. A soft moan slipped from her, and she parted her lips to him, curious as to what would happen. *Pleasure.* What happened was a shock of undiluted delight, pulsing through her veins as he thrust his tongue into her mouth and conquered.

He squeezed her body tightly to his, moving his lips over hers with sensual force.

She pulled from him, breathless. "Tobias."

"Good God, you taste even better than I imagined," he said gruffly.

Livvie was speechless, never in her wildest fancy could she have imagined such pleasure or the soft sensual tones he used. He disliked her, didn't he? "You've…thought of kissing me?"

"Every night since I've met you, utter madness."

"That was my very first kiss," she admitted shyly. What were they doing? Confusion clouded her mind and a protest welled against her lips, which was smothered by another kiss. He drowned all her thoughts under the sweetest bliss she had ever felt.

He dragged his lips along the curve of her throat. "I cannot stop tasting you." He sounded half strangled.

He excited her and made her nervous in the same breath. Tobias took another step forward, crowding her back against the linen shelves. He lowered his head to recapture her mouth. It was incredibly wonderful. In between hot kisses, he whispered sensual promises and praise, and kept up his tender assault on her senses. There was a tug on her dress and then her breasts filled his palms. Her nipples puckered painfully as pleasure sharp and sweet stirred in her blood. One of his hands left her aching breast, and she trembled as he slid his palm up to her knee, past her garter, up to where she was aching and damp.

Shock echoed along her body and she went completely rigid on him.

"You are so damn sweet and perfect. How I've craved you, Olivia, day and night. Open for me." His soothing, sensual tone was irresistible.

Her legs parted under his mastery and his decadent touch became even more wicked. Her body was filled with sudden exquisite tension and she desperately wanted a firmer touch. "Tobias," she moaned, shivering. "I need…"

"What do you need?"

"I do not know…but I crave."

The heavy length of his arousal pressed against her stomach, shocking and rousing her senses. He touched her with exquisite gentleness as the tip of his fingers parted her womanly flesh. She jerked in shock as arousal jolted through her body. Then his wicked, sinful fingers stroked inside.

It was indecent, the way he was holding her, touching her, kissing her…and Livvie never wanted him to stop.

• • •

Olivia's passion perfumed the air as slick, wet heat greeted his fingers.

She was beguiling, infuriating, and he couldn't help kissing her, tasting her, inhaling her moans and desire that flowed over his fingers. Tobias had told himself his curiosity would be appeased with a kiss. He'd been sure he knew what she would taste like, and it would be ordinary and normal. How wrong he had been. The scent of her had already soaked into his lungs, deep where he knew he'd never eradicate her. What a fool he was.

She is...incredible.

He could feel the wild tempo of her heartbeat underneath his thumb pressed into the curve of her throat. Tobias's discipline deserted him and he felt powerless against the attraction he felt for Olivia. He badly wanted to ruck her dress up to her waist, open his fly, and thrust his cock into what he knew would be the tightest clasp. Without releasing her lips, he withdrew his finger and glided it over the folds of her sex until he found the knot of her pleasure and pressed. She gave a tiny moan, of protest or pleasure, he wasn't sure which. But when he made to pull away, her hands tightened on his nape and her lips clung even more sweetly to his.

Thank Christ.

For he did not have the willpower to let her go. He lifted her and placed her on a small table. She widened her legs without his encouragement and more of his control slipped from him. A distant warning bell rang somewhere in his fevered brain, but he was too far gone to pay it any heed. He worked her clitoris until she trembled in his arms, then he slid two fingers down and thrust them deep.

She whimpered and he froze, then he groaned when she shivered. Olivia wrenched her lips from his, panting. "Tobias..."

"Yes?"

Then silence. The dark pressed in on them, cocooning them in intimacy and secrecy to just be. It shocked Tobias to acknowledge how alive she made him feel in this moment. His cock ached…painfully, a state he had never felt in all his years of life on earth. A whisper of a kiss feathered over his jaw and he closed his eyes against the sensations.

"I've always loved your scent."

And I yours.

Before he could assess the startling thought, her lips settled once again on his, but without the earlier shyness. Now she kissed him like the hoyden he knew, bold, reckless, and with wet carnality.

And he responded.

He pushed her gown up to her waist and stepped between her legs. Arousal rode him hard, and with each whimper and sigh she released, he lost a bit more of himself. He dragged his mouth from her, and kissed along her neck. She arched, giving him delightful access. "We should stop," he growled.

"Yes," she said, sounding dazed, needy, and hungry. "In a bit…kiss me again."

She gripped a fistful of his hair and dragged his lips back to hers. They feasted on each other in the dark, the need rioting in his blood, strong enough where he could release without even entering her. With fumbling movements he released the fly of his breeches, hooked her legs on his waist, and notched the head of his cock at her scalding entrance without releasing her lips. He slid his hand around to her buttocks, lifted her slightly so he could have a firmer purchase, and flexed his hips, driving deep inside her.

She jolted, a pained whimper escaping her lips, before she bit into his bottom lip.

She was so wonderfully tight; sweat beaded on his brows. "Shhh," he soothed. "You are wet enough to take me." And God, she was wet. She soaked his cock and in the same breath, resisted his invasion.

"Tobias?" Her voice was husky with arousal and

uncertainty.

"Relax," he whispered against her lips, trying to move. "You are so damn tight, Olivia."

She pressed a kiss to the corner of his lips. "Am I supposed to be this…this…tight?"

"Oh yes," he groaned. "Hold on to me and do not let go."

"Never," she assured him with a soft sigh.

The promise had his mouth drying, then she shivered, her tightness rippling over him and crumbling his control. He withdrew and surged back in, deeply but with restraint. Her flesh became even more pliant to his cock, sheathing it as if it were made specifically for his thickness and length. She flinched, and he took her lips in a tender kiss. Using one hand, Tobias combed through her curls until he found her knot of pleasure. He held himself buried deep while he flicked and caressed it, teasing and tempting her to relax more. She grew slicker, and he took her lips again with a low groan of satisfaction. He slid his hands up to cup her breasts gently, his thumb caressing her hardened nipples through her thin chemisette.

"Tobias," she gasped, her husky wail filled with rioting need.

Claiming her lips in a mimicry of his thrusting hips, he hitched her legs higher around his waist and thrust even deeper. She convulsed, tightening even more around his length. With a soft cry, she surrendered, and with a groan, Tobias emptied his seed in her.

Their harsh breathing rasped against his skin in the darkened closet, and his heart was a war drum in his ear. He wished there was a light so he could see her face. What was she thinking? *Hell*, what had he been thinking? And that was the problem. He *hadn't* been thinking, only feeling and experiencing the utter delight of being in her arms.

He'd completely lost his self-control and the notion froze

his soul. Tobias had to marry her, but how could he marry a woman who had completely destroyed his restraint in such a regard? He had made love to her in a linen closet in his home, which currently held over a hundred guests, his mother, sister...and his mistress.

Good God.

He gently pulled himself from Olivia, fishing his handkerchief from his pocket and tenderly cleaning her.

She gasped and grabbed on to his wrists. "I can do this myself," she muttered.

He cupped her cheek with his other hand and from the heat he surmised she was blushing. "Olivia—"

"No," she hissed fiercely. "I know what you are thinking and I assure you it is not necessary. No one but us knows and we shall keep it that way. The world cannot know I've been *ruined*."

He rocked back on his heels, completely stunned. He waited for relief to fill him, but only felt annoyance that she would reject his offer before he'd even made it. Anger filled his veins. She shimmied off the small table, and he winced when a sob caught in her throat.

"What was I thinking?" she whispered almost to herself. A finger jabbed his chest hard. "You don't even *like* me."

A true enough statement. He had no defense and Tobias was almost afraid to analyze the manner in which she ensnared his desires.

"And I am quite certain you do not like me," he rebutted softly. Then why had she given herself to him so sweetly, so wantonly? Why was he craving her touch even now, her taste?

Another soft exhalation filled the air. "Excuse me, I must get to my chamber right away," she muttered and wrenched the door open.

Damnation. In her haste, she'd not thought to ensure the hallway was clear. He hurried after her, grateful there were no guests in the corridor. He had to make his position clear. Honor demanded they wed, and even now she could be with his child. He stumbled and the hand he scrubbed over his face shook. The vision of Olivia swollen with his child was… frightfully appealing.

"Olivia, wait," he snapped.

She ignored him, almost running in her haste to get away from him. He felt like a heel. How in God's name had they lost such control over their passions? How had *he* lost such control? He was the one with the experience…he should have been more protective and considerate with her burgeoning passion. Instead, he had stoked the flames and ruthlessly used her inexperience to satiate his lust.

He infused cold command in his voice. "Lady Olivia, wait!"

She jerked to a halt, and as he reached her he realized it was because his mother, his sister, and unluckily, Lady Peabody were frozen staring at Olivia. His mother looked back and forth between them and awareness dawned on her face. It was not the timing of them being seeing together in the corridor alone but the fact that Olivia's hair was a mess, most of the pins having been dislodged. Her dress was obviously crumpled and her lips were red and swollen from his kisses. He had no notion of what his appearance was like, but she had gripped his hair and his jacket several times. There was no escaping the fact that they had been *very* intimate.

"Upon my word!" Lady Peabody exclaimed, speculation, glee, and then pity crossing her face. "Are you not the young lady whose father *killed* himself?"

Olivia's eyes became shadowed and a flush of angry embarrassment colored her cheeks. "And what of it?" she demanded staunchly.

Lady Peabody narrowed her eyes. "You are very decisive, aren't you?"

"That I am, my lady, and I will make no apology for it."

"How unseemly!"

Francie hurried over to Livvie's side and gripped her hand.

Lady Peabody squared her shoulders. "Your father—"

"You will hold your tongue in all matters relating to my intended," Tobias bit out with dangerous softness. "Or you will experience the full measure of my displeasure, Lady Peabody."

His mother's lips trembled and disapproval flashed in her gaze, and even Lady Peabody appeared stunned. Of course, it was expected that he would walk away, for Olivia was inferior to him in connections, wealth, and bloodlines. There was no doubt the second that Lady Peabody had her first drawing room meeting, the gossip would start to circulate. Olivia would be irrevocably ruined because of his loss of control. Scandal would touch the Blade name because of his weakness.

"There was no announcement," Lady Peabody said primly.

"I've just made it," he said flatly.

She gasped, and his mother paled.

"Tobias—"

"Mother, please," Francie interjected. "Livvie and I will be downstairs shortly. She must freshen up."

Olivia's face was so pale he feared she was in danger of fainting. Without waiting for the dowager countess's response, Olivia walked past them with her head held high, but he could see the fine trembling of her hands at her side. Regret twisted in his gut like a knife. Once again his loss of control over his passions had ruined someone's life, and invited scandal to his family. Intolerable. He had to make it right.

"You cannot think to marry her, Tobias," his mother gasped quite dramatically, affecting a swoon. Lady Peabody rushed to offer her shoulder as a prop.

He remained unaffected by her theatrics. "Should we take this someplace private?" he asked smoothly, strolling past them. A few minutes later, he entered the library without encountering any more guests. He should have allowed Olivia to leave the closet alone, then sought her out after he was sure the guests were abed. Though she would have still been ruined, considering her disheveled and ravished appearance. They would simply not have known the gentleman to affix the deed to. Somehow, he knew that she would never have revealed his name.

The door closed with a slam and he repressed a sigh. His mother would not do anything to temper her wayward emotions.

He faced her. "What of Lady Peabody?"

His mother flushed. "She is my dear friend, and I have asked her to be as circumspect as possible. She has retired to her chamber, no doubt from the shock of witnessing such licentiousness."

Tobias smiled and he was aware of its unpleasant nature from his mother's wince. "Lady Peabody will not open her mouth and breathe a word of what she believes she witnessed. If she makes any steps to ruin Olivia, I will ensure her husband will be closed to all investments from my circle."

He moved over to the mantle and poured brandy in a glass, which he consumed in three long swallows.

His mother moved farther into the library, anger evident in her posture. "You go too far, Tobias. Such threats are not necessary."

"I haven't even begun."

She dealt him a considering glance. "If you are going to extend your influence and squash all scandal, there is no need to insist on marrying Lady Olivia. You are a Blade, and she… she…" After a heavy sigh she said, "You are ill suited. She is inferior in wealth and connection. She is too opinionated and rebels against my directions in how a young lady's carriage and elegance ought—"

"Mother?"

Anger flushed her cheeks at being interrupted, but thankfully she did not release her vitriol. "Yes, my dear?"

"I *will* marry her."

She frowned. "No one knows, Tobias, you do not need to be honorable," she said in a long-suffering manner. "You have proven you can walk away from gossip unscathed and society will still love you. Surely we can successfully deflect—"

"No." Never would he have imagined weeks ago that he would make an announcement that he had offered for Olivia's hand, but he knew how far he had taken his madness. There was the possibility of a child…

Christ.

His mother's hand fluttered to her throat. "But what of Lady Willa? She is perfect for you, Tobias."

"I have no interest in her. You like her because you are of like mind. Whatever resentment you feel toward Olivia is because you cannot control her. And I know you, Mother, you despise that which you cannot manipulate."

The door jerked open and Grayson entered. He faltered, glancing from Tobias to his mother. "I did not realize the room was taken," he said softly, as was his way whenever he was in the company of the dowager countess. His mere presence normally sent her into fits of anger and fainting spells, all in hopes of manipulating Tobias to send his father's by-blow from his life.

"Well come in," she said. "Perhaps you can speak some sense into your brother. He is insisting on marrying a young lady who is very unsuitable for our distinguished title." An invitation that indicated how truly rattled she was at the thought of him marrying Olivia. His mother had never been civil to Grayson before.

Tobias walked to the oak desk and sat on the edge, droning out his mother's voice as she launched into her version of the damning event. He needed to concentrate on how to convince Olivia to be his countess, a feat he was sure would require a most arduous effort.

Chapter Nine

Livvie had been thoroughly ravished by a man reputed to be ruthless and cuttingly cold, yet he had burned with wild passion and it had all been for her. She had been so painfully alive for a glorious few minutes and now she was ruined. Tobias had kissed her, and all her thoughts had dissolved under his sensual mastery. She suddenly felt a swell of pity for all the debutantes who had fallen for the seductive charms and kisses of a seasoned rake. How weak she had been to his touch, but how wickedly delightful it had been to be in his arms.

The raw, painful emotions tearing through her were wholly unexpected, and it was not because she had been caught in such a thoroughly compromising position. It was the idea that Tobias could have touched her with such care, such tenderness, such passion, and he did not even like her. She had been seduced by a scoundrel and she had allowed him. Her mind raced from one frightening thought to another. She was entirely without prospects and was most assuredly ruined.

Was she no better than her father?

She pulled herself together with an effort of will. With quick motions, she caught her mess of hair into a simple chignon. She had already changed into a pale peach gown and slid her feet into more comfortable slippers, moving with quick efficiency, and doing her best to ignore the tenderness between her thighs. There would be no delaying speaking with the earl and his mother. With a heavy heart, she stood up from the chair in front of her dressing table.

Francie was waiting patiently by the door, her eyes alight with sympathy. "My brother is willing to do the honorable thing, but I can see from your expression you are going to be stubborn."

Livvie flinched. The *ton* considered Tobias a prime catch. He possessed wealth, connections, and power. She had given him her virtue in a rush of blind passion, and dare she admit it, she liked the man. He disliked her intensely, and the very idea of forming a lifelong commitment without any tender sentiments or regard was heart wrenching. She desired him, but her esteem was not returned. How could she endure such a marriage?

Her papa had not been contented with her mother and he'd been unable to live without his mistress when it should have been Mamma he felt such intensity of emotions for. What if she had a similar marriage? What if Tobias disliked her so intensely he would take mistresses when they married? The pain and humiliation would be unendurable.

"Tonight was the first time your brother has ever been anything but coldly polite. I am still at a loss as to what happened. One minute I wanted to kick his shin...and then the next all I wanted was for him to *never* stop kissing me," she confessed softly.

Her friend's eyes widened and a blush climbed her cheeks. "Was that all he did?"

"Francie!"

"It hardly matters. You will need the respectability of marriage to weather the storm to come."

The inevitability of another scandal pressed in on Livvie. A weight that was too heavy for her to bear alone. Once Lady Peabody's lips were loosed, her mistake would spread through the country and then on to London like wildfire. Did Tobias truly wish to wed her? She thought of the animosity between them and winced. No, he would not. She was without connections and had nothing to recommend her.

"Perhaps a scandal can be avoided. We are, after all, in the country and we were not seen doing anything."

Francie hurried over and clasped her hands. "Dear Livvie, please think on my brother's offer. I assure you, Lady Peabody will spread the gossip of what she saw and the scandal will be terrible. Though he is…he is different from other men, he is honorable. Mother and Tobias are awaiting us."

Livvie allowed a small smile to touch her lips. It was all she could manage. She tried to see the benefits of marriage to the earl and her mind was frightfully blank. They exited her chamber and walked at a brisk pace downstairs. Holding her head high, she marched down the hallway. Many of the guests were still at the ball and in the card rooms. She could hear the faint din of laughter and the soft chords of a waltz floating up from below. When they reached the library, she lifted her hand to knock and hesitated. The dowager countess's voice rose. "Why are you being so stubborn, Tobias?" she asked, a hint of admonition in her words.

"I've been told it's my nature to be pigheaded. It is why I have such support and success in the House of Lords," he said drily.

"And what if she deliberately trapped you? My cousin's estate isn't doing well and she only comes with two thousand, and from what I have seen of her wild ways, it is entirely possible."

Livvie stiffened in outrage.

"I do not care for such things," Tobias countered, mild annoyance evident in his tone. "This conversation is a waste of time as my mind is my own and it has decided on marrying Lady Olivia."

Her heart eased a bit.

"She is without decorum or any proper polish to become the Countess of Blade."

Francie gasped. "Oh, Livvie, do not take her words to heart, Mamma is…"

Then Tobias spoke, "Yet she will be the new countess. You will also make arrangements to open up the dower house for your future residence."

There was a flurry of sounds and Livvie managed to lurch back as the door was flung open and then slammed. The dowager countess vibrated with anger, and Livvie's heart broke a little more. The countess gave her a bitter look of tearful condemnation.

"Come along, Francie. It is terrible manners to eavesdrop. I taught you better."

She gripped her daughter's arm and walked away without acknowledging Livvie. It was certainly ridiculous to feel such hurt but she did. She lifted her hand to knock once again and faltered as another voice spoke.

"Is it Lady Olivia's character that has the frown on your face, or the countess's disapproval?"

She stiffened.

"Mother's disproval has no bearing on my decision. She will cry and rant bitterly that I have no respect for her nerves and tender feelings, I daresay she will even faint a few times. Women use tears and fainting spells solely to manipulate and bend a man to their will, and Mother is an expert. She will be leaving Grangeville Park for the dower house within the week, for I do not have the tolerance for the tantrum I can predict she will unleash."

"Ah, so it's the beauty. I know you have no aversion to marriage, so what could be your possible objection to such a charming beauty?"

He thinks me a charming beauty?

"Unfortunately, she is not the tractable and biddable sort of female."

There was a low chuckle and murmur she was unable to ascertain.

"You must admit it, man, Lady Olivia's charms are delightful. You would be bored with any other young lady, especially the tractable sorts."

There was a low grunt from Tobias.

"I think I will send the hoyden to the farthest estate of mine, in Scotland…hell, maybe the West Indies," Tobias drawled with amusement coloring his tone.

A strange numbness spread in her chest. The wretched, insufferable man. Narrowing her eyes, she rapped her knuckles on the door, then entered without waiting for a response.

• • •

Grayson launched to his feet as Olivia stalked into the library. Relief filled Tobias that her face wasn't wet with tears and that she'd possessed the strength to return below stairs instead of sequestering herself in her chamber with smelling salts.

"I would not marry you if you were the last man in England," she said by way of greeting.

Tobias smiled.

She turned to his brother and dipped into a shallow curtsy. "How charming to see you again, Grayson."

"Lady Olivia, I offer you my heartiest congratulations on your upcoming nuptials."

She gave him a pointed glare, before she softened with

a beautiful agreeable smile. His brother flushed and tugged at his cravat. "Thank you, Grayson, though such sentiments at this time are unwarranted. I would appreciate a private audience with the earl," she said with such charm that Tobias frowned, instantly suspicious.

Grayson grinned and after a short bow toward Olivia, exited.

She clasped her arm across her middle and faced him, her eyes alight with defiance. "If a carriage could be ordered for me, I would appreciate the kindness. At dawn, I would return to my stepfather's estate." Her gaze did not meet his, instead she glared at the point above his left shoulder.

Her lips were delightfully swollen from his kisses. It was still evident they had been cavorting. Yet she was refusing his hand. He'd known she was not the type of woman to succumb to persuasion, and instead of it filling him with irritation, he admired her.

"I will return with you and have a word with Lord Bathhurst," Tobias said smoothly.

Her flashing eyes snapped to his. "You truly cannot be entertaining marriage between us."

"Yes."

"My lord, I—"

"Tobias…Olivia. I believe we can dispense with all formalities after all we've shared, don't you agree?"

Looking slightly overwhelmed, she nodded. "Very well, Tobias. We do not like each other."

"We did well enough in the linen closet."

Her cheeks went red, and she glared at him. "I still cannot marry you."

"You are being silly," he said when he wanted to rattle her. Did she not realize how precarious her situation was? "Are you delusional about your current position in society?"

She gave a disdainful flick of her head. "I am fully aware.

We were not seen embracing intimately. Lady Peabody and your mother only observed me strolling down the hallway with you a few paces behind. Hardly damning. It does not require you to sacrifice your bachelorhood to a lady you deem to be your inferior and who you have no tendre for."

Tobias almost smiled. *Hardly damning.* Olivia was ruined and trying to act blasé. Being pretentious did not suit her. He could see the curl of fright in her eyes, and something more. He could not place the emotions that trembled on her lips or caused the soft sheen glistening in her eyes, but it made his heart soften, halting the blistering retort. He sucked in a harsh breath when he realized it was vulnerability.

She had always seemed so sure, possessing an acerbic tongue, disdainful of the *ton*'s mores, never afraid to voice her opinion, even when it was unsolicited. He forgot that she was only twenty-two years of age. "I do not believe you to be inferior to me in any regard, Olivia."

Her eyes narrowed. "You called me a hoyden."

He splayed his legs in a more casual repose and folded his arms across his chest. "And?"

"And such an opinion does not imply arrogant superiority on your part? After all, am I not a hoyden in your eyes because I swim and ride astride as you do?" She raised her chin a fraction higher. "You hold such an opinion of me and expect me to marry you?" Her tongue was cutting. "I would rather my reputation be ruined than marry a man who does not like me and wishes to restrict me."

Interesting. "And what of your sister's reputation?"

She froze, indecision flashing in her eyes. "Ophelia is eight years of age. When her time is near, nothing will mar her come out."

"Come now, we both know the power of scandal and its longevity. Your father killed himself years ago, and mine brought the Blade name into shocking disrepute and our estates to the brink of ruin. Society still judges us by their actions. How do you think your sister—and mine—will fare when our scandal roars through the *ton*?"

Shock settled on her face before she lowered her gaze, hiding her emotions from him. He waited for her to speak but she remained mute. Ah, he would need to be more ruthless.

"You could be with child as we speak," he said, watching her every expression.

Her head snapped up, and her eyes widened. "I ne…nev—" She paled. "A child? Of course…a child. I never knew…" Her hand instinctively settled on her stomach. "Surely one act of intimacy cannot conceive a child?"

"It can."

"I pray that isn't the case!"

"Do you find the thought so distasteful?" he asked icily, remembering his mother's tears and screams at his father for wanting another child.

"No…I must admit, a child, a family of my own was never something I had given much thought to until my stepfather and mother thrust the notion upon me. Yes, it would be an eventual desire but not now…and not one conceived in a bit of passion."

Bit of passion? She had damned near ruined his cock for anyone else. He could still taste her on his tongue, feel the ripple of her release. It irritated him that she should have such a hold over his passion. He'd never had any reason to reminisce on a lover's response as he had done with hers. How he had wished he had been able to see her eyes, see the wet glisten of her lips from his kisses, part her legs and look at her swollen folds. Sudden impatience bit him. "It only takes the one occurrence. It would be foolish to waste time to see if you are indeed increasing. By then, the rumors of your downfall will be rampant. I will arrange for a special license."

Her eyes flashed fire. "I have not consented."

"I am sure Lord Bathhurst will take care of such formalities for you when I inform him you may even now carry my heir."

She gasped, spluttered, and then paled. "Surely you would not be so ungentlemanly."

He arched a brow. "Most assuredly I would."

"And if he should challenge you?"

"I would spare you the pain of accepting."

Her green eyes were wary. "I heard your unflattering remark to your brother." She cocked her head quite gracefully to the side, observing him. "Do you hold any tender regards toward me?" she asked quietly.

It was the last question Tobias ever expected her to ask. But of course, he should have known that beneath the wildness beat a romantic heart like in all young ladies. Hell, maybe she would soon expect him to read poetry to her. "No."

She nodded. "Then I will not marry you. I've always vowed to only marry for love."

"Why?"

Amusement gleamed in her eyes and he was unaccountably pleased to see it.

"To be contrary. All my life, Mother has impressed on me the many reasons for marriage and not once has she spoken of the more tender sentiments."

"Sensible woman."

Olivia sauntered closer to him, and he restrained the urge to tug her to him and rub soothing circles on her shoulders.

"And because I despaired of hearing the *M* word so much, I took pleasure in insisting I'd only marry a man who admires all of me. I found the idea grew on me." A dimple appeared in her cheek as her smile widened. "What manner of man would actually love the fact that I may ride, shoot, and fence better than he? I have made money from my paintings, and I am quite determined to create a reputation as a reputable painter. My passions and virtues are not ones gentlemen of society seem to admire. Your mother has made that clear to me several times and it is quite disheartening to think I must pretend to have false likes and interests for a man to admire me. Even you, my lord, take some joy in calling me a *hoyden* and avoided me at every turn. If not for…" Her face reddened. "You would not be proposing marriage if not for…" She visibly gritted her teeth. "You know of which I speak. I do not pretend to be extraordinary, but I am not lacking."

I've avoided you because night upon night I have dreamed of you tangled in my sheets with me riding you to ecstasy.

He was desperate to get his wayward thoughts under control.

"It seems as if you are against marriage and not me in particular."

"I believe, my lord, you should imagine the simple pleasures you take for granted—riding astride, swimming in the lake—being forbidden to you and you are encouraged to only do needlework, take long walks, and play the pianoforte."

"Life would be dreadfully boring if I conceded to such expectations."

She laughed and it enchanted him. "I am gratified to hear you say so, Tobias." Then she sobered. "If you had some sentiments for me, I would marry you," she ended softly with a wistful smile. "Now I shall not even consider it lightly."

It was then that he truly appreciated how different she was from the many ladies of the *ton*. All would have been filled with glee for trapping him so thoroughly, but not her.

"I do not believe in the constricting emotion of love. Nor do I believe in anger, jealously, or bemoaning one's fate. That invariably leads to an excess of ruinous emotions."

The tempestuous clashes between his parents that had sometimes turned violent had evoked within Tobias a deep longing for calm and a strict control over one's emotions. The day he had learned to compartmentalize his mother's tears and fits of rage and his father's virulent fury one minute and then his unbridled happiness the next, life became simpler and had stayed so. And he would damn well do nothing to jeopardize that.

He had vowed he would never allow intimacy with a woman who had the power to shift the ground from underneath him, to test the restraints he had on his emotions, namely anger, jealously, and that frenzied obsession which disguised itself as love. The gossipmongers and even a few who called themselves friends named him cynical, coldhearted, and too detached to appreciate the sentiments involved in loving a woman. But he was certain on what needed to be done and would never be swayed to act rashly.

"Are you implying you do not feel? Though I can well credit such an assertion."

"I feel, Olivia, but feelings must always be tempered with logic and rational thought before one acts. When that is done, it should be quite evident the ridiculous ways in which people oftentimes behave are not required. I took the opportunity to speak with you instead of making my offer to your father. I tried to make allowances for your sensibility, which I can see was foolish of me to do. You are determined to be pigheaded."

She gasped, clearly affronted. "I simply do not wish for a husband to dictate my life."

"Yet you will have one within the week. I will not allow gossips to once more stain the Blade name. I will *not* allow scandal to taint my sister's future prospect. I expect you to be a countess with good sense and temperance." The very idea of stifling her vivacity and fieriness had discomfort churning in his gut. He swiftly buried the feelings, knowing it was best for their marriage if she understood his expectations. Though a part of him wondered what he truly wanted. *Lady O* was the very likeness of Olivia, never had he written of a heroine with such strong alluring complexities and vulnerabilities. "And I do expect all inappropriate behavior to end."

"And I expect you can kiss my backside," she said sweetly.

Her vulgar tongue had arousal singing through his blood. "I will. On our wedding night, I will kiss all of you. I regret that I did not love you as I wanted to earlier. I assure you, my oversight will be rectified."

Her eyes widened and her face turned an alarming shade of red. Then she turned and darted from the library.

Tobias chuckled. Life with her as his countess would never be boring or predictable, but he would have to be ruthless in ensuring he did not fall into the trap of all previous Blade men. Those who fell in love invariably lost all of their honor along with their senses.

Chapter Ten

After several hours of staring at the ceiling in the dark, Livvie slipped from the bed. She tugged on her robe, thrust her feet into her slippers, and left her room. She moved along the corridor in the dark, finding her way to the east wing by memory. Propriety dictated she wait until in the morning to speak with Tobias, but the thoughts and anxiety dominating her mind would not allow her to sleep a wink. The day had been dreadful. Lady Peabody had wasted no time informing a few selected friends of Livvie's mishap. The croquet match on the front lawn had been intolerable, as everyone had stared and whispered. Worse, the dowager countess had summoned Livvie's stepfather and mother to Grangeville Park. She wanted all to be settled with her and Tobias before her parents arrived.

Panting slightly from climbing the winding stairs so rapidly, she paused on the landing and took several steadying breaths. The oppressive dark would be disquieting to most but not to her. She hurried along the hallway and as she drew closer to Tobias's chamber, a single candelabrum provided a slice of light. Murmurings reached her ears and she slowed her steps.

"Please, Tobias, you cannot mean to leave me here in the hall, guests may happen upon us at any time."

Livvie's mouth went dry.

"I am in the doorway of my chamber, Arabella, and you are in the hallway, if anyone should happen along it is your own doing."

"You are refusing to let me in!"

"I did not invite you to my chambers."

Relief made Livvie's knees wobble.

"My darling, please, you cannot be serious in your earlier assertions that you are ending our relationship. Please let me in, so we may discuss the matter in a more *intimate* fashion," she said throatily.

"No. Whatever relationship we had is most certainly over. I am being generous in allowing you to remain at Grangeville Park until morning after your behavior. I expect you to depart then with no fuss or I shall have you forcibly removed."

She moaned low in her throat and swooned. Instead of catching her, Tobias's lips curved in disgust and he closed the door. The lady he had referred to as Arabella stiffened, then stomped her feet. A look of calculation settled on her face. She gripped her nightgown and stormed away, thankfully in the other direction.

A few seconds later Livvie was once again plunged into the dark as the lady took her candle with her. Taking a deep breath, she marched over to Tobias's door and knocked firmly. "It's Livvie," she whispered.

Before she could knock again, the door was flung open and he tugged her inside. "I can see you take pleasure in courting total ruination," he said, his face inscrutable as he stared down at her.

Despite it being summer, the fire was lit and the room

was nicely warm. She moved closer to the roaring fireplace. "I could not sleep…and I have been thinking on your offer."

"Go on."

"I would like us to reach a happy agreement before my parents arrive. My stepfather was grievously ill a few weeks past and I do not want to upset him much, and my mother can be over anxious." At his nod, she continued, "I have terms before…before I will consent to be your wife."

He smiled with deceptive charm. "Of course. I'd not expected anything else."

"As you are aware, I objected to marriage, not just to you, but to any man." She started to pace before the fire. "There are no advantages in marriage for a woman, in my opinion. You will control all aspects of my life, what little I own will no longer be my own…you have the right to beat me for imagined hoydenish ways and then when you are finished, you can cast me aside for any number of mistresses and I will have no recourse," she said, halting to face him.

He said nothing, and she forced herself to endure his unfathomable gaze for what felt like an eternity. There was no way around it. She took a deep breath and exhaled. "I understand you have a mistress," she said bluntly, driving to the heart of what had kept her awake and restless. Livvie wondered if the lady he'd just turned away was his mistress. Satisfaction rushed through her that he'd been honorable.

An arrogant brow arched. "I had not imagined such gossip would have reached your ears."

"I am quite attentive whenever the coldest earl London has ever seen is mentioned in whispered tones," she said with an inelegant shrug of her shoulders.

He sat on the edge of a small oak desk by the windows, sprawled his leg outward in the most improper fashion, and folded his arms, considering her. "There is a lady I had some attachment toward."

"Only the one?"

"Yes."

Her throat tightened and she folded her arms across her stomach. "I...I expect whatever attachments you have with her to end. My father...my father abandoned me and my mother to fend for ourselves, in a world that made it evident it has no use for women...on account of how desperately he loved his mistress, Lady Prudence Mayberry."

The earl's face went impassive. "I have no intention of keeping a mistress once we are married. I would never dishonor you in such a manner."

She searched his face intently. He seemed sincere, and a modicum of the tension left her body. "Thank you."

He nodded. "In fact, I ended whatever liaison I had today."

"Was it the lady I just saw at your door?"

He regarded her with cool challenge in his eyes. Dear Lord, surely he was not thinking she overstepped. She struggled for equanimity.

His gaze searched her face. "Yes."

"Good."

"Now—"

"Please, I have more, Tobias."

His mouth curved faintly, and he positively radiated power and leashed sensuality. "Pray, continue."

"Whenever we are in the country, when I ride, I will do so astride. When in Town, I will use the required side-saddle." Her heart drummed as she waited for his firm denial.

"Done."

"I...I...done?" She had braced herself for his flat refusal.

"Yes."

She took a deep breath, pleased with how their negotiations were progressing. "I have been told by many, my choices for reading are not delicate or of the sort of material and tracts a young lady should read. I would like to select my own reading material and not be confined in such a regard."

"Done."

She froze.

Why is he being so accommodating?

"I will not be abandoned in the country, Scotland, or the West Indies."

Amusement gleamed in his gaze. "If that is your wish?"

His capitulations were alarming her. "Most assuredly." What would he say to her final demand?

"You're awfully accommodating," she said suspiciously.

"I'm a reasonable man."

Hope surged hotly in her breast. "I want it in our…our marriage contract that…that I will be allowed to continue my work."

He appeared riveted, then he scrubbed a hand over his face. "Work?"

Livvie swallowed, appreciative of the shaky ground upon which she stood. "Yes, my lord…I paint."

"I know, and your talent is something wonderful. I have never witnessed such skill in one so young."

Dizzying pleasure filled her. "Thank you."

"I would not begrudge you any hobby. I have my own interests."

Her heart raced. "It is not a hobby, Tobias. I sold my last painting for twenty guineas to Squire Wentworth. I…I made his acquaintance in Bath a few months ago, and he admired my work most ardently."

For an instant, he looked totally nonplussed. "The Countess of Blade will not *work*."

She rushed over to him. "I…I cannot give up painting. It is as integral as breathing to me," she said softly. "I took up my first brush at three years of age and I have never stopped painting since."

His features softened. "Then do not stop. Convert entire rooms at all of our houses if you will for your work space."

"Oh! Thank you, Tobias, I—"

"However, you will not advertise your talent for sale. I will set aside an allowance for you of two hundred guineas monthly. I trust that will suffice?"

She had sold over thirty paintings in the past year and had not managed to save such an amount. "I...yes, my lord, that is beyond generous." Would he understand her need to earn something for herself and not to be solely dependent on his goodwill and income? She held back the words begging to tumble from her lips. She had achieved some victories tonight, more than she had ever hoped for. One day at a time.

"Are you now prepared to hear my terms?"

She nodded. It was subtle, but the easygoing, relaxing man vanished. "There will be no scandal, tantrums, or tears." He regarded her with measured, glittering eyes. "The last thing I expect to hear is gossip about my wife, *ever*. Is that very clear?"

She looked thoughtfully across at him. "I will endeavor to comport myself to your expectations." She would be a paragon of grace, modesty, and demureness...even if it killed her.

"Do not ever change, Livvie."

She suppressed the ghost of her father's whisper. The earl would have no cause to regret marrying her. Livvie was not only marrying him for her sake but for her family. However... "I cannot promise you no tears. There may be a time—"

"None. Tears, tantrums, and fainting spells are a mere form of manipulation and deception utilized by the wielder. Women use tears as artfully as fans are used for flirting. If you ever approach me in such a manner, I promise you, the very next day you will be at another estate."

"I will do all in my power to be as expected."

There was an odd flicker in his eyes, as if he was disappointed by her answer. Certainly she was mistaken.

"See that you do. The guests will be departing tomorrow, and I will procure a special license. We shall be married by next week. I trust this is acceptable."

"That…that is very soon." His eyes dropped deliberately to her stomach and she blushed. "And what if I am not with child?"

He studied her with unnerving calm. "I pride myself on my control and strict temperance over my passions, Olivia. For the first time in years, I acted without regard for another, a thing I had promised never to do again. I kissed you and I lost my damned senses. Even if you are without child, I *ruined* you. I stole your virtue, and your future husband would have felt its loss. And I assure you, Lady Peabody is already speaking of your supposed disgrace."

Livvie was still stuck on *I kissed you and I lost my damned sense*. "I…I lost a bit of me when you kissed me as well."

He stared at her, and she wished she had not spoken with such boldness. Silence stretched on for what seemed like an eternity. "Let me assure you, I will never be so reckless again."

"I do not mind…when we are married, of course."

He made no answer and her heart started a slow thud. What did he truly mean?

"Are we to have a normal marriage?"

"Yes, of course."

She now wondered what was truly normal. The farce of a marriage many in the *ton* had? Blank stares and cold touches, where one or both parties eventually sought a lover? Her stomach cramped at the very idea of Tobias betraying her in such a manner. "Good night, my lord."

"Tobias."

She allowed a smile to touch her lips and bury all the uncertainty she felt. "Tobias."

He pushed from the desk and walked over to her with easy grace and cupped her cheeks. He tilted her head and pressed a kiss against her forehead. His touch and gentleness was so unexpected, she froze.

"Sleep well, Olivia," he murmured and stepped back.

With a nod, she fairly ran from his chambers to hers, wondering what had just happened.

Chapter Eleven

Lady Sophie Rayburn, Viscountess Wimple, the woman Tobias had once been engaged to, was perfectly groomed, her slender figure sheathed in a high-waisted pale pink gown. Her long supple fingers clutched the folds of Tobias's jacket and her pouting lips pressed to his.

Livvie felt as if she were suffocating. It was through a veil of anger and pain she noticed Tobias's eyes were open and glued to her, frozen at the threshold of his library. Without flickering a lid, he gripped the lady's shoulders firmly and pushed her from him.

"Oh, Tobias, I've missed you so, darling. I cannot credit why you have ended the house party and dismissed all the guests. Only you would be so *rude*, and yet be admired for your actions. Everyone was positively atwitter at the announcement. Invite me to stay for a few more days and—"

Livvie slammed the door, and Lady Wimple jerked and spun around. Her delicate hands fluttered to her throat, but her brown eyes gleamed with cunning and spite. It was then Livvie realized this was all a contrived show and this harpy wanted her to feel the distressing jealously now surging though her veins. Her anger spiked and she walked farther into the library.

"To what do I owe your interruption, Olivia?"

Oooh, as if she had not caught another woman pressed against him. It was just last night she had visited his chambers and he had reassured her he would end all liaisons. He stared at her now with a chilling sort of watchfulness and she wanted to slap the icy reserve from his features. He despised emotional tantrums, but she wanted to indulge in one that very moment. But she needed to be *ladylike*.

The viscountess smiled. "Please do excuse us, Lady Olivia, but I was having a private meeting with the earl."

Her control wavered.

"Well?" Lady Wimple demanded haughtily, looking down her thin but very elegant nose.

Livvie smiled. "You will pack your belongings and depart within the hour. I will order a carriage for you, and you will not be invited to Grangeville Park again."

Shock slackened the viscountess's features. It was evident she had not expected Livvie to be so bold and decisive. They both knew she had no real power and that Tobias could veto any of her edicts.

The viscountess walked a few paces forward and then angled her body toward Tobias so her breasts were shown to their best advantage. "Jealousy does not become your future countess does it, darling," she drawled. "I did hear she was a bit…unconventional."

"No, it does not." His tone was icy, and the slender teeter Livvie had on her temper snapped.

She cast him an irritated glance. "You will be quiet, my lord, or I will…I will… Pails of snails will be the least you have to fear."

His mien shuttered even further, and Lady Wimple's

tinkling laughter echoed in the library.

Livvie rounded on her. "I fail to understand your amusement. Your husband is in residence. I feel no reservations about marching to him and letting your shameful behavior be known."

The viscountess spluttered. "I…I never—"

Livvie waved her hand. "Though Lord Blade may not like it, I am quite possessive and in that regard I certainly have no intention of adjusting my attitude or my expectations. I would have no compunction about grabbing your exquisite coiffeur in my hands and dragging you from what will be my home in a few days' time, then dropping you on your fundament outside. I may be small, but I am quite ferocious."

The viscountess paled. "Tobias! Will you allow her to speak to me in this fashion? I am only here to speak of business and she has insulted me."

Livvie glanced at him. He stood transfixed and her breath seized on the amusement glittering in his dark green eyes. He was not angry? Even though she had acted in a manner he found unbecoming.

"You heard my fiancée, Sophie."

"But…but what about our business—"

Livvie took deep, calming breaths in an effort to hold on to her emotions. "I am sure you will find some other man who will be grateful for your attentions. In the event it had escaped your notice, Lord Blade was unaffected by your advances. Now, you have an hour to depart from my home and I think I am being overly generous."

The viscountess marched from the room, anger evident in every line of her posture. The silence that remained was not a calm or relaxing one. Though she felt some measure of satisfaction, Livvie's anger had not subsided. "Why did you allow her to kiss you?"

He blinked, all traces of amusement vanishing. "I will not

countenance jealous fits."

Jealous fits? She curled her hands into a tight fist. "I expect loyalty."

"I am loyal."

"Then—"

"And I expect *trust*. I ended all liaisons when I decided to marry you. I will not have a marriage where I have to explain every damned encounter I have with a woman. I will not try and rationalize the actions of someone, when I hardly know what the hell she could have been thinking. I will not be met with jealously or anger. I've had enough for a lifetime," he snapped, his voice a sharp cutting blade.

Her heart jerked in alarm. She had never seen him show such passion before. *Except in the closet*, a tiny voice reminded her. "Then if you ever come upon a man pawing me, I shall expect the same trust with no explanations from me. Good day, my lord."

She walked away with calm serenity, wanting to rail, but knowing her passionate nature would only repulse him more. He had been very clear in his demands last night, and it might be foolish of her, but she wanted their eventual marriage to work. They were on rocky, ill formed grounds and any tiny thing could make either party break their promises, despite the possibility of a dreadful scandal…and a baby. Her hand touched the door handle, and the sudden heat of a solid wall behind her froze her. She had not heard him move.

"I would not question your honor if I ever saw such a thing, but be assured whichever man touches you, whether it was by your invitation or not, I would break him," he said, dangerously soft. "He would lose wealth, his friends, certainly the use of a limb or two, for even thinking to touch you, much less doing so."

The cold implacability of his tone sent a shiver through her, and what was even worse, she believed him to be ruthless enough to destroy any man who would have the temerity to kiss, or attempt to seduce her.

She wriggled, wanting a bit of room to turn. He eased back slightly, and she spun to face him. She allowed a smile to tip her lips. "I am gratified you understand my emotions, my lord. I would hate to have to challenge Lady Wimple for her audacity and dishonorable behavior today. Although everything in me clamored to. You announced our engagement this morning!"

His lips twitched and some of the tension eased from his shoulders. "You are not a man, Olivia."

Her brow wrinkled. "Dishonor is dishonor. She attempted to disrespect and shame me. And I am a crack shot, and if not pistols, I would only give her a tiny nick with my foil."

He unexpectedly chuckled, and the sound vibrated to the core of her.

"We were speaking of investments, and when she heard footsteps outside, suddenly she was pressed against me, her lips on mine. You entered before I even had a chance to react."

Sweet relief filled her. "I thank you for the explanation."

"I fear I must. I would hate for you to actually challenge the woman and create an even greater scandal than the one we are currently contending with."

"I overstepped when I ordered her from your home. Forgive me."

"There is nothing to forgive. It is your home now."

"In five days' time," she said softly, curious at his lack of anger. "She was your fiancée once."

The hard planes of his darkly handsome features shuttered. "Yes."

"You ended the attachment?"

"Yes."

"Because she created a scene?"

"You are well-informed."

"I had thought that must be a ghastly rumor."

"I cannot abide tears and screeching at the top of one's lungs."

Oh. "Forgive the harsh way in which I spoke to her."

"I quite like your decisiveness."

She smiled. "I believe I have found something you actually like about me, my lord."

"There are several things I enjoy about you."

Her heart stuttered and a strange sort of exhilaration pumped through her blood. "Such as?" she demanded.

"Your lips."

Her heart began to pound with such strength she felt faint.

His eyes warmed with interest…and desire. "Your taste, scent, and your smile, they are all the same…captivating."

"I would have you more intrigued by my character," she said softly.

Her earl's lips twitched and she tried not to stare helplessly at his sensual mouth.

"You expect me to appreciate your opinionated willful ways?"

She stiffened.

He leaned in even closer. "I assure you, you are growing on me."

"That makes me sound like a wart, very unflattering."

"Now that you mentioned it…"

The desire to touch him, to kiss his lips, was as overwhelming as it was inexplicable. Giving into a reckless impulse, she tipped and pressed her lips to his. She expected him to take command as he'd done in the closet, but instead he cradled her jaw in his large hands, keeping their kiss light and shatteringly sweet. Though their lips barely met, a thrilling sense of anticipation poured through her. With a soft groan, he deepened their embrace ever so slightly and ravished her mouth with a skilled eroticism that was spellbinding.

He lifted his head. "Why did you come to the library?"

"My parents are here. They arrived a few minutes ago and they are taking tea in the parlor with Lady Blade. I...I... excused myself to speak with you."

"Ah."

He dragged his thumb across her bottom lips. "And what did you wish to speak of?"

"I will marry you, as I promised last night, and I thank you for the offer," she said tremulously. "I do not wish for you to burden my stepfather with the possibility of a child. I want nothing to distress him. The very hint of impropriety and scandal will be painful enough—"

"You have my word, Olivia."

Relief filled her. "Thank you. My stepfather and mother are eager to speak with you...with us."

"I will be there shortly."

Still, there was something bothering her. She searched his eyes. "Why were you in the closet?"

An awkward silence ensued.

"Is it important to know?"

Livvie frowned. "No, I am but curious."

"My former lover wanted me to pursue her by searching my chambers, the gazebo, and the closet. It is a lover's game we had indulged in before. For some reason she thought it was appropriate here. She thought wrong."

Her eyes widened. "You thought I was her?"

"Only for a second."

A thought occurred to her. "Do you expect me to play such games?"

"Good God, no."

She was affronted at his appalled tone. "And why not? Do you not believe I am adventurous?"

He arched an imperious brow. "Are we going to argue?"

Livvie chuckled. She pressed a kiss to the corner of his lips, ignoring his surprised inhalation. She slipped from the cage of his arms, and hurried down the hallway to the drawing room feeling quite happy indeed about their upcoming nuptials.

· · ·

The meeting with Lady Olivia's parents had been as Tobias had expected. There was no anger or recriminations, only hearty congratulations and well wishes from Lord and Lady Bathhurst. Speculation had been rife in their gazes, but of course, they had been too polite to question if there had been any impropriety. A few brows had been raised when he informed everyone he was in the process of obtaining a special license, and Olivia had blushed furiously.

After an hour of tea and pleasantries, Tobias was now alone with the viscount in the library, finalizing the marriage contract. The viscount had a frown on his face, and Tobias surmised he was at the section that included his stepdaughter's demands.

He met Tobias's gaze with a grimace. "Livvie has her own opinions and isn't afraid to voice them," he murmured.

Tobias reclined in his chair in a deliberately casual pose. "So I've discovered."

"And what will you do with your…discovery?"

"There is nothing to be done."

"Many men would say she is unruly, headstrong, and disobedient. In need of a firm guiding hand."

Was the man trying to persuade him to call off the rushed engagement? "Olivia is not a horse and I am not other men."

Speculation swirled in the Viscount's eyes. "No, you are not. Then what would you say she is?"

"A bit reckless and high-spirited, a brilliant painter, intelligent, witty, and quite stubborn."

"And this does not…dissuade you?"

His lips twitched. "No." It should have, but instead he was

frustratingly enticed. He would have to be careful he did not lose himself to her. It would have been palatable if he were only roused sexually. But what if she tugged at his jealously? His rage? What if he lost control with her or because of her? Never had he worried about being reckless with another woman before, but it was as if her willful nature tempted him to be more…relaxed with his feelings and tempers.

Dangerous.

Tobias's mother was beautiful, high-strung, and had been very reckless in her younger days. His father had fought several duels for her, sometimes the offense had simply been another man staring for a little longer than what was deemed proper. His mother, of course, had gloried in the scandals and the passionate possessiveness of her husband. What she had not realized was that his father's possessive jealousy would bloom into him using his fists or riding crop against her whenever he succumbed to his fits of rage.

Bile coated Tobias's tongue and his gut clenched when he remembered the visceral reaction he'd had earlier, when Olivia had merely suggested being in another man's arms to make a point.

He launched from the chair and walked over to the windows. His promise to break any man who would dare touch her had been instinctive and appalling. He had done everything in his power to show an unaffected mien to his ridiculous assertions, but he had been disturbed, for surely he had sounded as demented as his father, who always vowed to his wife to defend her honor by crushing whoever dared.

God's blood.

Olivia was the wrong type of woman to marry. His gut and brain knew it, but his blasted body and honor had other ideas.

"Is everything well, Blade?" the Viscount queried.

Tobias nodded, watching the many carriages pulling away

down the long driveway. He had dismissed all the guests to his mother's distress, ending the house party days earlier than had been originally intended. He did not care. The guests were nosy gossipers and he felt like he was a bug under a microscope in his own home. He would not have it. Worse, he'd fielded veiled insinuations from several gentlemen. He'd done the right thing by sending in the engagement announcement to the papers this morning. By tomorrow, all of England would be agog with the news, the scandal would spread, and the furor would begin. But none of it would be under his roof.

The viscount moved to stand beside him. "Livvie has made a sound match by aligning with your family, and I could not have hoped for her to do better," Bathurst said.

Tobias made no answer.

The man inhaled. "I know of your reputation, Blade. You are not a man to trifle with, and I know you can be ruthless in your business dealings. Outside of that, I have no knowledge of you."

Tobias shifted and faced the viscount.

Worry glowed in the man's eyes and his hands were fisted at his side. "Why is there a need for a special license? Her mother had always envisioned a particular wedding for Livvie."

Tobias hesitated. "It is best we wed sooner than later."

Knowledge flared in the viscount's eyes and he froze for a few seconds before he spoke, "Your honor does you credit. I love her as my own. I would like your promise that you will treat her kindly, Blade."

He nodded. "You will have nothing to worry about once she is my wife."

Lord Bathhurst inhaled softly. "Your father—"

"I am *not* my father," Tobias said with chilling softness. He knew what the viscount was about to hint at. The rumors that had floated in society of his father's volatile tempers, the many nights he had dragged his wife from a ball with the *ton* watching in horrified glee.

"I know it is the law but I will not countenance you beating Livvie."

Cold anger sliced through his blood.

The viscount tugged at his cravat. "I meant no insult but the stories about your father — "

"I will not say this again, Bathhurst. I am not my father."

The memory of his father's riding crop biting into his mother's skin roiled through Tobias. His mother's screams had echoed through the house and all of the servants had been scared to speak out or act in her defense. He glanced at his hand. He had been without thought and conscience as he had mercilessly beaten his father. Then he had acted with even worse disregard of others when he'd marched to the town house of his mother's lover, raw with anger, and challenged him to a duel.

Christ.

The very memory had his stomach twisting in painful knots. He needed to get on the exercise mat and have a good round of boxing until he found his center calm. It would be necessary in the upcoming days.

"I will protect your daughter and cherish the gift you are relinquishing to me, Bathhurst," Tobias said smoothly. "If you will excuse me, there are matters I must attend to." He nodded to the papers in the man's hands. "I trust all is well?"

"It is," the viscount said.

"Good. You and your viscountess are invited to stay until after the wedding. Make yourself completely at home. The lake is teeming with fish."

With a polite nod, he exited the library, eager to spar with Grayson and release the tension building in his gut. What in damnation had he signed up for? And why, amidst the uncertainty, was he feeling such a profound sense of eager anticipation?

Chapter Twelve

Four days after losing her virtue to Tobias, Livvie was the Countess of Blade. She pinched herself again, yet she did not jerk from a dream. She was indeed married to Tobias and had been for exactly nine hours. After her parents had descended on Grangeville Park, everything had moved with shocking speed. He had insisted on a small, intimate wedding in the estate's chapel. She had understood the urgency, especially under the circumstances.

Her parents had been a bit flustered with the rush, but somehow Livvie felt as if her mother knew. She blushed even now, remembering when her mother had taken her aside and asked if she needed to discuss the delicate points of the wedding night. She had been mortified, but she had said no. Her mother and stepfather were well pleased with the match, and her mother even praised her on her ingenuity in compromising such a worthy husband.

A few weeks ago, she'd never imagined she would now be a wife and a countess. Though forming a connection would have been inevitable, she'd never given much thought to the state of being married. What was she to do with her time? Would she still paint and try to sell her work? Her heart shouted yes. Her mother had spoken to her about the finer points of being a countess. Planning balls and hosting parties, from the frivolous types to political ones. She had even been advised to find a few charities to give money to.

Livvie closed her eyes with a soft sigh. She needed to find her way in this world she had been thrown into by her own reckless heart. And she needed to learn her new husband's ways so their situation could be comfortable. Hopefully the tension of the past few days would fade as they became more familiar with each other's likes and dislikes. Moving from the window overlooking the splendid grounds, she sat down on the edge of the bed and closed her eyes.

I'm married.

Her heart was suddenly pounding a furious beat and she struggled to breathe evenly. Her mother had told her it was her duty to ensure she pleased Tobias well enough, so he would give up his mistress permanently. Mortified, she'd staunchly informed her mother all such liaisons had been terminated, and she had been dealt such a look of pity her heart had cracked. Thinking about her husband kissing any other woman made Livvie's stomach hurt and it infuriated her to think his loyalty hinged on her...her what? She had hardly understood her mother's reasoning. Launching to her feet, she grabbed the letter her mother had given her.

Livvie Dearest,

You will succeed splendidly at your new station. You have attained more than I ever dreamed—you are now the Countess of Blade. I offer you these insights gained from my two marriages, and I urge you to take them to heart for I know how important loyalty and mutual regard in a relationship is to you.

Never argue with your husband.

Never smile too long at other men.

Ensure the household runs smoothly, at all times.

Do not prick your earl's temper, and I encourage you to obey his directions at all times.

Love the foods that he adores and read the articles he writes.

Compliment your earl often. Men like their vanity to be praised.

Livvie crumpled the note in her fist, unable to read farther, but recalling her mother had mentioned twice that it was Livvie's duty to provide Tobias with an heir…at all costs. Tears burned the backs of her eyes and she blinked fiercely. She was doomed to fail at her marriage if she needed to do all those things to ensure Tobias was affectionate and faithful. How her mother could urge Livvie to go against her character was beyond her. Her stomach felt hollow at the thought that the love her mother showed her viscount was all contrived, all to ensure he did not abandon her as her first husband had done.

What if the love she thought her mother found with the viscount was all fake? What if Livvie couldn't be a good wife? What good was it trying to find impossible answers to these *frustrating* questions?

There was a knock, then the doorknob rattled. She threw the note into the fireplace and it was quickly consumed by the flames. Francie walked in, and Livvie smiled. "Francie, I never expected you."

"Oh, Livvie, you look so pale. Are you terribly afraid?"

"Only anxious. Everything has happened so fast. What are you doing here? I expected your brother," she admitted with a blush.

"Tobias is swimming in the lake. The heat is sweltering. Mother says she cannot remember a summer being this dreadfully hot."

"You do not have to excuse your brother's absence."

Francie flushed, confirming Livvie's suspicion. She pushed the hurt down deep. Was it that he did not want them to have a wedding night? She was unsure if the idea filled her with relief or anger. Her friend closed the door and leaned against it. "I…I wanted to see you before…" Regret and anxiety coated her lovely features.

Alarm skittered through Livvie, and she strolled over to her friend. "Before what, Francie?"

Her lips flattened. "Why did you marry my brother?"

"I—"

"I know your stubborn nature and I do not believe you were coerced. You would never allow anyone to persuade you against your desires, at least not in marriage. I know your romantic heart, so please tell me the truth."

Livvie frowned, instinctively realizing this was more than what truly prompted her to marry Tobias. "If I did not desire your brother, nothing could have persuaded me to wed him, even with our compromised state," she answered truthfully. "He makes me angry at times, but he also fascinates me. I… like him."

Francie wilted in obvious relief.

"What is this about?"

Hot hope glowed in her eyes as she took a tentative step forward. "I have the deepest affection for someone, and I know he adores me, Livvie. He has asked me to marry him, and though I said yes, I know Mother and Tobias will object to our union. I have been in an agony of doubt for most of today, wondering what decision to make. Do I accept the man my mother has selected for me? A viscount whom I am sure Tobias will approve? Or do I follow my heart?"

"Oh, Francie, I am terribly sorry." Livvie tugged her close and they hugged fiercely. "I am very sure your brother loves you, and I encourage you to speak with him and share what is in your heart. Tell him of your gentleman's proposal."

"And if he objects and bundles me away to Scotland or a nunnery?"

"Then you list all the reasons you love and respect your gentleman. And let Tobias meet him so he can see those qualities for himself. If you cannot live without him, convince your bother of your mutual affections, but do not wed where you will not be happy."

Francie pulled back and smiled. "Thank you, Livvie. I shall not be persuaded away from him."

"Good. Are you now able to share his name and family connections with me?"

"I wish to speak with Tobias first. I cannot trust you would not be tempted to tell him before I get the chance."

"Francie! I would never betray your confidence."

"Forgive me, but I must be careful, you do not know Tobias like I do." Then she pressed a quick kiss to Livvie's cheek and left.

She was still unsure if she had relieved her friend's heart. The only thing she was certain of was that Tobias was avoiding her. She suddenly felt very inadequate and horribly embarrassed. It was clear the night in the closet was an aberration. He did not truly desire her. She was just the undesirable connection he felt honor bound to marry.

She was confronted with the daunting task of persuading Tobias to accept and possibly fall in love with her as she was—romantic and oftentimes reckless. Livvie despised the way her heart ached.

She closed her eyes, fighting tears. They were useless and she would not indulge herself. She reminded herself that she and Tobias had a lifetime to learn about each other and form an attachment based on mutual respect and genuine tender regards.

She exited her chamber and hurried below stairs to the library. After a quick knock to ensure it was empty, she entered and strolled over to the vast selection of books that lined an entire wall. The fireplace was lit and she enjoyed the inviting glow of the room. She would spend the night here reading. Ignoring the disappointment lumping in her throat, she selected a thin leather volume. The door opened and she spun around.

Tobias jerked to a halt when he saw her and stood stock-still for a few seconds before entering the room. His shirt was plastered to his chest in some places, and his hair was obviously damp. His chest was layered with well-defined muscle, and Livvie doubted she'd ever seen such a magnificent sight in all her life. Her eyes widened when she spied his bare feet.

"I did not expect anyone to be here," he said. "I thought you would be asleep by now."

She stared into his eyes for a long moment, hating how distant they seemed. "You've been swimming."

"Yes. And it did not work."

"What did not work?"

"I still want you."

Her heart was in her throat. She had not expected such honesty. "That is why you've been swimming…because you desire me?"

"Yes."

"And is that so terrible?"

"Evidently."

She worked to contain her emotions. "*Why?*"

"I have never hungered for another woman the way I do you," he said. "I do not like it."

Elation surged through her blood. "It seems a bit foolish to be reserved with our passions…we are man and wife, I cannot think of a more permanent union."

"No, I cannot," he said thoughtfully.

He closed the door with a firm *snick* and prowled over to her until he was fairly crowding her against the desk. He nudged her legs apart and gripped her nightgown, pushing it up until he cupped the suddenly aching center of her. Nothing could have prepared Livvie for such a fierce jolt of desire. His throat worked on a swallow, and he closed his eyes as if trying to control whatever he was feeling. She did not give him the chance and instead leaned into him, causing his palm to press against her nub of pleasure. She shivered violently and an answering groan was ripped from him. "Kiss me, Tobias."

The words were barely from her lips when he claimed her mouth in a deep carnal kiss. His mouth slanted over hers again and again.

She arched against him, seeking more of the incredible sensations. He pulled the pins out, and the weight of her hair tumbled to her shoulders. Livvie tugged at his shirt, and with eager touches, tugs, and pulls, Tobias's shirt was discarded. Before she could appreciate his magnificent form, he knelt in front of her, cupped her buttocks, and roughly pulled her up against his mouth.

Dear God, his tongue was rubbing against her most intimate part. Tremors of pleasure coursed through her body, and she bit into her lip to stop the cries wanting to erupt from her. He licked her deep, and Livvie screamed silently and fisted his hair with strength. Her heart pounded, and her knees trembled. Everything seemed as if it was spiraling out of control. His tongue flicked, and then his teeth scraped against her nub of pleasure. If Tobias didn't have such a firm hold on her, she would have collapsed.

He stood, lifted her, and then seated her on the oak desk, spreading her thighs in one powerful motion. A very blunt but wonderful pressure notched at her slick entrance.

"You're so wet," he murmured, his dark green eyes glittering with emotions she could not decipher.

"I can't help it," she whispered on a half groan, needing him to fill her.

With a powerful surge he entered her, and Livvie cried out, gripping his shoulders. Holding her gaze, Tobias glided back and drove forward repeatedly, at times shallow, and then wonderfully hard and deep, filling her with bliss until she climaxed with soul-searing intensity. He kissed her and seconds later he hugged her into a tight embrace, and with a groan, found his own release.

They stayed like that for a few seconds and she became aware she was the only one breathing so erratically. His were even and controlled. Though she had felt such wonderful pleasure, tonight felt different from their night in the closet. In the dark, they had been free, wild, and without restraint.

He pulled from her and she gasped softly. Her core was achy and tender.

"Did I hurt you?"

She found it hard to meet his eyes. "No."

He straightened himself and fished a handkerchief from his pockets and pressed it to her. Livvie fought a blush, staring into the fireplace. They had consummated their vows on a desk in his library. He removed his hands and the cloth and gently tugged her nightgown down so it fluttered to her ankles. At the silence, she turned her head to him. He was staring at her, and Livvie could do nothing but return his regard. His arms went around her waist, gathering her close. Her heart tripped in delight and she all but melted against his bare chest.

"Hello…wife," he said softly, a decidedly puzzled and fascinated vein in his tone.

"Hello…husband," she replied even softer, biting her lower lip to stop its tremble.

His forehead dropped against hers. "My behavior is inexcusable. I pounced on you like a starving man. I should have escorted you to our chambers and—"

"Is there a rule that says wedding nights are most enjoyable in one's chambers?"

"No."

"Then I think we are doing well."

A slow, lazy smile swept across Tobias's face. "You are beautiful, wife," he said, quite unexpectedly.

It felt as if a fist closed over her heart. "I…thank you."

He skimmed his fingers over her cheek almost tentative in his exploration. Then he pressed a kiss to the corner of her lips. It was light, tender, sweet, and soothing. Emotions clogged her throat and a craving for something more surged through her.

"I find I do not want to release you."

Her heart kicked into a furious rhythm. "Then don't."

His eyes bore into hers. "Normally, I would be writing, practicing my fighting arts, or if in Town, visiting one of my clubs."

"I would be painting. I want to paint you…as you are now, so raw and beautiful."

Another slow grin, heartbreakingly sensual, tugged at his lips. Livvie was at a loss as to what was happening…but it felt as if invisible strings were drawing them closer together. She was still seated on the edge of his desk and he was wonderfully close. The intimacy of their situation had a sweet tension pooling through her veins.

"Would you like to play a game of chess?"

Pleasure filled her. "Are you not afraid I will trounce

you?"

His left brow climbed arrogantly. "I accept this challenge."

He lifted her from the desk.

"I was quite capable of dismounting without assistance."

"I like touching you."

"Oh." The very notion pleased her to her toes. There was hope for their marriage after all.

With a grin, she sauntered over to the small table that held the chess set and sat. He joined her and in short order they were engrossed in the game. Thirty minutes later, she murmured, "Checkmate."

Tobias chuckled. "I am fascinated by your strategy. At times reckless, and at other times masterfully brilliant."

The praise stunned her, and acting on instinct, she leaned over and kissed his chin.

They both went absolutely still.

"Did you by chance, countess, miss my lips?"

"No…this arrogant cleft is right where I wanted my mouth," she said huskily.

He smiled and her heart lightened. She wasn't about to wallow in misery. Life could only move forward and she resolved to make the best of her marriage. In time, affection and trust would surely develop between her and the earl. In fact, she would work to ensure it.

Chapter Thirteen

Tobias dipped the tip of the quill into the inkwell for the last time. Deep into the fictional world he had created, it took him a few moments to realize there was a steady knocking at the door of his library. He frowned. The entire staff knew that right after breaking his fast, he ensconced himself in his library for at least two hours writing his novels, before facing the duties he had to deal with for his many estates. "Who is it?"

"It's Livvie."

A blast of pleasure filled him. He froze. Unusual indeed. He had been trying his damnedest to not recall their wedding night and the depth of strength it had taken not to lose himself in her as he had done in the closet. Her fragrance lingered on his fingers, her taste on his lips, and in the deep recesses of his heart, he wished he had been untamed with her. "Enter."

The handle twisted and when she appeared, his mouth dried. Her loveliness was very fresh and appealing. Her dark red tresses were caught in a simple chignon, and a few tendrils caressed her cheeks. She wore a pale blue high-waisted dress, and she had a book clasped in her hands. His heart jolted when he saw it was a copy of *In the Service of the Crown*. "You read the work of Aikens?"

A wide smile stretched her lips. "Yes, do you?" she asked excitedly. "It's clever and intriguing, and I highly recommend it."

He grunted noncommittally, but raw pleasure blasted through him. She liked his writing. "I see."

"Aikens's work is quite wonderful," she gushed, more earnest than ever. "I urge you to read *In the Service of the Crown*. I have the first eight volumes with me, if you wish to borrow them."

Masking his delight at her praise, he casually leaned back in his chair. "I'd not thought such books were suitable for a young lady."

She rolled her eyes. "I daresay if men can read it, women can. There is nothing there to shock and traumatize us delicate young ladies. Unless you count the few kisses and seduction Wrotham has employed to retrieve secrets?"

Good God. Kisses and seduction? Tobias knew damn well he wrote more scandalous encounters than mere kisses.

"Which volume are you?"

"I am at volume seven."

It was volume eight and nine that dealt with the ruthless art of seduction. Should he allow her to read further? He recalled promising not to censure her reading choices.

"What are you writing?"

He glanced down at the loose sheaf of papers and quickly organized them into a pile, then opened his top drawer, laid them down neatly, and locked it with a key. He did not share his writing with anyone but his publisher. He did not consent to interviews, nor to public appearances. He was truly anonymous and his publisher was bound by a very strict and ironclad contract to never reveal that the Earl of Blade was

Theodore Aikens. As a child, he'd been desperate to escape the violence in his home, and he'd found his sanctuary in books. When the stories in his library had no longer offered Tobias the comfort he sought, he'd created the world he craved, a world where he had complete and utter control of all characters, emotions, and situations. It was such a private part of him, he wondered then if he would ever be able to share such an intimate side of him with his countess. *Perhaps never.*

After pocketing the key, he glanced up.

Wicked laughter danced in her eyes. "It's a secret. I like secrets, and it's quite evident, my lord, you possess one." She sauntered over to the desk, trailing the tip of her finger across the hardwood desk.

Just looking at her made him ache to touch her, to take her. He pushed from the chair and stood. "Then it's best I take care to hide my key."

She chuckled, then sobered. It was then he spied the wariness in her eyes and understood. He had been struggling to find his equilibrium since she had entered his life, how unsettling things must be for her as well. He now had a *wife*… and he was at a loss as what to do with her. His days were structured to write, manage his estates, write motions for parliament, practice his fighting forms, and, if he needed, visit a lover in London. A tightness settled in his chest. Olivia was truly his wife. He had to learn to share his time and interests.

"Mrs. Potter gave me a tour of the estate. I tried to tell her I have been living here for weeks, but she was not deterred. Grangeville Park is very happily situated and it is a wonderful estate."

Five years ago, the estate had been crumbling. He'd spent thousands of pounds to restore it to such beauty, and he liked the admiration he spied in her gaze. "Thank you."

"I was advised by Mother to take an interest in several

charities. I find I am very keen on the idea," she said with a smile. "But I have no notion where to start." She cleared her throat. "Would you...would you like to take a stroll through the gardens and discuss the merits of which charities would benefit from my patronage? I confess, I do not like the dowager countess's recommendation, and I shall not heed her advice," she said with evident pleasure.

"A stroll?"

"It is a beautiful day out."

He considered her. "I am involved in a project with the Marquess of Westfall. We are working on building homes and schools for the more poor and destitute of our society. Buildings are being constructed as we speak. There is one that will be finished in a few weeks. It would be good if you could produce some paintings to brighten the house."

Pleasure lit her eyes and the smile she gave him was so brilliant, he was rendered momentarily speechless.

"That would be wonderful, Tobias. And when you say the more vulnerable of our society...women and children?"

"Yes...those who were rescued from brutal situations. Orphans. The homeless. Invalided soldiers."

There was a sharp knock on the door. "Yes?"

The knob twisted and their butler, Ferguson, entered with what appeared to be a letter on a slaver. "This was left for you by Lady Francie, my lord. She gave strict instructions that it was not to be delivered before ten a.m."

Tobias took it, and the butler excused himself. He retrieved the letter opener from his desk and slit the seal. He read the note, then read it over again, sure it must be a jest on Francie's part.

"Tobias, is all well?"

Dear Tobias,

Please do not berate me too harshly when you receive my missive. I instructed it to be delivered when I was well away from the estate, and in truth, by now I am sure I am Mrs. Browning. I've run away to Gretna Green with Mr. Jasper Browning, your steward.

Tobias was even more certain now that this could only be an elaborate ruse. He glanced at his wife. "Did you put Francie up to this nonsense?"

Olivia's brow arched. "I have not seen Francie since last night, and I assure you, I have not put her up to anything."

The confusion in his wife's voice had foreboding slithering through Tobias. "Her note is dated yesterday."

Olivia leaned over. "May I?"

He nodded and she plucked the note from his grasp. She started to read and then paled alarmingly.

Cold fury surged through his veins. This was not a jest. "Read aloud," he bit coldly, pointing to where she should resume.

The hands holding the letter trembled. "Tobias, I—"

"Aloud, countess."

She shifted with perceptible uneasiness. Smoothing the edges of the paper, she read, "I love Jasper, but I knew you would not hear of my affections for him. He is romantic, a poetic soul who loves everything about me. I've been in love with him for several months now. I had doubts, but in confiding in Livvie, I saw how much I must follow my own heart and to not be misled by society's opinion or my family's dictate to wed a gentleman of their choice. Jasper is the man of my dreams and I have followed it. Livvie assured me if I married my heart, you would not be cruel enough to remove me from my inheritance. I only pray that she is right. I have her love and approval, and upon our return, I pray to have yours and Mamma's."

His wife's fingers tightened on the letter, then she glanced up. "Oh dear."

Oh dear?

• • •

Cold rage leaped in Tobias's eyes, riveting Livvie to the spot. Instincts told her the remainder of the morning would not unfold how she had imagined—strolling by the lake while discussing what's next in this unexpectedly thrilling but very frightening adventure they'd embarked upon.

Oh, Francie, what were you thinking?

He gave her a sharp, impatient look. "I await your explanation, wife."

She had never seen him this angry before, and for some unfathomable reason, his quality of stillness made her unaccountably nervous. She walked away from him, needing the space from his imposing presence to think. *God*, what had Francie been thinking? To elope?

"I knew Francie was in love with someone and that she was worried about your reaction. I thought he was a younger son of a lord or an impoverished lord. I…I never imagined he was your steward."

Tobias strolled to the side mantle and poured himself a splash of brandy, which he downed in one swallow, then he poured another before walking over to his desk. He lowered himself onto the edge with his legs sprawled. Livvie was not fooled. She could feel the tension vibrating from him. She was grateful for his restraint.

"My sister is now *ruined* and *you* encouraged her in her fancy," he murmured.

"The letter says they are to be married," she said softly, though her heart was twisting. How would they weather the scandal to come? What if someone had recognized her before they were married? Livvie pressed fingers to her pounding forehead. Even when they were recovered it would be perceived as a disaster. The daughter of an earl married to a commoner.

She met Tobias's gaze and faltered. He was glaring at her with accusation and what seemed like contempt. "Their marriage—"

His hard mouth curved faintly. "And are you naive enough to believe marriage will render my sister respectable after she slipped away in the night with...Mr. Browning, a man who is obviously a debauched fortune hunter, unchaperoned?" The glass filled with amber liquid snapped between Tobias's fingers, betraying the depth of his fury. With cool aplomb, he dusted away the shards, placed the remnants of the broken glass on the desk beside him, then withdrew a handkerchief and cleaned his bloody fingers.

Her heart jolted at the controlled anger evident in his actions. She looked to the broken crystal and swallowed. The rumors she had heard hinted at a terrible temper, though she had yet to see it. Not that she believed him to be good-natured and amiable, but certainly not as fearsome as a few of the ladies had hinted at behind their fans at the last ball. In fact, the man before her now appeared as if his emotions were locked away in a cold, remote place inside of him. "You're bleeding, Tobias," she said as ruby drops settled on the peach carpet.

"It's negligible."

She glanced up into dark eyes. "Let me assist you."

"A small cut is not important in the circumstances, countess."

"I am truly regretful Francie acted in such a ruinous manner. I do believe her to genuinely love Mr. Browning and that he holds a strong attachment for her. I cannot credit she could—"

"Since our acquaintance, you have continually courted the edge of propriety. With her willful action, my sister has shown she has little respect for her stance in society or the power of scandal that has already gutted our family. Your stupidity in believing in love and fairytales are what prompted my sister to act in such a wanton and reckless manner."

Anger stirred in Livvie's breast. "I—"

He pushed from the desk and prowled closer. "From the moment I saw your reckless and unseemly influence I should have moved to reduce your effect on her," he snapped.

Tears burned in her eyes, and she brushed aside the uneasiness his words triggered. "I assure you, I did nothing but advise your sister to act according to her heart. I told her to inform you of the attachment she formed. I never imagined she would elope. I would have advised her against it, Tobias."

The coldest green eyes considered her. "The deed has been done. Now I must once again work to fix my family's foolish behavior."

"If they are already married—"

"I assure you, I will not allow such a marriage to stand. I will ensure a legal declaration is made to a solicitor of law and then the magistrate will sign all relevant documents." He was, in this moment, the epitome of a man sure of his strength.

"And if Francie truly loves him and he her?"

"Without her inheritance or monetary support from her family, his supposed love will wither," he said with cutting scorn.

A pang sliced through her heart as she recalled one of Francie's passionate assurances as she'd spoken about her mysterious suitor.

He loves me, Livvie, truly. We are two souls connecting as one.

"Would you prefer your sister to be trapped in a loveless marriage, one without any genuine affections and respect? Is it truly better for Francie to be wedded to a man who has no regard for her beyond her fortune, but because he is a lord, the marriage is a good match?" Livvie demanded, shocked by his pronouncement.

"Yes."

She jerked. "You are cruel. It was ill judged of Francie to act in such a ruinous manner, but I believe she was being true to her heart. Mr. Browning has been your steward for some time. Should you not know the manner of man he is, and know whether Francie will be cared for?"

A hard, cynical smile twisted his lips. "I know exactly the kind of man he is, and I am still trying to decide if I will kill him when I recover my sister."

Alarm filled her. "Please tell me what you know."

"I am leaving. I must find my sister, have the ridiculous marriage annulled, and squash a scandal. It's best when I return that you are at another of my estates."

She recoiled. *What?* "You're sending me away?"

"It is wise, countess, for you to be elsewhere for a while. Your presence is not calming or reassuring, for I have been envisioning wringing your pretty little neck and am doing my damnedest to convince myself otherwise," he growled, the anger burning his eyes even greener.

Then he marched away and closed the door with a soft *snick*.

Livvie sucked in a deep breath and hurried after Tobias. His long strides took him up the stairs and it was as if the household exploded into a flurry of action as he clipped orders and they acted with alacrity to obey. She lifted her dress and dashed up the stairs. Upon reaching his chamber, she burst in. His valet, Mr. Ackers, lifted a startled glance in her direction.

"If you will excuse us, Mr. Ackers, I would confer with the earl in privacy."

Tobias did not spare her a glance. Instead, he continued

shrugging into his jacket without the aid of his valet.

"I…I am traveling with you. Francie will need me."

He took a greatcoat from the armoire and dragged it on, then placed his hat firmly on his head. "No."

"I must accompany you, Tobias, please."

"No."

"I will order the carriage and travel to Francie on my own. I cannot in good conscience abandon her now."

His lips twitched, but she did not think he was amused. "It seems you have forgotten that we are married. Let me enlighten you, countess. I can give orders for you to not leave the estate and it will be enforced."

Good Lord, was he serious? Livvie suppressed her outrage and glowered at him. It was important that Francie have an ally when he caught up to her. Though she had the boldness to elope, Tobias's personality was so forceful and ruthless, neither she nor Mr. Browning would stand a chance in the face of his resolve to procure an annulment. If Livvie could convince him on the trip to Scotland that what his sister felt was genuine love and not some foolish fancy, then maybe Francie would have a chance at happiness.

"You are being wretched. Your sister…I know you love her and her heart will be greatly relieved if I am with you when you catch up with them. My presence will be a comfort to her. I can only imagine how uncertain she is at this very moment."

"No."

"Tobias, please—"

"I have no intention of traveling by coach. I will be taking my fastest and strongest stallion and in a few hours I shall be in Scotland. The way I intend to travel is no way for a lady."

She steeled herself against his anger. "I am just as skilled as you at riding horses. Think of how good such a journey would be for us as well, we can get to know each other."

"I see you have forgotten that my thoughts are filled with wringing your neck."

She pursed her lips. *This man!* "I believe I know where Francie and Mr. Browning are headed."

The intensity in his look almost frightened her.

"You are truly in denial of your position, aren't you?" Then he took a menacing step toward her.

She backed up warily and he froze.

"Are you afraid of me?"

He held himself so still that she recognized her answer was of crucial importance to him. "You can appear intimidating, but I am not afraid."

A soft sigh of what sounded like relief slipped from him.

"Pack lightly. I will order a coach with a team of two for you."

A strong sense of relief washed through her. "It will only be a few hours to cross the border, I am happy to ride beside you on my horse."

Cold eyes caressed her face, before a fleeting smile touched his lips. "Is that so?"

"Yes, do you think me unequal to the task?"

"Perhaps."

"I have ridden past the River Eske before into Scotland with my papa before he died. I was *ten*. It is one of my fonder memories of him. I assure you, I am an excellent rider and that way, we shall be in Scotland in only a few hours and at the Rose Cottage before nightfall."

His eyes as he stared were piercing, and she suddenly felt vulnerable. Why had she mentioned her father? She hardly ever spoke of her memories of him with anyone.

"I should have known...the Rose Cottage. We visited several times when our grandmother was alive."

"Francie never confided in me that she was running away there, but she often spoke of it with love and wistfulness. I also know she has not been there in years and it…it seems likely to me she would head there with Mr. Browning instead of an inn surrounded by strangers."

"Be ready within the hour, wife."

He grabbed a cane from his armoire, and strode from the room, no doubt heading to the stables.

She hurriedly rang the bell for her lady's maid.

Exactly an hour after the news of Francie's elopement, Livvie was packed lightly but sensibly for a trip to Scotland. Her hair had been plaited in a very tight coronet and she dressed in her finest and most practical riding habit with a pleated skirt, comfortable sturdy riding boots, and a dark blue velvet over jacket. She hurried down to the stables to see two of the most magnificent stallions in the earl's stables saddled and ready. Tobias was already seated atop his horse.

"You are allowing me to ride Arius?"

"Yes."

She glanced at his fittings. "Astride?"

"I have observed you riding several times, you are a capable rider."

She fisted a hand on her hip. "*Capable*?"

"In truth, I have never seen a better horsewoman."

Pleasure warmed her. "Thank you, Tobias."

He launched from his horse and strolled over to her. He took the small valise and secured it at the back of her horse, then gripped her waist and helped her astride. "Are you comfortable?"

She smiled, happy he was not cold or snarling. If he was still angry, it was carefully buried. "I am."

The housekeeper hurried outside with a tightly wrapped bundle. She handed it to Livvie.

"Just something to tide you over milady. Bread, cheese, a few apples, and a flask of wine."

"Thank you, Mrs. Potter," Livvie said warmly, and the

housekeeper glowed.

After ensuring the food was properly secured, she grabbed Arius's reins and cantered off, following Tobias. She said a swift prayer, hoping they would indeed find Francie and her lover at the Rose Cottage. She didn't want to think of how Tobias would react if they didn't.

Chapter Fourteen

Lust was making a mockery out of his will to be in control in all aspects of his life with his new countess. Tobias never imagined he could be so…well, *weak* with a female. This did not bode well for the future state of their marriage. He rode ahead on his horse, not trusting himself to ride alongside her.

Somehow during their argument, he had deemed it safer for his wife to accompany him in retrieving his sister. Olivia had not manipulated him with tears and tantrums. Instead, she had only been kind. She had been worried about Francie, a sentiment he shared only too well. He'd finally realized she would need the comfort of a woman, especially if the bounder had seduced and abandon her, as most cads in society did to the young ladies they preyed on.

Tobias had been at a loss where to start his search, only knowing to head to Gretna Green first. Hopefully a few coins tossed here and there would provide a trail as to where she had headed with his steward. He feared it was already too late to prevent the marriage, but by God if they traveled without stopping, they should make it to Rose Cottage before their consummation of the vow.

Tobias thought of the possible scandals and the influence he would have to exert to protect Francie. She would be cut by all who had called her their friend and she would no longer be welcomed in any drawing room. He wondered if she had even considered the full consequences of her actions before she decided to elope. It was damn likely not, for no doubt she had convinced herself she was acting with her bloody heart. *Stupid chit.* What in God's name had she been thinking? Tobias fought down his rising uneasiness. Nothing good was ever accomplished by giving into rash emotions.

There was a clatter of hooves and his countess appeared beside him. He fished his watch from the top pocket of his coat. Olivia had managed to last two hours riding in silence. He was impressed. He glanced at her and softly sucked in a breath. She glowed. It was then he realized she was in her element. In the ballroom she had seemed so restricted, but now…a smile bloomed on her lips, her posture on the horse was one of supreme confidence, and there was joy in her face. A yearning to truly know her welled within him. "Tell me about your father."

She shot him a startled glance. "My father?"

"Yes."

"Why?"

"I am curious about you."

Her eyes widened. "I am not sure if the best place to start is with Papa."

"I find that we tend to be defined by the actions of our fathers. So I say it is a good place to start."

"Do you speak from experience?

He exhaled slowly. "I do."

She considered him for a brief moment. "My father was the Baron Harcourt, and I am sure you know the scandal surrounding his name."

"From time to time I may hear rumors, but I do not listen to them."

One of her shoulders lifted in an inelegant shrug. "Papa did not love my mother. He married her because she was an heiress and he needed her money. He gambled and whored it away," she said bluntly. "He met someone he loved dearly. They had an affair. When her husband threatened to take her children if she did not end the affair, she agreed. He killed himself," she ended flatly. "And he left me and Mamma to face his debts and the horrid scandal alone. According to the *ton*, I have the taint of his blood in my veins."

Tobias considered the manner in which her fingers clenched and unclenched on the reins.

"Do you have good memories?" he asked softly, remembering each time someone asked of his father, they had only desired to hear the worst, not the good that had been present. Good memories never made for salacious and ruinous gossip.

A shadow crossed her face. "I...I loved him," she said defiantly. "And there are days when I feel I still do."

He arched a brow. "It is usual for one to love their father. Mine was a reckless libertine, a wastrel, and yet, for years, I wanted to emulate him." He'd never said that aloud to anyone in his life.

The horses slowed to a more even canter and her thighs brushed against his as they rode with companionable ease. It was peaceful, and he was suddenly glad for her company. The last thing he desired in this moment was to be in his own head, imagining the varied ways he would gut his steward. Perhaps burying his body in an isolated cave, except surely his family would want his remains to bury.

"My father taught me to ride, fish, swim, and the rudiments of fencing," she finally said wistfully. "Papa never regretted that he did not have a son. He treated me like I was cherished, and I was allowed to run wild, though most of the neighbors complained. Of course, if I had been a boy, my behavior would not have been considered outrageous. He simply loved me for me."

"He sounds admirable."

She stiffened, pain darkening her pale catlike eyes. "He was…he was wonderful and a hero in my eyes, until…until he left us. The pain of his betrayal overshadowed everything else in our lives for months, years," she said, her breath hitching on a soft sob.

He nudged his horse even closer to hers. Her eyes were red, and if he was not mistaken, she was valiantly holding on to her tears. Regret soured his tongue. "Forgive my questions, Olivia, you do not have to speak of it. I can see it still pains you."

She tossed her head. "I am well. Now you tell me of your father."

It was his turn to be discomfited. "My father was jealous and obsessed with my mother."

He felt the caress of her gaze on his face, but he did not look at her. "He was?"

"Yes."

His heart started to pound as the memories started to swirl.

"What happened?" Olivia questioned softly.

"Every man who admired Mother was a threat. Father would be wild with jealousy if another man dared to dance with her. I remember at my first ball, Father dragged her from the ballroom, out of Lord Gresham's arms. She threw champagne in his face and he slung her over his shoulder. That scandal roared through the *ton* for weeks. Everywhere I went there was pointing and whispers."

She gasped. "I cannot credit it!"

"I had known of my father's temper and my mother's

fieriness, but I never knew society was also aware of their volatility."

"Is that why you are so…reserved with your feelings? You dread being similar?"

He met her curious eyes then. "Yes," he said, burying the darker part of his legacy behind a small smile. "I strive to not be as careless with my tempers." If she only knew what he worked to bury. He glanced up at the swirling dark clouds. Rain was imminent. "We need to find shelter."

"Are we not close to the Rose Cottage?"

"At least an hour's hard ride."

"I can take a hard ride, Tobias."

The illicit images of giving his wife a very hard ride, and the brutal desires her words evoked, robbed him of breath.

He cleared his throat. "We will not beat the rain. If my memory serves, there is an old hunting cottage a few minutes east of here." He glanced around him. "Stay here, in the open plain. I will check to ensure there are no occupants."

"I shall follow you."

Exasperation rushed through him. "No. Anyone could be using the cottage as a refuge. It would be better if I am allowed to assume the risk to investigate."

"And I am safe here?" she demanded incredulously, her eyes sweeping the land far and wide.

"Yes," he said drily. "You can see if anyone approaches for miles out. Ride in my direction if you feel threatened."

She pouted but nodded in acquiescence. Stifling his grin, he urged his horse in the direction where he knew the cottage to be. A few minutes later, he broke through a thicket into a clearing. There were brambles and wild flowers on the forest floor and the place had an air of abandonment. He launched off the horse and allowed the reins to dangle. The trees there were so thick, the horses should have some relief from the icy rain that was about to come.

He marched up the three steps leading to the cottage and tested the handle. It opened. Inside was empty but very dusty. It would have to do. A quick check showed there was a stockpile of logs and a lantern on the small wooden table beneath the window.

Thunder rumbled, and Tobias moved with quick efficiency and in a short time had the lantern lit and the fireplace kindling. The fire would be roaring by the time he returned with Olivia. He went outside and whistled for his horse. He mounted and rode off back to where he left his wife. In the distance, he saw Arius unmounted. He slowed to a canter. Tobias stilled, certain he heard voices.

"I will most certainly not allow you to search my person. I will not hesitate to box your ears," a clipped voice said sternly.

The woman sounded like his countess, but the idea was so ludicrous it did not bear contemplation. He had told her to wait while he investigated the cottage. Silently dismounting and lowering the reins, he slipped his hand inside his coat and gripped the curved handle of his dagger. Then he padded quietly toward the voice.

A loud crack sounded, and he belatedly realized it was a slap from the curse spilling from the man.

"Ouch, lass. Yer a strong one, mon."

"How dare you, sir. You touched my bosoms. I assure you, I have no hidden jewels in my décolletage, and when my husband, the Earl of Blade, hears about this, you will sorely regret it."

God's blood.

Tobias scrubbed a hand over his face in disbelief. Silly woman did not realize it was best to pretend to have no connections.

"An earl, ye said?" the man asked speculatively.

"Yes, and he has a fearsome and terrifying temper. I assure you, sir, he will be very displeased that you have accosted his countess."

Fearsome and terrifying temper? What had his wife heard about him? He assessed the robber, noting he was more a boy than a full-grown man. He appeared lean, of a similar height to Olivia, and had a cloth covering his face partially. Tobias knew better than to underestimate him because of his young years.

The robber rubbed his chin. "Countess, ye say?"

With a sigh, Tobias strolled forward from behind the trees. He was still at loss if he should be amused or infuriated. When she spied him, her eyes lighted with pleasure and relief. The daft woman had no notion of the depth of trouble she was in.

"Oh, thank heavens, Tobias."

The robber spun around, his aim steady with the pistol pointing at Tobias. "You be the earl?"

"I am," he answered, standing so the dagger was held close to his sleeve.

"A rich earl?"

"Yes."

Delight widened the highwayman's eyes, then they narrowed in suspicion. "Yer awfully accommodating, aren't you?" he asked, taking a few steps back from Tobias and toward Olivia. He knew his size was not reassuring and the boy grew jittery after his thorough inspection of Tobias.

"A bit." He did not want to alarm the already nervous boy, because he might accidentally harm Olivia. The very idea of any injury befalling his reckless lady had a bitter taste filling his mouth. "I have several gold coins you may have. And a dagger. Its handle is encrusted with emeralds. Take them and leave."

The boy's eyes narrowed in speculation and greed.

Olivia gasped, and spluttered, fisting a hand on her hip. "And you call me reckless? Have you not read Samuel Johnson's *A Journey to the Western Islands of Scotland*? It is never wise to travel with a fortune because of fellows like this," she said, waving her hand toward the highwayman. "Also—"

"Be quiet," Tobias said.

She glared at him but obeyed.

"I may be wantin' more than what ye offerin'," the boy said with a touch of uncertainty.

"That is not possible."

The boy waved toward Olivia. "Or I may have to do something unpleasant to her," he said, taking a threatening step in her direction.

"That would not be wise," Tobias said, going cold. The boy was now pointing the pistol in the direction of his countess. Why the hell had Tobias agreed to take her with him? Who the hell would have expected a bandit on this less traveled and remote country road?

"Listen 'ere—"

Tobias allowed his dagger to fly from his hand with precision. It buried itself in the boy's arm, and with a bellow, he dropped the pistol. Before he could recover, Tobias was on him. He kicked his legs from underneath him, straddled him, and dragged off the makeshift mask.

"Christ."

He couldn't be more than fourteen summers.

"Help me," the boy pleaded toward Olivia.

She swiftly ran over. Without Tobias saying anything, she grabbed the cloth the boy had used to cover his face and tied it around his wound. He wailed, his arm twitching.

"Shut up," Tobias growled.

"There is a very large knife sticking out of his shoulder," she said faintly. "And he is in pain, Tobias."

"He deserves to be in pain. He is very fortunate I did not kill him. In fact, I may very well slit his throat for inconveniencing me."

The boy wailed even louder.

She shot him an irritated look. "Hush now," she said sympathetically. "He does not mean it."

Tobias glared at her. "If you'd stayed where I told you, this would have been avoided."

"I was saving you," she gasped.

Anger and annoyance snapped through him in equal measure. "No, you were being reckless and rebellious!"

Her eyes flashed. "I saw this…this…I have no clue what he is, creeping in the direction of where you headed and I decided to warn you. He looked very alarming with the cloth over his face and the pistol in his hand, I could not allow him to come upon you unaware. My only thoughts were of protecting you, Tobias! Not deliberately being willful and… reckless. Somehow he noticed me, and well, you know the rest."

Protecting me? Though his heart jerked at the notion, he was not mollified. The fear that had torn through his heart when he'd realized the bounder had a pistol pointed to her heart had been a brutal punch to his system. "He could have shot you…or done worse, countess. Abducted you, robbed and slit your throat before you could sound an alert. But I can see it was truly ridiculous of me to expect you to act in an obedient or ladylike manner."

It was never more evident to him that he could not truly rely on his wife to behave in the expected manner. Her temper was too uncertain, and she was too willful.

She winced, and if he was not mistaken, hurt darkened her eyes.

"I'm bleeding to death here," the boy grumbled. "A wee bit of attention on me wouldn't be bad."

Tobias hauled him up quite roughly, and the boy swayed.

His wife scrambled to her feet. "What are you going to do with him?"

"Take him to the law."

The boy paled, and his countess gasped.

She touched his arms fleetingly, a frown on her face. "Tobias, he is just a boy."

"This *boy* had a pistol pointed at you a few minutes ago and threatened to shoot you."

"I dinna mean it, mon," he said, staring at Tobias with wide eyes. "Surely I dinna mean it. She is a countess, I dinna want to be hanged, so I bluffed."

"See," Olivia said eagerly. "He meant me—us—no harm. He was bluffing, weren't you?" she said with a pointed glare.

The boy nodded vigorously, clutching his arm.

Tobias pushed him away and the boy stumbled. "Get out of here."

He turned and started scampering toward a small dappled horse.

"Wait," Olivia called out.

"What in God's name should he wait for?" Tobias snapped.

She turned to him. "Will you still give him the coins? I am sure he would not have attempted a robbery if he was not in need."

After a gape of apparent disbelief, the boy nodded his agreement most ardently.

Surely she was jesting. "He should be grateful I did not thrash him."

Disappointment flashed across her face. Tobias tipped his head to the sky and pinched the bridge of his nose. It confounded him that he wanted to please her when she had so disgruntled him with her willful ways. Stifling a sigh, he threw the small bag of gold he had to robber. The boy darted and grabbed it with speed. When he felt its weight, his eyes widened. "Thank ye, I willna forget yer kindness," he muttered, then ran to his horse and rode away.

Pleasure gleamed in his wife's gaze. "Thank you, Tobias."

The sky chose that moment to open with biting cold rain. He whistled for the horses. "This way," he yelled, grabbing his countess's arm and running in the direction of the cottage. She ran beside him, surprisingly keeping pace. A few minutes later they broke through the thicket and the cottage came into view. As they scrambled up the step, Olivia slipped. With a grunt, he tried to prevent her fall, but failed miserably. He twisted, tumbling with her so that she landed on him with a soft *oof* against the forest floor.

They scrambled to their feet and instead of dashing up the step and into the cottage, they stood in the rain, staring at each other. A wide grin stretched her beguiling mouth and it was a brilliant, dazzling smile. He was utterly perplexed what to do about the sensations winding through his heart. The damn organ jerked and a weak feeling suffused his pores. He was desperate to taste her again, to feel her wet, tight heat clamped on his cock. *Damnation*. That was an unfamiliar experience.

Her grin stretched even wider and then a full-throated laugh escaped her. Tobias stared in bemusement, wondering why in this moment she looked so damned beautiful, so perfect. *His wife*. Her hair spilled in waves about her shoulders, and she had a few twigs perched atop her glorious mess.

"Come on," he muttered, grabbing her hand, "for if you fall ill and die, I'll simply lay you to rest here in these woods."

They scrambled up the steps with care, her giggling the entire way and him thinking he was very glad indeed he had brought her with him.

• • •

Livvie was somewhat warm, startlingly aroused, and most contented. Heavy rain whipped against the grimy window. The cottage was very tiny, but so cozy and delightful. She was in her chemise only, as most of their clothes hung on the small grate by the fire drying.

"Wouldn't it be wonderful to live somewhere like this?"

"No."

She threw her husband a withering glare. "You are still being churlish because I tried to rescue you?"

"What I should have done the minute we reached the cottage was turn you over my knees and tan your backside. It is evident you were in sore need of discipline growing up."

Instead, she was sitting in his lap because everywhere else was too dusty and they had dragged the one great chair close to the fireplace. She was most comfortably situated atop his very obvious reaction to her nearness. Her earl desired her. Livvie grinned and wiggled in his lap, and he cursed.

"You little minx, you did that deliberately."

"I believe I did."

"You would not be so smug if I tossed up your skirt right here in this chair and took you, amongst the dust and all," he growled.

"Is that possible?"

He stiffened.

"You must show me, Tobias," she purred, deliberately sliding her bottom against his arousal.

His soft chuckle sounded strained. "No. The latch on the door is broken and we must be vigilant. I also promised myself the next time I seduced my wife, it would be in a bed."

She relaxed into him even more, soaking up the warmth from this body. She swore the heat from him was even more delicious than that coming from the fireplace. "Do you think the boy will return?"

"If he is foolish, mayhap. But he should be contented with the gold I gave him. It was quite hefty."

"Thank you for being so kind."

He grunted.

She smiled. "Is it not odd we are sitting here, me in your lap, and dare I say it, we are contented?"

"I am still thinking of wringing your neck, Olivia," he said, then pressed a soft kiss to the spot where he must have been imagining wrapping his fingers.

She twisted and glared at him. He was smiling, and his relaxed charm drove the air from her lungs. She leaned in and pressed a kiss to his lips. With a sigh, she deepened the kiss and moaned when he responded. She withdrew and stared into his eyes, which glowed with unreserved passion. "Tobias?"

"Hmmm?"

"I ache."

The tension in the room shot up perceptibly. "Do not tempt me, Olivia."

A laugh caught in her throat. "I will endeavor to behave."

"Do more than try, wife, succeed."

"Thank you for taking me with you. I know it could not have been easy with you wanting to…gently clasp my neck between your hands," she said with an unrepentant grin.

He smiled, and it was so sensually charming her breath caught. "Thank you for accompanying me. Your presence kept the demons from my head."

She pressed her forehead against his. "I truly believe Francie will be well. Mr. Browning—"

Tobias's hands tightened on her hips, almost painfully, and his dark brows came together in a harsh forbidding line. "He is a vile seducer who can possess no true regard for my sister. He has exposed her to scandal, ridicule, and scorn. If he held genuine affections he would have approached me for her hand."

"And would you not have denied him?"

A scowl darkened his face.

"I am not defending Mr. Browning's actions," she hurriedly assured Tobias. "I am only hoping you can understand what may have prompted them to not declare themselves. Francie admires and loves you above all else. I would hate to see her grievously injured by your anger and disappointment."

His face shuttered.

Livvie encircled his neck with her hand, gently playing with the curl of hair at his nape. "I enjoy cream of parsnip soup, boiled duck in apricot sauce, and gooseberries," she said lightly, hoping to distract him from the dark thoughts she could see gathering in his eyes. If she could not seduce him, the best way to pass the time was to learn of each other. She was rather looking forward to it.

For a timeless moment, he said nothing, and the steady drumming of the rain on the roof and against the windows were the only sounds echoing in the small room.

"I like beef á la royale and Bakewell tarts."

Pleasure burst inside of her, and she quickly shared something else. "One of my greatest desires is to establish myself as a respected painter."

He frowned. "Selling your work?"

"Yes."

"All that I own is yours. You have no need to work."

"Wrong," she said softly, unable to resist the temptation of kissing the cleft on his chin. "All that you own belongs to your heir…our son, if we are blessed enough in that regard. And even if I were the richest woman in the world, I would still desire to see my paintings gracing many homes and even a gallery. I've also thought about attending the Royal Academy."

His breathing changed, roughening when she kissed the corner of his lips.

"For many years I dreamed of having my own money and not being dependent on a man, whether he be my father or a husband."

Her earl tipped back his head, his dark gaze searching

hers. "And why is that?"

"The months following my father's suicide were the worst I have ever experienced. It was as if I had passed over, into a fantastical caricature of what my life had been. In this new life, misfortune and hunger were frequent companions. And this had all happened at the whim of a man, a husband, a father. All my mother could do was cry and put herself at the mercy of another man to improve our situation."

"I see."

"I never wanted to endure that. I wanted to be able to support myself with a comfortable living."

He gathered her even closer. "The first thing I did the morning we married was notify my attorney to open an account in your name. A sum of twenty thousand pounds was deposited and an annuity will be added. When I die, I promise you, countess, you will be well situated financially. I also want you to select two of my un-entailed estates when we return, and they will be a part of your widow's portion."

Livvie could only stare at him in shock. "I...thank you."

A disquieting silence lingered. She had never expected him to be so protective and generous. "We suffered the degradation of poverty...so says my mother. But were we truly poor? I've read of the slums in the newspapers, the calls for reform to help those suffering. I cannot imagine living in such squalor as what is reported. There are so many homeless children. I visited London once with Mamma while our troops were fighting Napoleon and dozens of children accosted us, begging." She shuddered. "They were so dirty, covered in soot and grime, and they stank. In their eyes, Tobias, I only saw emptiness, despair. No hope for the future or a better tomorrow. I have been reading your arguments on how society needs to pull together and render assistance to those whom England has abandoned and...you have my deepest admiration," she ended softly.

A glint entered his eyes, and he had the most arrested expression. "Most of the *ton* thinks I am foolish."

"But not all, and those are the ones we should concentrate upon to gain their support for the thousands so in need."

A decidedly arrogant brow arched. "We?"

"Yes…I want to help in every way I can," she declared loyally.

"Then I will be sure to include you in Westfall's and my next meeting."

"I've heard rumors of the marquess. His daughter…"

Shadows darkened Tobias's eyes. "She was once one of those poor and abandoned children of England. No more. The *ton* may not claim her, but she is loved by the marquess and his true friends."

Livvie smiled. "I'm glad."

His head bent and he kissed the side of her neck. Though she wanted to dally in pleasure, she feared never getting such an opportunity where they spoke with such relaxed frankness. "Tell me more of your family."

He stilled and lifted his head. A faint sound of amusement slipped from him, though his eyes blanked. "No."

"All I am privy to is rumors, I daresay that is not the way to gain knowledge of my new family. Did your parents love each other, despite everything?"

He slanted her a considering glance. "On many occasion my father beat my mother, quite harshly. Yet perplexingly, she loved him."

"I do hope you are aware that you are nothing like that."

He cocked his head and her stomach tightened to see the doubt lingering in his gaze. How could he believe such a thing?

"For years, I dreaded being like him. I was quick to temper and volatile. I got in many fights in my younger days and he was proud to say how alike we were. Father would have been even prouder if I had become a debauched rake like himself."

Her heart thudded at his revelation. "I am so very sorry, Tobias."

"Francie was afraid of him and it was my job to protect her. It is still my job and will always be my duty to care and protect her." His jaw visibly clenched. "Mother started an affair because she learned of Grayson's existence. Our father discovered and his rage knew no bounds. He beat our mother with a riding crop most severely. Francie was beside herself with tears and in a bid to silence her hysteria, he hurt her. My father and I fought…and I revealed in my character that I was just as volatile and merciless as he." Every word he uttered was wrapped in a layer of ice and contempt.

"What did you do?"

His eyes darkened to jade. "I broke my father's hands, then I traveled to the house of my mother's lover and challenged him to a duel."

Her stomach cramped. "What happened?"

"My mother's lover…a Viscount, met me at Battersea Fields, sword in hand with his seconds. I ruined his life. The scandal after was terrible. His wife and daughters were grievously injured by all our actions, by my thoughtless anger. Until I stormed their town house, his family had no notion of the affair. I was the person who brought it all to the attention of the *ton* with my unrestrained anger."

It was a testament to his influence that the few occasions she'd had to be in society she had not heard those rumors. "Did you…did you kill him, your mother's lover?"

"No."

"I'm glad."

"You are tenderhearted."

"Yes…but it is also balanced by my ferocity."

A smile tugged at his lips. "My family is notorious for their tempers, which have been a plague to the Blade's name.

My father, grandfather, and great-grandfather have caused endless scandals. I vowed to be different, my sons will be different."

"How?"

"By simply not being a damned fool. By not loving a woman so much that I would do stupid and reckless things for her and because of her. I will squash any scandal that attempts to affect my family. I will teach my children to control their tempers and restrain their emotions so they are always thoughtful of how society and others are affected by their actions."

She sent him a reproachful glance. "I do not believe love caused grown men to act with such foolhardy and wanton disregard of others' sensibilities."

He stroked his thumb back and forth along her cheek. "And what would you know about love?"

Awareness pierced her heart and an electrifying thrill arced through her. *Enough to know I am falling in love with you.* "Charity suffereth long, and is kind; charity envieth not."

He had an arrested look on his face. "Did you just quote the Bible?"

She grinned. "I did, and I believe it, too. Charity is love, so your father could not have loved your mother…ever."

His mien grew serious and she ached to know what went on behind his blank stare. "From time to time, I write… poetry," he said, effectively shifting the topic of discourse.

She blinked. "*You* dabble in poetry?"

His lips twitched. "Yes."

She tapped on her chin with a finger. "To contemplation's sober eye, such is the race of Man; and they that creep, and they that fly, shall end where they began. Alike the Busy and the Gay, but flutter thro' life's little day, in fortune's varying colors drest:—"

"Brushed by the hand of rough Mischance, or chilled by

Age, their airy dance, they leave, in dust to rest," he ended. "Do not expect me to write you any," he warned in a gruff tone.

She grinned. "I love dogs."

"I love snakes."

She found that most remarkable. "You jest!"

"I had a pet snake once."

"Oh, Tobias, the very notion of a snake in the house is wretchedly intolerable. They are…well, creepy."

"Now I know the manner of my revenge. Be aware, countess, one day you will be greeted with one of my friends beneath the bed sheets."

She laughed, delighted by his somewhat playful mood after such a serious turn a few seconds past. "I think you should be more worried about my reaction."

He arched a quizzical brow.

"I may very well burst into tears and swoon. My hysteria would last for days, and you would have to contend with my deplorable screeching atop my lungs."

He narrowed his eyes. "You wouldn't dare."

She nodded most empathically. "I most assuredly would." Then she winked. "I admit it, there are times my nerves are quite delicate."

Tobias scowled.

"What happened to him?"

"Who?"

"The snake."

"It was a she."

"Your pet snake was a she?"

His eyes brightened.

"Are you teasing me, Tobias?"

Without answering he kissed her deep and hard, then slow and sensuous. When he lifted his head, they were both panting.

"The rain has stopped," he murmured, pressing another kiss to her lips. "We ride out now."

"I agree, but first..." She gripped his hair and tugged his mouth to hers. His head slanted, and he deepened their embrace. Heat stirred low in her belly and she twisted in his lap, eager to sit astride and relieve the ache in her center.

She rose on her knees so they pressed into his thighs.

He pulled from their kiss. "Your knees are perilously close to my manhood."

She glanced down at the very impressive bulge, leaned in slightly, and lowered one of her hands from his nape to cup his wonderful hardness. "Is that what this is? A manhood?" she asked huskily.

"Yes."

"A very strange name."

"Hmmm, some call it plugtail or tallywag."

Tallywag? Livvie dissolved into fits of laughter.

Tobias's eyes gleamed with amusement. "Find that humorous, do you?"

She nodded, mirth bringing tears to her eyes. "I absolutely refuse...plug..." She hiccupped on a laugh. "Plugtail."

His eyes hooded. "I myself prefer cock," he said with such dark, sensual intent she sobered, drawn by the carnal need glowing in his emerald eyes. He tugged her to him, knocking the point of her knees from his thighs, but catching her before she tumbled from his lap.

He smiled faintly and shook his head. "You tempt me, wife, to lose myself in you here and now, but we must leave. Francie needs us."

Livvie slid from his lap, and they dressed in companionable silence. She hoped the easy camaraderie they'd formed would last. And she mentally chucked out her mother's list. The way to her earl's heart was not by flattering his vanity or being pretentious.

For the first time, she felt it was possible for someone to admire and love her...well, for her. She held the sweet hope filling her close inside, and prayed she wasn't leading her reckless heart to pain and disappointment.

Chapter Fifteen

After less than an hour of hard riding, Tobias and Livvie stopped at a beautiful two-story stone cottage with a thatched roof, surrounded by lovely birch, pine, and oak trees. It looked homey, comfortable, and welcoming.

She felt dusty and travel weary, and was in need of tea. "What if Francie is not here?"

He glanced around. "She is here, I can feel it."

"Now who is being fanciful?" she said, hoping to tease him into relaxing. His tension had climbed the closer they drew to the cottage.

He said nothing, and her stomach knotted. Hopefully then he would give Francie and Mr. Browning a credible chance to explain their decision. Tobias dismounted, strolled over, and assisted her from the horse. A crunch of boot on gravel had them turning around. A short rotund man came into view. A smile wreathed his leathery face when he spied them. "Milord, I was of a mind you would show up soon."

Tobias's eyes lit with pleasure. "Samuel, good to see you." He greeted the man by hugging him close, before releasing him. "How are Glenda and the children?"

"They are right fine, milord, right fine," the man replied with a proud smile.

"May I present my countess, Lady Blade. Samuel here taught me all I know of fishing and training horses. He and his wife are the caretakers of Rose Cottage. My sister and I have spent many summers here."

"Your ladyship," Samuel said with a bow. "Verra pleased to meet such a bonny lass."

"I'm delighted to make your acquaintance as well, Samuel."

"Is Lady Francie inside?" Tobias queried coolly.

Samuel must have detected that something was amiss, for he backed up, a look of caution settling on his face.

"Aye, with her husband, a Mr. Jasper Browning, a fine fellow, though a bit shady as to where his family is from."

Tobias smiled and it chilled Livvie.

"Is aught amiss, milord?"

"Not at all, Samuel. I will escort my wife inside, please see the horses to the stables. They need a good rub down for they have been ridden well."

"Yes, my lord," the caretaker answered with a quick bow.

Tobias gripped her hand, fairly dragging her across the gravelled pathway to the entrance of the fairy-tale-like cottage. Without knocking, he opened the cottage door and gestured for her to precede him. She entered into a small hallway. There was music and muted laughter echoing from an open door to the left. Ignoring the stairs and a few more doors, Tobias moved like a stalking predator toward the revelry. Livvie followed him, and stifled her gasp at the very intimate and telling scene they encountered. Francie was seated closely beside Mr. Browning in front of the pianoforte by the window, and they played together. They appeared besotted, and Livvie dearly hoped Tobias saw the mutual admiration.

"How charming," he drawled with biting sarcasm.

Francie and Mr. Browning jerked around. She hurriedly shifted apart. "Tobias? Livvie?" she gasped, her hand fluttering to her throat. All of her earlier merriment had been wiped away. "I...I'd not expected you to follow me. How did you know I would be here?"

"You left me a note to say that you ran away with a man I am sure you have no knowledge of and expected me to let you be on your merry way with a fortune hunter?" Tobias demanded, striding inside and closing the door softly.

Mr. Browning hobbled to his feet and it was then Livvie saw he was injured. A big swathe of crème-colored bandage covered from his knee to his shin and he had to use a stick for support. He forced himself to stand, leaning heavily on his stick, but he somehow squared his shoulders, determination darkening his gaze. He was very handsome with light brown hair, gray eyes, and a very slim and elegant build. His overall countenance was sufficiently pleasing. Livvie understood how he attracted Francie, who seemed to like the poetic and romantic sorts.

"Jasper loves *me*, Tobias...not my connections and wealth."

"I most assuredly do, my lord," Mr. Browning said earnestly, lacing his fingers with Francie's and giving her a tender smile.

Tobias did not even deign to glance in his direction, and Livvie winced in sympathy.

"A man who loves you would not have exposed you to ridicule and scandal. He would have approached me and asked for your hand in marriage," he said. "Gather your things, we depart in an hour."

Francie paled. "Don't hate me, Tobias," she said in a hushed voice, her eyes glistening with tears and distress.

"I cannot leave...we are well and truly married." A blush reddened her cheeks and she clasped her hand around her middle, the implication clear.

Mr. Browning released her and stepped forward haltingly, clenching and unclenching his fist at his side. His cheeks were flushed and caution glowed from his eyes. "My lord," he started. "If we could speak in private as gentlemen—"

"Silence." Tobias's tone brooked no argument, but Livvie was gratified to see that neither Francie nor her husband was wilting under the force of his contained anger.

Mr. Browning took Francie's arm in his. The love and concern on his face for her regard spoke volumes. Tobias observed them in silence, his presence dwarfing everything else in the room. Livvie badly wanted to kick his shins. Couldn't he see how petrified and uncertain his sister was?

"Shall we ring for tea and cake or perhaps sandwiches?" Livvie asked, hoping to defuse the coiled tension.

Francie nodded eagerly and threw her a grateful glance, and assisted her husband to the sofa in the left corner, strategically away from her brother. Still ignoring Mr. Browning, Tobias walked up to the couple and caught his sister in a warm embrace, and Francie promptly burst into loud sobs.

"F-forgive me," she gulped.

He closed his eyes, resting his chin on top of her head, stroking her back in soothing motions. "Wipe your tears, I do not like them," he said gruffly. It was then Livvie saw the love and concern.

Francie gripped the back of his coat in a tight fist. "I never meant to disappoint you, Tobias. The scandal will be horrendous, I—"

"Let me worry about the scandal. Now dry your tears," he ordered.

With a sniffle, Francie swiped at her cheeks. "I love him,

Tobias, and he truly loves me."

He murmured something too low for Livvie to discern and Francie nodded before producing a watery smile. Mr. Browning looked on almost helplessly, clearly wanting to be the one to comfort his weeping wife. Tobias released her and then looked at Mr. Browning, who appeared most anxious.

"Retire with me to the library. We have much to discuss."

"Tobias, please," Francie rushed out. "We can all meet—"

He made a sharp, slicing sweep of his hand.

She faltered, squared her shoulders, setting her lips together mutinously. "I know you, brother. I want to be privy to all conversation in regard to me and my husband. I am no longer a child. Please, let us sit here," she entreated.

"There are things best said with Mr. Browning alone."

Her eyes flashed, and she fisted a hand on her hip. "I will not countenance it. I am determined to be a part of all discourse."

Tobias strolled to stand by the window overlooking a small but charming garden. He seemed tensed. Livvie's feelings of disaster increased.

Francie hurried over to her. "Thank you for coming, Livvie, though it was not necessary."

Livvie hugged her. "I knew you would need me, think nothing of it."

"Did you marry in a church?" Tobias asked without shifting from where he stood.

His sister frowned, and Mr. Browning tensed, anger and something elusive but somehow menacing shifted in the depth of his eyes. Something was wrong. Livvie tugged Francie over to the pale-yellow sofa and they lowered themselves onto the cushions.

"Answer me, Francie."

"Lady Francie is my wife," Mr. Browning blustered. "We have been alone for a day without a chaperon," he ended a bit smugly.

"No, Tobias. I…it was over the anvil and our vows were performed by the village's blacksmith. We planned to be married properly when we returned to England, with your blessing, then we had the carriage accident."

"Accident?"

"We lost a wheel on the way to Rose Cottage and Jasper was injured."

"I love Francie, and she is my wife. Nothing you can say will rip us apart," Mr. Browning said defiantly.

"Is she?" Tobias murmured coolly, a dangerous glint in his eyes.

"Yes!"

"Yet you will relinquish your claim and never breathe a word as to how you spent the last twenty-four hours."

"You cannot—"

"Or I will see you hanged," Tobias incised ruthlessly.

Francie gasped and surged to her feet. "Tobias!"

"That's preposterous, my lord! I have done nothing."

"I am the Earl of Blade and it seemed you forgot that salient fact when you kidnapped my sister."

The steward stiffened, his eyes going wide. "Kidnapped?"

"Of course. Francie is a sheltered and mild-mannered girl. She was taken advantage of by a heartless bounder who only has an interest in her fortune. You have two choices, the hangman's noose or a press gang."

Tobias wielded his power with awful precision and instinctively Livvie knew he was not even unleashing the full force of his personality. It was as if the air vibrated around him, so taut he was from keeping a tight leash on his temper.

"I will not be persuaded to separate from my wife!"

Tobias finally turned. "Do you not mean her fortune?"

"You are being wretched, Tobias! Jasper cares nothing for my fortune," Francie said, hurrying to stand beside her brother. "I need you to trust me on this."

Tobias considered her, and Livvie could see the keen regret glittering in his gaze. She braced herself, recognizing whatever he had to say would devastate his sister.

"Forgive me for the hurt I am about to cause, I would spare you this pain if I could."

Francie wetted her lips, a nervous gesture. "I beg your pardon?"

"Did he tell you of his wife and three children in Bedfordshire?"

Tobias's words caught Livvie sharply in the chest. Dear God, she felt faint. *How could this be?*

Mr. Browning went white as a sheet, and Francie stood motionless, staring at her brother incomprehensibly.

"*Wife*?" she muttered through bloodless lips.

Mr. Browning struggled to stand, and Tobias casually walked over and sank onto the sofa beside his steward. Tobias gripped his shin, right above the bandage and squeezed.

A hoarse scream of pain echoed from Mr. Browning, and Francie flinched.

"Do you wish to grant us privacy now?" Tobias asked her with quiet menace.

Tears glittered on her lids and she trembled, but she shook her head. "No…I need to hear this, please."

"Darling, please…" The rest of the words strangled in Mr. Browning's throat as Tobias applied more pressure to the wounded area.

"Did you believe I would have hired you without having you investigated? That I would have a man living under my roof, with my family, without knowing his background?"

The steward paled alarmingly and sweat beaded his brow.

"Are you already married?" Francie asked, her voice a mere whisper.

"No, I—"

Tobias bore down with pressure and the steward screamed. His leg was released and he gulped audibly.

"I was...was married but not anymore, I swear, my darling!"

"Lady Francie—you will only refer to her as Lady Francie," Tobias murmured with such menace and barely suppressed savagery that Livvie felt discomfited. "And if you utter another lie, I will take you out back and slit your throat."

Dear Lord.

The steward's eyes bulged and desperation settled on his face. "Yes, yes of course, my lady, I...I am married."

Francie swayed. Livvie rushed over to her and clasped her hands, offering silent support. She could all but feel her friend's pain and confusion.

"And...and you have children?"

"Yes."

"I see."

It was painful for Livvie to watch the disappointment and hurt darkening Francie's eyes. "I cannot understand why you pursued me so ardently," she said, tears trickling down her face. "You wrote me such beautiful poems and letters and... you are married? I cannot credit it."

"I do not believe Mr. Browning considered a hasty marriage over the anvil a real marriage, hence he would not worry overmuch about the legality of being a bigamist." Tobias captured the man's eyes with his. "What was it going to be? Blackmail letter? A request from Francie for money urgently?"

Mr. Browning shot a pleading glance at Francie. "I love you, Francie, it was never about the money. It was *you*. My wife...she is dreadfully ill, taken over by the consumption, and she is not expected to make it. I...I...once she passed I was going to allow for us to marry in the church in England. It was never about your wealth," he ended hoarsely. "I admire you most ardently. I fell in love with you, and I wanted to be your husband and your protector. I could not tell you of Catherine, but I knew she would not live long and I would be free. When you suggested elopement instead of a long courtship, how could I refuse? On what grounds could I reasonably delay you without rousing your suspicion and risk losing your affections? You are my heart. Please forgive me."

"I never want to see you again," she said softly, tears streaming down her face.

"Please do not say that." He struggled to rise from the chair and Tobias stood and rested a hand on Mr. Browning's left shoulder. It appeared a casual touch, but from the strain on the steward's face, Livvie knew Tobias was rendering some hurt.

"You are a heartless bounder to pursue me so ardently when you knew your heart was engaged and it was impossible for you to wed another. Your wife is ill...*dying*, your children left alone to face such a burden." There was bleak desperation in Francie's eyes. "You are not the man I thought you were... you were never that man."

On a sob, she hurried from the room. At the door, she halted and shifted to face Tobias. "I...I am so deeply sorry. I was so very foolish. I thought...I truly believed he loved and respected me. *Oh*, Tobias, the scandal will be horrifying."

"There will be no scandal," he said, cold purpose echoing in his tone. "No one in England truly knows and I will deal with those who are aware here. I promise you, not a word of this mishap will be uttered."

She nodded, trust glowing in her eyes. "I...we..." Pink bloomed on her cheeks. "He kissed me a few times, but we never consummated our farce of a marriage. I wanted to wait until we were wed in the church before...and then the accident and..."

"I understand, Francie, say no more."

She inhaled deeply. "I must. We planned together to say we had been intimate when we returned and ask for your blessing to wed in a church. It was wrong of me to imply when you arrived that I might be increasing. I am deeply regretful, please forgive me."

Tobias nodded, his eyes dark with unnamed emotions.

"Do you desire my company?" Livvie asked, stepping forward, concern curling through her at the wounded look in her friend's eyes.

"Please, no, I wish to be alone. I will retire to my room." Then she fled as if the devil was on her heels.

The silence that remained was painful and the unblinking gaze with which her husband was watching Mr. Browning did not bode well.

"You will disappear from Francie's life. Either you go to the West Indies with an escort of mine, or your body will be found on the road heading north. Your choice."

In that moment, Tobias scared her, for she could see the chilling resolve within him. He was quite capable of killing his steward. "Tobias, I—"

He glanced at her, and his face was etched in a hard, unforgiving manner. "Mr. Browning and I have much to discuss, countess. I would appreciate your discretion at this moment."

Livvie hesitated, and then with a nod, exited. Could she have prevented all this heartache? Was it really her wild heart that had influenced Francie to be so reckless? Would Tobias forgive her?

Chapter Sixteen

Moonlight bathed the land in an ethereal glow. From the window of their small but tastefully furnished chamber, Livvie watched Tobias with utmost discreetness. She did not want him to know she ogled him in such a blatant and wanton manner. It had only been a few hours since he had booted Mr. Browning from their lives.

Tobias had been generous enough to offer him a place at one of his estates in the West Indies as the steward. Mr. Browning could take his family to Jamaica, and perhaps the sun and lack of England's cruel winters may give his wife a chance of life. Livvie also surmised her earl wanted the man as far away from England and from his sister as possible. But he had been generous indeed, for with his wealth and undeniable influence he could have sentenced the steward to the press gang or worse, death, and not an eyelash would flicker. Tobias had then announced there was no scandal, and they would treat it as a jaunt to Scotland and nothing more.

A simple dinner of baked trout and potatoes was had, and after several minutes of strained conversation, Francie fled in tears. Tobias had been bitingly polite as he excused himself and disappeared from the cottage.

It was after Livvie had taken a bath and was perched by the window that she had seen him in the distance, stripped to the waist, his feet dancing lightly, his hands punching and jabbing the air as he boxed with an unseen opponent in a primal rhythm. Need stirred hot and deep inside as she observed the play of muscles across his back and shoulders. Her husband was a powerfully made man, a gorgeous one. To look at him was immensely pleasurable and tenderness stirred in her heart.

He spun gracefully and her breath hitched. Did he see her? His hands flowed, and the expanse of his chest twisted like a snake as he moved to an invisible rhythm. Acting on impulse, she shrugged on her riding coat, and slipped her feet into slippers and hurried down the stairs. The cottage was silent, and only the crackle of the fireplace in the small drawing room could be heard. She headed through the kitchen and opened the latch on the backdoor and clambered down a few cobbled steps. Livvie moved carefully through a small back garden and around to the glen where she had spied Tobias. She faltered when, as she broke the corner, they came face-to-face.

"I…hello," she said, somewhat breathlessly.

He was silent, watching her with icy green eyes.

"Wife."

Her eyes took in the light sheen of sweat on his skin, the beauty of his body, his appealing maleness. "You are quite magnificent, husband." The brutal power of his body, all muscle and sinew, was the most appealing image she had ever seen. Her fingers itched for a paintbrush and canvas to capture the raw, beautiful imagery of her husband. "I want to paint you," she said huskily. "Just like this." Livvie trailed her fingers over his chest.

He stared at her, seemingly transfixed, and he didn't make a sound.

She moved closer to him. "What is it that you are practicing?"

At first, she thought he would ignore her, then he exhaled and tugged her to him.

"Boxing."

He spun, his movements so fluid and graceful, so that she was facing away from him and her back nestled against his chest. He dipped his head and inhaled at her neck, and her heart tripped in pleasure.

"Whenever I...I feel with too much intensity, I find a quiet place and I practice." He nuzzled her neck.

"Will you teach me?"

She felt his smile against her.

"Perhaps," he murmured.

He shaped her fingers so that she spread her hands wide with his. Tobias pushed her forward and flowed in a rhythm, controlling her movements. It felt natural to dip with him, to allow him to lead her in the gentle but somehow sensual and provocative movements.

"I feel as if we are dancing," she said softly.

They moved together for a few minutes until her motions seemed more fluid. She tipped her head to the night sky, the chill in the air forgotten as a slow burn started to build in her blood. She felt relaxed and stirred in the same breath. "Have you forgiven Francie?"

"Is there truly anything to forgive?"

"Perhaps not. It is sad she is so heartbroken. I could hear her weeping from her chamber. It takes bravery to go against family and society's expectation for love."

He sighed.

"No blistering retort declaring that love is nonsense?"

He spun her to face him. "No. There is something between

my sister and Mr. Browning. Is it love? I do not know. When I first saw them in the parlor, a part of me wished I could leave them be. Even though I wanted to crush him for the heartache I knew she would endure. I desperately wished his circumstances had changed in the three years since I hired him, as I realized Francie would be content to live with him here for the rest of their lives."

"The poor misguided fool," Livvie said softly.

"He wept when I informed him he could never see my sister or speak with her again, he wept unashamedly," Tobias murmured.

"And…and how will the scandal be weathered?"

"As how I've weathered all of them since I understood the cogs that kept society turning. With power, influence, and a good deal of thick hide."

She rested the side of her face against his chest. "And I shall weather it with you."

"I am glad you came with me."

"You are?"

"Yes, I am certain If I had been alone, I would have beaten Mr. Browning to a pulp and then discarded his body somewhere," he said lightly.

"And I am certain you are underestimating your honor. I do not think you have to fear from your temper. The very fact that you want to guard others against your anger, speaks much of your character."

He framed her face with his powerful hands and tugged her closer. He kissed her thoroughly, and Livvie responded with helpless greed, desire roaring though her veins. He lifted her with easy strength, walking through the beaten-down path to the back door of the cottage, never releasing her from his drugging and somewhat violent kisses. Sensations cascaded through her quickly and so intensely she quaked in his arms. Somehow they reached their chamber, and he tumbled her to the bed with a satisfied groan that reverberated to the core of her.

She ached so desperately. With swift motions, he stripped her until she was gloriously naked, then he eased from her and removed his trousers and for the first time, she got a perfect look at her husband from the soft glow of moonlight spilling through the windows. He was so physically arresting her breath seized.

He came over her, blanketing her body with his, nudging her thighs apart. She wrapped her arms around him and pulled him even closer. Livvie savored the feel of his hard, sleek muscles underneath the tips of her fingers. Hunger twisted through her veins, hardening her nipples to painful points.

"How I want you, Tobias. Kiss me."

His hot hungry lips found hers in the dark, and he made love to her mouth with soul-searing intensity. He released her lips, trailing kisses over her cheeks, neck, blazing a trail of fire lower. She trembled and made no protest as she was splayed wantonly wide.

He rose to his knees, his eyes drifting down to the intimate heart of her. Her entire body went hot at the lust that tightened his savagely beautiful features. Then he dipped his head and licked along her already wet slit. Livvie cried out in unbridled arousal. She dropped her head back against the silken sheets, moaning as she lifted herself against his delightfully wicked lips.

"Oh, yes, please, yes."

Wonderful minutes passed in complete bliss, and with a final rake of his teeth over her aching nub, she shattered, a hoarse moan slipping from her as acute pleasure swamped her senses. Seconds later, she felt a heavy, invading pressure and then he was deep inside of her. They froze. He buried his face in her neck. When he moved he was so slow, tension and an awfully intense sensation twisted low in her stomach. "Tobias"—she gasped—"harder…"

"No. Slowly…we have all night."

She nipped his shoulders in retaliation and he chuckled, low and heated, before sliding back and thrusting deeply. Livvie arched on a gasp, glorying in the shocking strength he made love to her with. He took her to ecstasy again and again with the most exacting and delightfully torturous gentle movements. She groaned, desperate for the intense rush, but never wanting the excruciating sweet pressure to end. Her hands roamed over his sweat-slicked back, and she bit into his shoulder.

Acting on wanton instincts, she raised her legs high above his back and rolled her hips, inviting him to burn faster with her. He froze and an answering groan was ripped from him. The bed squeaked from his sudden hard thrusts. His groans blended with her whimpers of pleasure.

"Tobias," she moaned, poised on the brink of ecstasy. He buried his face against her neck as he slammed into her over and over. She clung to her husband and let the ecstasy consume her, unknowing that she could experience such contentment in marriage.

Finished, he rolled with her so she was splayed atop his chest.

"Do we return to Grangeville Park tomorrow?" she asked, still drowsy from arousal.

"No. I believe it best we remain here for a few days. I will need to speak with Francie in detail to ensure she was not seen. If she was, I need to know who and exactly where she was spied."

"And what will you do?"

"Offer bribes."

"And if bribes are not welcomed?"

"Threats and blackmail will be effective."

She shifted, placing her hands on his chest and reared so she could observe his expression. "Is this how you've dealt with scandal in the past?"

"No. In the past, I have quashed rumormongering where I can, or I ignore the *ton's* reaction. My wealth and influence has seen my perceived infractions forgiven, time and time again. However, society will not be so kind to Francie if her indiscretion is revealed. I must do all in my power to protect her."

Warmth filled Livvie's chest. "I should be appalled, but I admire your will to see her safe."

"Do you?"

"Hmm," she murmured, pressing a kiss to his lips.

"I will take you fishing tomorrow, do you believe yourself up to the challenge?"

Shock rolled over her like a tidal wave. "*Fishing*?"

"Yes."

The oddest tugging sensation roared up and burst inside her chest. *Happiness.* In a daze, she accepted she felt happy. "I am more than ready for such a challenge."

"Then I will happily trounce you at fencing the day after. I will not be so easily vanquished as Lord Muir."

She shoved at his shoulder playfully and was delighted when he twisted with her. He rested his powerful body between her spread legs and brought his mouth down on hers. A slow burst of heat spread from her aching breast to her throbbing center.

Yes…she quite liked being married to her earl.

• • •

Four days later, Livvie returned to England with Tobias and Francie. They reentered without much fanfare, and as far as Livvie could see, none seemed the wiser about her friend's elopement. The dowager countess had opened the dowager manor and had retired there, and Francie went to visit her this morning. Hopefully a visit with her mother would rally her spirits even further.

The past few days had been a honeymoon of sorts for Livvie and Tobias. They had spent the time fishing, swimming together in the lake, and ripping each other's clothes off with every opportunity that presented itself. He'd even showed her a few boxing moves, to her utter delight. At first she had felt deep discomfort to be so happy when her dearest friend was so miserable. But dear brave Francie had rallied, and had joined Livvie and Tobias for all the meals and even strolled with them across the countryside that last evening.

Upon their return yesterday afternoon, Livvie had been beyond thrilled to receive a warm and pleasant note from the Duchess of Wolverton, who insisted she call her Adel. The duchess was considering commissioning her to make portraits of her twin sons who were only a few months old. Livvie would call on the duchess on Friday, which gave her two days to select her best pieces to show.

Livvie was now comfortably situated in her workroom, painting the beauty she remembered of the lowlands of Scotland.

A knock on the door had her lifting her head. "Yes?"

The housekeeper strolled in. "Good afternoon, your ladyship, a letter for you from Riverhill Manor. The lad that delivered it is in the kitchen drinking milk and eating a sandwich. He's awaiting yer reply."

With a grin, Livvie carefully replaced her brushes in their boxes, stood, and removed the apron she wore whenever she painted. "Thank you, Mrs. Potter."

Livvie walked over to the small walnut desk in the left corner and grabbed a letter knife. Slitting the seal open, she quickly scanned the note.

Dearest Livvie,

How we miss you at Riverhill. We sent around on Sunday, inviting you and Lord Blade to dine with us, and learned of your departure to Scotland. News abounded that you've returned, and I urge you to visit your father. Though he does not complain often, he misses you dreadfully, and a quick visit would not be amiss.

Your mother.
Helena

"I shall be traveling to Riverhill for luncheon with my parents. You can send the boy with a reply that I will visit, but I shall be right behind him. Please also inform Mr. Wilson to ready a carriage."

The housekeeper smiled. "Shall I also inform Lord Blade and Lord Westfall you will not be with joining them for the afternoon luncheon?"

Livvie glanced through the side windows in the direction of the lake, where the gentlemen were fishing. The Marquess of Westfall had arrived at Grangeville Park only a few hours after they had returned from Scotland. The man had been icily polite as he took her measure, and she had not imagined the distaste in his eyes when he looked down on her. The marquess possessed an aura of quiet, self-contained power that would have been intimidating if she was the frail sort.

Lord Westfall had also brought his seven-year-old daughter, Emily, who was the sweetest child. When she had bounded around the corner with a puppy hurtling behind her, the marquess's entire demeanor had changed. He had smiled, swinging her into his arms and then into the air to the child's delight. Livvie had been shocked when the little lady had calmly announced she was his bastard daughter and made an enquiry as to who Livvie was.

The entire meeting had possessed an air of unreality, but Tobias had smoothed the tension with surprising charm, and luncheon had been quite entertaining and pleasantly diverting, when she had found herself liking Lord Westfall's dry wit. His daughter was delightful, and it wasn't till after she had told him so, that the man had bent and kissed Livvie's cheek, welcoming her to the family. That evening, she had instructed Mrs. Potter to make sure they were properly welcomed as she hoped they would stay.

"Yes, please do inform the earl."

"Yes, my lady," Mrs. Potter said and left.

Livvie hurried from the parlor and bounded up the stairs. Her stepfather's home was less than an hour by carriage. She would visit and return home in time for dinner. It felt like a lifetime since she had last seen him, and she wondered if he was truly well. Was there a new worry hidden between her mother's lines? With the aid of her lady's maid, Livvie dressed in a pale lavender carriage dress with a matching bonnet and gloves and donned walking boots. She would encourage her father to wander with her through the lovely gardens of Riverhill.

After leaving a quick note for Tobias, she summoned the carriage and departed to visit her parents. She was quite happy that they lived in such close proximity, and in truth, she could easily visit her parents once per week.

She shifted in her seat, making herself comfortable before opening *In the Service of the Crown*. Within seconds, she was drawn into the world of intrigue and murder, and her heart raced along with Wrotham as he investigated who in his cadre betrayed secrets to France. About half an hour later, the coach pulled into the forecourt of her parents' home, and she reluctantly closed the leather volume. She was assisted by the footmen who greeted her with pleasure, and she fairly sailed through the entrance.

"Your ladyship," the butler Emerson said on a deep bow.

She grinned and inclined her head. "Where are Father and Mother, Emerson?"

"His lordship is in his study and her ladyship is in the gardens, my lady."

"No need to announce me, I will intrude upon Father in his study. However, please inform Mother I've come to call."

"Very well, my lady."

She handed him her coat and then walked briskly down the hall. At her father's study, she knocked twice, then waited.

"Come in."

With a smile, she opened the door. "Good morning, Father." Livvie untied her bonnet strings.

Her father pushed from behind his desk and walked over to engulf her in a warm hug. "You did not send word you were coming."

"Mother sent over a note. I'm sure she is quite aware and wanted my visit to be a surprise for you. It's quite convenient that we live in such close proximity and I shamelessly took the opportunity to pay you a visit."

His eyes widened in undisguised alarm. "Good God, you did not leave your husband, did you?"

She chuckled. "No, Father, I simply wanted to see my family."

He patted her shoulder. "Come, luncheon will soon be served and it will be pleasant for all of us to gather once more. William is here as well, with Lady Louisa. They return to Town next week."

Distaste curled through Livvie, and she strove to show an unaffected mien. She had not seen William since the occasion when he had accosted her. Of course, he would have heard the news she was now a countess. Should she now tell her father, since he had recovered, of the despicable manner in which his son had acted? She looped her hand through his arms as they exited the study and made their way to the gardens. "Are you well, Father? It has been over a week since we last spoke. Are you on the mend?"

"Dear girl," he said with a smile. "I daresay I should stop referring to you as dear girl, you are a countess now."

"Oh, pish, Father."

He chortled and her heart lifted with happiness. To think that three months ago she had thought she would lose him to death.

"I am recovering quite well, my dear. Your mother, bless her heart, is with me every step of the way. It was just last week that I put away the walking stick. I still tire and do not indulge in long walks, but in no time, I shall be mended in its entirety."

"I'm glad."

He patted her hand where it rested against his arms. "Tell me, Livvie, are you happy?"

She cast him a quick glance. "Of course."

His shoulders relaxed. "I am relieved. While Lord Blade is not an unpleasant man, he has a reputation of being cold."

Her heart twisted. "Father, I—"

Her sister's shrieks of joy were an effective distraction from further conversation. With a light laugh, Livvie pulled away and ran down the well-tended pathway that led to the garden to greet Ophelia and her mother. They spent a pleasant hour together chatting about the gossip in the area, namely the momentous occasion of Squire Wentworth marrying the Dowager Duchess of Wolverton last week in a small, intimate ceremony at Rosette Park. The vicar had also been caught in an awkward situation with the butcher's daughter and was being pressured by the bishop to take her as his wife. Surprisingly, he was staunchly denying any wrongdoing and refusing to offer for the girl. His congregation was not taking kindly to the news, as most were insisting he marry the girl. It was feared that he would lose his position.

Laughing, Livvie gasped, "I never thought the vicar had it in him."

"It is rubbish if you ask me," her father growled. "The vicar had his arm on the girl's shoulder as she cried. It's his duty to offer comfort when needed. There is certainly no cause for a marriage as her family is demanding."

"They were alone in a closed vestibule. I daresay her papa is doing the right thing in demanding the vicar to act with honor," her mother sniffed.

"By the by, Livvie, I have in my possession the latest volume of *In the Service of the Crown*. The delivery came yesterday. I thought with your hasty wedding and everything, you would not have gotten a chance to place your order," her father said with a wink.

She almost combusted on the spot. "It is here?"

He smiled indulgently. "Yes, my dear."

She jumped to her feet from the garden bench, and hurried away to the house. His laughter followed her as she all but ran through the hallway to the library. She swept inside and hurried over to the large oak desk where a small brown parcel was atop it. With impatience, she tore through the package and a smile burst on her lips when she spied the familiar leather volume. The door to the library closed with a *snick* and she spun around.

"Oh, Father—" Livvie's words faltered and she instinctively retreated a step.

William. Her stepbrother leaned against the door watching her like a silent predator.

"Why have you closed the door?" she asked with cool aplomb.

"I saw you from my window when you arrived. I watched

you in the gardens with Father. How you glowed. You look ravishing, Livvie. I can see you are a woman now," he said thickly.

He prowled over to the windows and alarm skittered thorough her when he drew the drapes closed so only a slice of sunlight came through the parted section.

"What in God's name are you doing, and where is Louisa?"

"My wife had been obliging enough to visit our neighbors. For all intents and purposes, we are alone…a state I have been most eager to get you in."

Fear sent chills down her spine. Without hesitation, she made a dash for the door, and halfway there, he grabbed her around the waist and flung her. She screamed and he chuckled.

"There is no one close by. I've ensured I assigned tasks to all the lingering footmen and maids. Father will remain in the garden as is customary for the better part of the afternoon and your whore of a mother will hover."

"Release me, William."

"You are a married woman now, Livvie. You have full knowledge of what goes on between a man and a woman." He pushed his hips against hers suggestively. "And you know what I want from you," he said, lust glittering in his eyes.

She tried to push at his chest and was met with staunch resistance. "You are being despicable," she hissed. "If you act on your foolish desires, imagine the pain you will cause Father. He trusts you."

"You will tell no one that I've had you. Your husband would beat and banish you. And Father…such stories from you would surely do him in. His heart is still weak, you know. Will you really burden him? I believe not." A light entered his eyes, and a charming smile tipped his lips. "There is no use resisting. Stay the night. Louisa has been complaining of melancholy and has been taking laudanum. It will be quite easy for me to visit you in your old chamber."

Livvie recoiled from him. "You insufferable ass! Your logic is beyond me. I am a married woman, and Tobias will be severely displeased when he learns of your conduct."

His charming facade slipped into a hard mask. "All of society knows Blade would never be reckless enough to duel over a woman. The man feels no passion and is a cold bastard. In fact...I can assure you he will be quite annoyed if you reveal anything that may lead his family's name into gossips and scandal," William said, looking extremely smug.

Her heart lodged in her throat as she stared at him. She lifted her hand and slapped him with all her strength. The crack echoed in the library and he glared at her with a look akin to stunned disbelief.

He grabbed her, and his lips assaulted her. She lifted her knee to his private area with all her strength. With a groan, he collapsed to the carpeted floor on his knees.

"You bitch," he gritted, tears streaming down his face.

She rushed to the door.

"I promise you, Livvie, I will have you underneath me before the month is out. And I will not promise that you will enjoy it." Ignoring him, she wrenched the door opened and hurried outside. Her emotions were in a chaos. The blasted blackguard! How dare he believe she would not report his disgusting behavior to her husband? Her heart squeezed. What if she told him and he did nothing because of the potential scandal?

It was clearly a matter of honor...*her honor*, and she would take care of William. *But how?* His unexpected assault clearly showed he was willing to attempt his forced seduction wherever and whenever he would see her. Even if she stayed away, she would encounter William at balls and garden parties, where there were ample dark corners, linen closets, and secluded spots in gardens he could drag her away to before she could sound an alarm.

And if she screamed for help, the scandal would be terrible. Tobias would never forgive her for allowing such a taint to touch his family's name after the ruthless way in which he had repaired their reputation.

Her breath hitched on a sob. She could not fail him in this, nor could she allow her lout of a brother to compromise the vow that she had promised to her husband.

"Livvie, are you well?" her father demanded.

She glanced up to see him leaning on his walking stick. Her heart lurched. "I thought you no longer had to use a stick for support?"

A tired smile creased his lips. "Only when I exhaust myself. I assure you, there is nothing to worry about, but if you do not mind terribly I am off to take a nap. Your mother and sister wore me out."

She hurried over to him and pressed a kiss to his cheek. "Of course not." Should she tell him? *And what if you do and the shock makes him even more ill?* Her stomach cramped at the notion.

"Your mother is planning a jaunt in to the village shops. Will you join her?"

"I must return to Grangeville Park. I will make my excuses. Have a good rest, Father."

Good Lord, what was she do to?

Chapter Seventeen

A few minutes after making her excuses, Livvie was headed home. She leaned her head back wearily against the squabs, her fingers gripping the padded seat in the carriage, her mind churning furiously. She would simply have to defend her own honor, discreetly. And when she had soundly trashed William, he would not breathe a word of his shame to anyone, but he would certainly acknowledge that she was not a woman to trifle with.

She swallowed heavily and wondered if her nerves would be completely shattered before the ordeal was over. The carriage sped home, but nothing she did could turn her mind from her determination to face William by herself. His size had been so frightening, the press of his lips against hers and the intent in his touch had been revolting. The mere memory made her feel ill to her stomach. The carriage rolled through the forecourt of the estate, and the footman aided her descent. She walked briskly through the door held open by the butler.

"Olivia?"

She faltered when she spied Tobias walking down the hall

toward the library with Lord Westfall. After saying something to the marquess she could not hear, Tobias walked toward her. Westfall went ahead to the library.

"I thought you and the marquess were to be fishing?"

He arched a brow at the noticeable tremble in her voice.

"We retired earlier than planned to complete discussion on the school and hospital we are building." Dark green eyes searched her face. "I understand from Mrs. Potter you visited your parents? Is the Viscount well? You seem a bit rattled."

His concern had tears prickling behind her lids. She so desperately wanted to rush into his arms and be comforted, but knew he would hate such a display of excessive passion. "Yes, Tobias," she said, walking toward the parlor. She breathed a soft sigh of relief as he followed her, a mild frown marring his handsome features.

They entered, and at the *snick* of the door, she spun around. And mortified herself by bursting into tears. "Oh! My nerves must be more unsettled than I realized, forgive me."

Instead of drawing her to him, he leaned on the door and folded his arms, a cold and cynical look shuttering his features. The hurt in her heart grew worse, and she valiantly tried to control the sobs.

"You are clearly upset," he said, "gather your composure, dry your tears, and try to speak sensibly."

Anger surged through her, and she welcomed the distraction from the memory of William's cruel touch. "You are being unfeeling!"

"I have no time for theatrics." His eyes took on a darker shade of green. "I am not given to indulging women in manipulative tears. You know how I feel on the matter, Olivia."

She was instantly flustered. "Not all tears are tools for manipulation, Tobias," she cried softly. "And I am not just some woman! I am your wife."

Impatience flashed in his eyes. "What has happened?"

"I…I…had a dreadful encounter with my stepbrother." Her heart pounded, and she was suddenly afraid of how much to reveal. And with despair, she realized it was because she was petrified he would truly say or do nothing. If she were to reveal the truth and Tobias remained unconcerned, she would be shattered, for she was more than halfway in love with her husband. If he showed he did not care, she would not be able to bear it.

Unable to voice her fears and anxiety or her mounting love, she marched over to him. She stretched up to him and grabbed his hair to pull his lips down to hers. Then she kissed him hard and passionately. With a muffled groan of surprise, he unfolded his arms and tugged her even closer to him. The kiss was hot, hungry, and demanding and as she shivered in his arms, she realized how badly she wanted Tobias's touch and taste to wipe away the vile threats of William.

Tobias gripped her hips and marched her backward toward the chaise lounge. They halted when the back of her shin hit the chaise, and his hand drifted around to cup her buttock into his large palm. She cried out softly when he tilted her and ground his hardness between her thighs.

He pulled his lips from hers, breathing raggedly. "You tempt me, countess, but Westfall awaits me with pressing business that must be sorted before he returns to Town this evening."

Her heart broke in denial. She needed this. "I…I… needed your kiss," she whispered half under her breath, feeling exposed and terribly vulnerable.

An unidentifiable emotion shifted in his eyes. "What has happened, Olivia?"

She remained muted, her heart beating a furious rhythm.

"Well?" he clipped, and she winced.

"Kiss me, Tobias, love me," she murmured pressing hot,

desperate kisses along his neck. She tugged frantically at his cravat, and as the silken cloth slid through her fingers, she parted his shirt and bit into the soft of his neck. He gripped her hands and clasped them gently. Dipping his head, he kissed the tip of her nose, her cheek, the corner of her mouth, and she curled into him, reveling in the tenderness he displayed.

"I must attend to business, I cannot dally."

She lifted her head from his chest and nodded with words trapped in her throat.

After pressing a kiss to her lips, he walked toward the door. He gripped the knob, before glancing back with a frown. "I do not like you being upset and in tears."

She tried to smile but it wobbled. "I am considerably eased," she answered truthfully. "Nor am I crying any longer."

"Good, I trust you will inform me after my meetings what has occurred?"

A throb of tension pulsed behind her temples. *Perhaps*. "I... Yes, though I may do so with tears."

His gaze searched her face intently. "Do you wish me to remain? I will inform Westfall—"

She hurried forward. "No, attend your business meeting. I shall retire to my chambers until we meet for dinner. The argument with William was quite unsettling, but I am fully capable of dealing with it and that had been my intention. Seeing you, I...I unraveled a bit but I am back to sorts."

"Are you certain, wife?"

"I am," she answered firmly.

With a small nod, he departed. Livvie was even more resolved now. She would settle the matter without being a bother to her husband.

• • •

Fifteen minutes after he'd left his wife in the parlor, Tobias frowned as he spied her riding away astride on Arius. It seemed whatever had distressed her had not abated if she would go for a long ride so soon. Should he have stayed and prodded her to reveal whatever had brought her to tears?

Tears.

He had always despised the weapon women used with such ruthlessness. Tears had never inspired anything in him but disgust. When he had seen the glisten in Olivia's eyes, his heart had jerked, then a cold resolve had filled him to destroy who ever had upset her. That had shocked him, the very idea that his countess had the power to torment him with tears, as his mother had done with his father. Their days since setting off to Scotland had been filled with their mutual sensual awareness. It had been delightful and he had been at peace. He had even come to appreciate and enjoy her cutting tongue more.

Last night, when he had sat down to write, his wife had completely colored the lenses of how he saw his heroine, and he had started to craft the perfect lady for Wrotham. When he wrote, it was an escape, a need, a pleasure, another life he could immerse himself in. The world of secrets, lies, and passion, where everything was as he made it, and regret, pain, fear held no sway. Yet last night, as if he had been controlled by another, Tobias had written his hero falling in love with the mysterious Lady O, a suspected traitor to the crown, and he had infused such intensity of emotions in his characters it had shaken him deeply.

Did that mean he was falling in love with his wife? The way he watched for her smile to brighten his day, the insatiable desire he had to kiss and make love to her, the way he anticipated her doing something reckless, not in dread... but in fascination. Was that love? Tobias was unsure, he only knew he had never endured the emotions she was stirring in his heart.

Why had she been crying?

It unnerved him to realize she had not been swooning and descending into great hysteria, but had simply demanded his kisses to soothe whatever emotions had been rioting inside. He was caught off guard by the pleasure rushing through him at that realization.

As Olivia nudged her horse into a canter, he felt a vague sense of unease. Where was she really off to?

He pushed from the winged back chair and strolled to the open windows for a closer look. Acting on instinct, he grabbed the telescope from off his desk, lengthened it, and brought it to his eyes.

She had one of his foils belted at her waist. *Good God.* What was she about? The fact that she chose to travel on horse and not in a carriage suggested she was not going far. Olivia nudged her horse into a gallop and he lost sight of her. Lowering the telescopic lens, Tobias considered her actions deeply. She'd said she had an argument with her brother, whom she encountered visiting her parents. An argument so severe it had brought her to tears, and she now returned with a weapon, one with which she was most proficient. Knowledge bloomed like a late flower in springtime. Without a doubt, she was heading back to her father's estate to settle whatever wrong her stepbrother had done to her.

Good God. The reckless hoyden!

Was she not aware of the magnitude of scandal that she could bring down on their family? They had barely escaped the past few days with Francie's reputation intact, and even then, he was just waiting for the first wave of rumors to start before using the full force of his power to squash all tattle.

He would tan Olivia's backside when he caught up with her.

"What is it?" Westfall finally asked, no doubt annoyed by his delay.

"I must leave. I will travel to Town tomorrow and conclude our business if need be. I understand you cannot stay any longer. But my wife needs me."

The marquess gave him a cynical glance. "Is she well?"

"She…she had been crying," he said gruffly. "And I should have known she was not the type of lady to be rattled by simple matters."

Westfall's lips curved, but he said nothing.

Tobias stormed from the room, his mind shifting through the possibilities. What would she really do with his foil? She was proficient, for they had sparred together to her delight in Scotland a few mornings. But surely she would not think to use a weapon on someone. Unable to walk sedately, he broke into a run for the stables, guilt and frustration worming its way through him.

His wife had needed him, and he had not probed deeply enough. He appreciated then, the control she had on her tempers. Because she had not been wailing and swooning as how females of his acquaintance had behaved before, he'd assumed whatever had upset her had been trifle.

Damnation.

Chapter Eighteen

Livvie returned to Riverhill Manor determined that today would be the last William would ever behave so disgustingly toward her. She was well pleased to learn her father was still abed resting, and her mother and sister had not yet returned from their jaunt in the village.

"Has my brother departed, Mrs. Billings?" Livvie enquired of the housekeeper.

"No, my lady. He is in the drawing room taking his evening tea. Dinner will be served at six. Shall I let the cook set a place for you?"

"No, thank you, I shall not be long." Livvie handed over her coat and untied her bonnet. "See to it that we are not disturbed."

"Yes, my lady."

First she went into her father's study and eyed the few foils he had arranged in a glass case. She searched for the keys in his desk and unlocked the case, selecting a fine foil. Gripping both foils in a death grip, she marched to the drawing room and entered without announcing her presence. She was very deliberate in her action as she closed the door, ensuring the latch turned, ensconcing them inside.

William's head jerked around. "Livvie," he breathed, a rare smile of pleasure and genuine affection lighting his eyes. "You have returned." He lowered his tea and the sandwich he had been consuming and pushed aside some papers he had been reading.

He stood, his eyes devouring her. The wretched man was truly pleased to see her.

"I knew you would come to your senses." A lascivious smile tipped his lips and bile rose in her throat. "Leave with me tonight for Town. I have reopened the town house in Mayfair, and we will be alone for the night save for a few servants."

Livvie said nothing when the wretched libertine sauntered to the sideboard where decanters and glasses were arranged. He poured amber liquid into two glasses. He turned to her and hesitated when he finally spied the foils in her hands.

"What do we have here?" he murmured, raising an enquiring brow.

She held the foils even more firmly in her hands. "I will not—"

"We will need to be discreet," he said, as if she had not spoken.

"William—"

"I will admit, your husband is reputed to be ruthless when crossed, so we must be careful. I'd prefer if we started our affair after you've whelped his heir, but it cannot be helped. I want you too much," he said thickly, a bulge rising at the front of his breeches.

She held the foils in her hands out toward him. When his attention riveted on the blades, she strolled to the center of the room.

"What in God's name are—" He gasped, the glasses

dropping from his hands to the carpet, as she pressed the end of the pointed foil to his throat. William stared at her in shocked disbelief. "Livvie—"

"Do not breathe my name, you despicable cad," she said with a calmness that she distantly admired. Her heart was a war drum in her ears, her stomach felt hollow, but her hand was steady, and that was all that mattered. "You have assaulted, insulted, and tried to dishonor me. You have no honor and I am here to defend mine. You promised, William, that you would have me before the month is out, and I promise you…I will kill you if you think to besmirch me and take what belongs only to my husband."

His eyes widened in shock before fury darkened his blue orbs. "Do you believe this will stand?" he growled.

"Most assuredly. Do not think I have any fear about running you through." Her stomach pitched and uncertainty tried to claim her, but she pushed it aside and pressed the blade firmer against his throat. "I have bruises on my arms! I am your *sister*…if not by blood, by law. I have known you for eleven years and have only thought of you as a brother. You have attacked me twice now, trying to steal kisses and touches that do not belong to you, and I can clearly see you have no intention of stopping your despicable behavior."

"I—"

"You thought I would be so afraid of my husband's reaction that I would not inform him of your licentious character. You are right, but nor will I allow you to incite fear in my heart."

She stepped back and threw the other foil to him, which he deftly caught. He looked at it blankly.

"While it is appealing to run you through and flee, I will give you a chance to defend your honor, William. I challenge you to a duel."

He smiled a faint, derisive smile. "You are not a man,

Livvie. And that has always been your problem. You do not know your place. I am going to teach you today where you belong, which is spread beneath me," he growled, and before she could blink, he lunged at her.

She parried his thrust with nimble speed and skill, and deliberately nicked his chin, letting blood.

He swore viciously.

"That was for the first time you kissed me."

Anger tautened his cheekbones, and he rushed at her without form. He was a brute of a man and as their foils came together, she felt the strength in him. She twisted away and lunged, slicing through his peach waistcoat and shirt, creating a thin line of blood across his stomach. He cried out in pain and stumbled back.

"Oh, do be quiet, it is nothing but a scratch."

"You've scarred me," he muttered faintly.

"That is for the terrible manner in which you assaulted me earlier. My honor has been satisfied. Do you swear, William, to never accost me again?" she demanded, pointing the blade at his heart.

"You bitch!"

They stared at each other in furious silence, before he nodded tersely. She lowered her sword. With speed and shocking strength, he lashed out and slapped her across the face. Livvie stumbled, a faint ringing sound buzzing in her head. A hand gripped her wrist and squeezed with such strength she feared her bones would be crushed. With a sharp cry, she dropped the sword, unprepared for the way he tumbled her to the sofa.

"I would have treated you with gentleness before, I would have, Livvie. I wanted you for years. I even asked Father for your hand in marriage and he stupidly told me we were brother and sister when we share no blood."

A sharp rip sounded as he tore the neckline of her riding

habit. He kissed her and she shredded his lips with her teeth. His yowl of pain filled her with savage satisfaction. He reared up above her and backhanded her. A coppery taste entered her mouth. She jerked both her knees up, swift and sure. He groaned and rolled off her, and she dived to the floor and grabbed her foil.

"I should have known you had no honor," she said, her heart breaking. Livvie had wanted to avoid devastating her father, but there was no hope for any other outcome now. William would not give up, and he would not recognize her defending her honor. "You have broken my heart…and you will destroy Father's."

Before he could respond, raised voices filtered through the door of the drawing room.

"I was given strict orders they are not to be disturbed, my lord!"

William's eyes widened, there was another shout in the hallway, and confident footsteps echoed before the doorknob twisted. Livvie did not want to risk taking her attention from her stepbrother, not even following the noise of several powerful slams. The door crashed open and her husband walked in, as calm as if he had not just kicked down the door.

She almost fainted.

With a sweeping glance, he took in the shambles of the drawing rooms, the cushions on the floor, and the glasses and liquor stain on the carpet. His piercing regard on her brother, a faint smile edged the grimness of Tobias's mouth. "Countess, I trust there is a reasonable explanation?" he asked calmly, never taking his predatory stare from William.

Alarm and relief filled her in equal measure at Tobias's presence.

William swallowed. "This is outrageous, I…"

He spluttered when she pressed the foil to his throat.

"Wife…" Tobias said warningly. "You are in enough

trouble as it is, best not to add murder to your repertoire."

"I had a nagging problem and instead of troubling you with my histrionics, I decided to handle the matter myself," she drawled smoothly.

A shadow passed over her earl's face. "I see."

William grimaced. "My lord, the countess—"

"Quiet." Tobias's voice cracked like a whip. "Olivia?"

"He has assaulted me twice now. Shortly before I met you, and earlier this morning, when I visited Mother and Father. He…he…cornered me in the library, kissed me, and tried to push his hands beneath my dress!"

"She wanted it! We are lovers…" William trailed away at the surge of fury that lit Tobias's eyes before he lowered his lashes.

Her stepbrother rallied quickly. "I swear on my honor, Lord Blade, Livvie and I have been lovers—"

She gasped, jerking back and lowering the blade. "He lies!"

Painful silence enveloped the room.

"Tobias?" The word seemed to get caught somewhere in her throat.

"Sheath your sword, wife. We will bid your father good-bye and depart."

She tried to pull her disjointed thoughts into some semblance of order. What was he thinking? Surely he did not believe this bounder?

Her stomach went hollow.

William tugged at his cravat and ran a hand through his hair. "I am sure we can sort this unpleasantness, Blade, as men. Livvie has been hounding me, before I even wed Louisa. Today, when I told her I was no longer interested in an affair, for my wife is increasing, she threw a tantrum. I, too, share a similar distaste for female vapors and machinations and told her so." He frowned convincingly and waved a hand. "I did not expect this."

She gaped.

Tobias's lips twitched, barely, and it chilled her. He walked farther into the room, not once glancing her way. Was it possible he believed her stepbrother and was too disgusted to look at her? A surge of fury sliced through her veins.

"You have grievously injured my countess and you will be made to understand the severity of your mistake," her husband said with terrible softness. "I have not excused your behavior."

Oh!

William narrowed his eyes. "My lord, I—"

Tobias smiled with icy civility. "You will name your seconds."

The room swam around her. He was going to fight a duel for her? "Tobias—"

"You will be quiet, wife."

William had blanched and even jerked back a few paces. "Blade, you cannot be serious. You would not do something as illegal as force a duel on me over…over…a woman?"

Not even Livvie could countenance such an assertion. The idea of Tobias facing such danger filled her with dread.

"My countess isn't just a woman."

Despite her revulsion at the situation, her heart quickened in pleasure. He was truly willing to fight for her. Did this mean he was growing attached to her in a similar regard?

"Good God, man, I shall not meet you. I do not care if I am dubbed a…a…coward, you are reputed to be a crack shot and are undefeated with a foil," William ended faintly, tugging at his cravat.

There was something about the stillness of Tobias's manner that made Livvie wary. Tension fairly vibrated from him like an aura, and it was as a fleeting smile touched his lips that she saw beneath his deceptive mien. He was beyond fury.

His control shook her…what would it be like if he were to ever lose the rigid control he held on to so ruthlessly.

"I will not kill you. I have no intention to flee to the continent or be judged by my peers for taking your life." He stepped closer, and William scrambled back until he was flush against the wall. "You touched my wife without her consent."

"I swear she was willing," her stepbrother babbled.

"And you insult her by insinuating she is without honor. Death would be a relief for you, as you would escape the consequences of your actions. I will ruin you. Your investors will no longer do business with you, your clubs will blackball you, you and your wife will no longer be accepted into any respectable drawing room."

It was impossible for William to even whiten further… but he did.

Livvie scrambled to stand beside her husband and touch his arms. "Tobias, I—"

She faltered as his face went white. He reached out his hand almost hesitantly and touched her cheek. She flinched.

"He hurt you," he said through bloodless lips. His eyes darkened, and she felt the latent violence surged through his body.

Her heart trembled, and she was filled with acute discomfort. "Let us depart this place. We will call on my father tomorrow—"

"Your lips bleed."

Livvie swallowed.

"Your riding habit and chemise is torn. There are bruises on your neck, your cheek," he said softly, as if he were simply reciting some inconsequential list.

He turned from her to her stepbrother.

William's lips sneered. "I already told you, I will not meet you at dawn. I did nothing she did not want, I—" His head snapped back with force as her husband backhanded him.

The violence was delivered with such calm brutality, Livvie jerked away from Tobias.

William crumpled, sliding against the wall to the floor. Tobias hauled him to his feet and delivered a powerful blow to his midsection. Her stepbrother gagged.

She recoiled. "Tobias, stop! Please."

But her husband showed no mercy. With each blow he delivered to William, she retreated more. She wanted her stepbrother to be punished, but this…this was too much. His face was a bloodied mess, and he lay limply on the ground, no sound issuing forth.

Her husband faced her and a visible jolt went through her. She watched him with a deep wariness, not liking the anger turning his eyes to jade. The silence seethed between them. What could she say? Minutes passed and his piercing unemotional regard was nerve-wracking. "Tobias, I…I think what just happened must be discussed."

"Do you?" His murmur was low and deadly, and she hated that he used that tone with her. "What manner of excuse do you have to explain your behavior?"

"Surely you must see I had to do what—"

"You naive, reckless…" The words exploded from him, shocking her with their ferocity.

Oh God, he is furious.

Her heart started a slow thud.

"If he had overpowered you…you cannot imagine what he may have done to you, countess. Once again, you were reckless and acted without thought or logic over your emotions. It would be an injustice if I do not tan your backside so that you will not be able to sit for days," he snarled. "He would have brutally beaten and raped you. Was it so hard to inform me of what was happening? Did you believe I would not have defended your honor? Do you have such little faith in me, wife?"

Her eyes widened. She had never seen him so...so... intimidating. "If you had made it possible to confide in you, I would not have been placed in such an untenable situation."

He jerked as if she had slapped him.

"I wanted to spare you from scandal...and in truth, I was not sure if you would give the matter any thought. I know how much you deplore emotional tantrums and tears, and I was afraid to tell my husband of my worries because I feared you would not approve of me!"

He stepped toward her, and Livvie turned and fled. She ran through the hallway, and out the door as if the devil were on her heels. She continued through the forecourt and on to the uneven country road until she slowed to a walk. She panted breathlessly, her throat tightening with tears. She knew what would happen now.

Scandal. Horrible scandal. The cook would tell her niece, who worked as an upstairs maid at another great house, and that niece will inform a cousin, and then it would spread to the drawing rooms and parlors of those most influential in the *ton*.

Her stomach cramped.

Worse, Tobias was indeed shocked at her behavior. A sob burst from her throat.

The pounding hooves of a horse sounded behind her. She stopped walking and waited for him to approach. He jumped off the horse before it fully halted, grabbed her around the waist, and seated her none too gentle in the saddle astride. He mounted behind her and urged the stallion into a powerful run.

They rode hard, and she felt every jolt on her backside. She would be sore later, but instead of protesting, she held on to the pommel, seething. They swept through the high walls leading to his lands, and he turned the horse toward a grotto, where he jerked to a halt. He pushed from the horse and handed her the reins.

She stared down at him dazedly and was shocked at the depth of rage and contempt she spied in his eyes. Pain tore through her heart. His knuckles were bruised and bloody. She ran a finger softly over the cuts. "Please, Tobias, we must discuss this."

"Return to the main house," he said with chilling calm. "I want you out of my sight."

She flinched. Then she scrambled from the horse, almost falling to the ground in her haste. She slapped the rump of the horse, and he cantered away before slowing to a walk.

"Why would you say this to me? How have I caused such an offense you would wish me from your very sight?"

"If you had been honest instead of manipulative, I would not have almost killed a man." He gazed at his hands in a daze, on the blood on his knuckles. "I gave you every opportunity to confide in me and instead you once again acted with reckless disregard for anyone but yourself."

"How dare you, Tobias. You did nothing to make me believe I could trust you with my emotions. I had to act for myself, as I did not believe my own husband would protect me at the cost of appearing emotional." Her voice shook. "Do you think I am not aware of the manner of man I have had the misfortune to fall in love with?"

His lips curved in a sneer, and her anger flared even hotter.

"Yes, Tobias, love! The emotion you seem to despise in equal measure along with anger and damnable tears. I am a woman! I am human, I cannot remain unfeeling and repress all the emotions I have because you have demanded it to be so. You are an arrogant and unfeeling lout!"

"This is what you think of me?"

"Can there be any other thought to be had?" she asked hoarsely. "From the moment we became intimate you've informed me I am not to cry, not to be angry, and heaven forbid I actually swoon. You want me to be cold and unfeeling. Do you deny it?"

He made no answer.

"Do you love me?"

His face shuttered. "You know my thoughts on the matter."

"Do I?"

"Yes," he ground out.

"We have known each other for several weeks. We have been as man and wife. Every opportunity you've had, you sought my presence, kissed me, introduced me to pleasure, came after me when you thought I was disturbed. You lost the rein on your famed temper because I had been threatened and hurt. Can you reflect on these things and say you have no attachment or tendre for me, Tobias?" she demanded, her voice breaking, and her heart trembling for she feared his answer.

The silence stretched, and then he spoke. "I only know that you are dangerous, and I regret staying in that closet with you."

She stumbled back with a soft cry. Then she ran from him. Her name floated on the wind, but she did not hesitate, only stumbled deeper into the thicket. Mere seconds later, a hand grabbed her waist and spun her around, and acting from a place of deep hurt, she lashed out. He caught her hand in a gentle grip so at odds with the raw emotions darkening his eyes to emerald.

"I cannot bear the thought of you in tears. It rips me in two and makes me want to slay whoever hurt you...even when it's myself. How do I know you are not manipulating me with them? How the hell do I know anything?"

"I have no cause to manipulate my husband."

"I wanted to kill him," he muttered fiercely. "I wanted to

break all of his bones for touching you. I am the very man my father was."

"Tobias, no, you—"

He dipped his head and slashed his mouth over hers in a fierce and unexpected kiss.

Chapter Nineteen

When had he gotten so obsessed with his wife's scent and taste? When had she snuck under his guard and owned his fucking soul? She whimpered into his kiss and wrenched away, trembling fingers going to her bruised lips, her eyes wide pools of desire and hurt. He vowed then that he would break William for what he had done. Hell, he would just kill him and be done with it.

Control. He had to fight for control. He was a rational man, and he was not ruled by emotions. Tobias jerked away from her and she moved with him, fisting his jacket and tugging his lips back to hers.

"I don't want to hurt you," he growled, kissing the corner of her lips. Her taste was honeyed intoxication and it was painful to admit he would never get enough.

Olivia stood on her toes and cupped his jaw in her delicate hands. "Then don't hurt me," she breathed. "Love me, hold me, and comfort me."

Her touch shattered him and a fierce surge of possessiveness shook him. With a deep groan, he kissed her tenderly, barely brushing his lips over hers, but his hands coasted over her body with fierceness. He pushed the skirt of her riding habit to her waist and pressed her against the tree. He gripped her thighs and lifted her, parting her legs so she straddled his waist.

Hands trembling with need, and blood pounding with furious emotions, he unfastened his breeches and pressed his hardened length against her already wet entrance. It was immediate penetration. He thrust deep and a wail of pleasure sounded from her lips, destroying the remnants of his self-control. He drove inside her harder, deeper, one hand on her hip holding her still, the other under her shoulders, arching her breasts to his devouring mouth. Her head fell back, a hard shudder wracking her body.

"Tobias," she gasped.

He was powerless to stop what was happening to him, and in that moment, he knew he would never be able to live with her. She made him lose all reason, all sense of his self and control. With her, he had no idea who he was and it chilled his soul.

"I love you," she cried, convulsing on his cock and bathing him in her scalding wetness.

He froze, unable to release, for he lingered on those three words.

"How I love you," she said, pressing a kiss to his neck.

She unraveled him and he gave a harsh cry and froze as he spent inside her. Tobias gently pulled from her and straightened her clothes. His hands trembled and he stilled, glaring at them. How was it that he was unable to be detached with her? From the moment she had entered his life, everything had been different, more turbulent. Nothing was calm.

They straightened themselves in silence, and he considered her bent head.

"When you ran from me earlier…were you afraid?" The question had haunted him the minute she fled. Everything had become dark and painful, and he had recalled the fear his mother felt when his father got angry. It had gutted him that he could have driven his wife to feel a similar emotion.

"No."

He searched her eyes for the truth and he was reassured by what he saw. "Good."

He turned and whistled, and a few seconds later, the horse broke through the cover. "Ride him home."

Her lower lip trembled. "Shall we ride together?"

"No."

"Why not?"

"I need to be alone."

Her eyes widened. "Tobias, I—"

"No, countess. Since I've met you, I have no idea who I am. You tie me in knots and the feelings are not pleasant. For the first time in my life, I truly believe I am just like my father. I felt everything when I realized you were in a room alone with your stepbrother. Unreasonable jealousy, possessiveness, rage. Before you, I've only experienced a shadow of such feelings."

"I love you," she said softly.

Once again, everything inside of him jolted at the words. Then his heart started a furious rhythm. He recalled her utterance that love was patient and kind. The violent emotions she roused in his heart, his obsessive need to brand her with his touch and kisses, felt no semblance of kindness or patience. He forced himself back under control.

"Do you have any affections for me?" she ask boldly, as was her way, jutting her chin, and damn if she was not staring him down.

"No."

She flinched.

"What I feel for you is beyond affection. At the crest of each dawn I think of being inside of you. I write and you crowd my thoughts. I sleep and you are the last person I think of, and damn me if when I wake, you are not the first person I fucking look for. I think that borders on obsession wife, not mere *affection*."

"Tobias, I—"

"I wanted to kill William for touching you. In fact, he may be walking in London sometime in the future and meet his demise with a footpad."

She gasped.

"You are dangerous to me, wife."

"No, I am not," she said most earnestly.

"I am leaving Grangeville Park."

She froze, indecisions flaring in her eyes. "For Town?"

"Yes."

"Shall I pack?"

"No."

He could see the pulse fluttering wildly in her throat.

"I see."

What did she see, exactly? Did she understand he needed to shore up his resolve and that it was impossible to do that in her presence? Would she understand that he felt out of sorts, so unlike himself, as if someone else had invaded his body and it was all because of her? No, and he would not burden her with his feelings, he would simply exorcise her and return to the man he was at peace with.

The man he had been before he lost his damn senses inside that linen closet.

• • •

Hours later, Livvie was unable to sleep. Kicking the twisted sheets from her legs in frustration, she launched from the bed. Marching to the armoire, she selected a simple gown and dressed herself. She headed to the room that she had converted to a painting studio, desperate to hold a brush in her hand. A few minutes later, she opened the door to the studio, calm filling her by simply being surrounded by her work.

Glancing through the window, she spied the sunrays as dawn broke. She wanted to ride across the mews to the grotto she had discovered and pour her confusion into painting, but the overcast sky warned her it was best to stay indoors. Livvie donned an apron, left the chilly studio, and strolled down the hallway to the parlor, grateful to see that a fire was already lit there. She arranged her easel and sheets toward the windows and then drew the drapes. The beauty of the rolling lawn stole her breath. Today, she would lose herself in painting, and nothing else. Perhaps something good would come from it, and she could send a few pieces to the shop she sold through in London and hopefully they would be snatched up as her other works had been.

She sat down, carefully opened her box, and started to paint. There was a knock on the parlor door, and Livvie reluctantly shifted her concentration from the easel. A quick glance at the pocket watch showed she had been painting for four hours.

"Yes?"

The door opened and in strolled Francie.

"Oh, Livvie," Francie said softly, rushing over. "Does your apparent misery have anything to do with Tobias departing for town?"

Her heart cracked. Memories of the many fights between her parents surfaced and her father's subsequent actions surfaced. "Do you suppose this means he will soon take a mistress?" she asked hoarsely.

"Livvie!" Francie snapped, fisting her hands on her hips.

"Tobias would never dishonor you so."

Livvie laughed without humor. "He has left for an unmentioned duration for Town. It seems the very thought of living with me is unbearable. Any gentleman as passionate as your brother would surely find it impossible to do without the more intimate areas of companionship after several weeks of estrangement from his wife."

Shock slackened her friend's jaw, and she stood speechless. "Your fight was…"

"Terrible," Livvie supplied with a smile that wobbled. "I own I was reckless and foolhardy, but I thought I was protecting him from potential scandal. Instead it seems I made a muck of it, and then he made an even worse muck. Now we again hate each other, and I fear I may never regain his good opinion. It enrages me that I so desperately want it and his adoration."

"Tell me what happened," Francie demanded.

As fast as possible, Livvie relayed the dreadful happenings.

"William *attacked* you?" Francie gasped, sinking onto the sofa.

"Yes."

"And you challenged him to a duel? Then Tobias came and…and…beat him?" she said incredulously.

"Yes," Livvie snapped.

"I cannot credit your assertions. Tobias would never fight or duel or act so scandalously."

"He did, and he hates me for it," she said on a sob.

"Oh, he must love you so much," Francie breathed in wonderment.

Livvie froze, even her heart felt as if it had stilled. "Love? Are you afflicted?"

Her mind churned in confusion, and what felt like hope blasted through her. She surged to her feet and started pacing. *Love?* Then she scoffed at the very notion. A man in love did not abandon his wife.

"He does not love me…he desires me, but there are no tender sentiments in his heart."

"Oh, Livvie, surely you must see how rattled he would have been by his rage. He is so composed and chilly, and for whatever reason you have been unraveling his knots."

"And he resents it."

"Or maybe he is just unsure?"

"He *left* me."

"I do not think he means to be away forever, think of the scandal when society learns of your estrangement."

"He does not care about society's opinion. In fact, he would be much relieved if I left for another of his estates and lived there until I am needed for his heir."

Francie shook her head as if in a daze and then her gaze landed on the canvas. She gasped and her fingers fluttered to her lips. It was then that Livvie glanced down at the painting she had rendered. It was of Tobias.

"It's beautiful," Francie said in a breathless tone. She stood and walked over to look at it, awe settling on her face.

The image was of Tobias standing on the cliff bluff at the far east of the estate. He looked raw, untamed, passionate, and free from constraint. Though she painted him immaculately dressed in riding breeches and jacket, hat and a crop dangling from his hand, his eyes and expressions were anything but proper. The wildness of the land around him and the fierceness of the man himself could not be denied.

"Is this how you see my brother?" Francie asked softly.

Livvie frowned. "This is how he is, this is Tobias, but he hides from his passion…"

Francie gripped her hand. "Have you decided which estate to depart to?"

"No!"

"Select one, go there, and give him time. It may take

several months, but I believe he will realize how much he adores you and—"

"You expect me to leave my home?" She tugged her hand away and fisted one on her hip.

"I—"

"I will not run with my tail tucked between my legs, nor will I mope and cry and suffer my heart to break more every day. I love your infuriating brother, more than I dreamed possible, but I will not allow such sentiments to…to…" She caught her breath on a frustrated sigh. After taking a deep breath, she continued, "The Season is in full swing and I will be traveling to Town."

"You are expressly disobeying him, Livvie. I do not think that is the way to win over Tobias."

Livvie steeled her resolved. "Who said anything about winning him over? I aim to show my earl that I will not wilt away without him, and if he adores me as you say, then he will recognize my worth. If he does not, then to hell with him," she said with a satisfied nod. Then she swept from the parlor, determined to heal her heart and not remain broken.

Though deep inside, she felt it was false bravado at best.

• • •

Livvie had been in London for two weeks, and her husband was quite aware. He had made no effort to call on her, and she would not visit the town house, though secretly she desired reconciliation.

"I thought you had determined to be merry," the duchess of Wolverton murmured to Livvie.

She smiled, desperately wanting the ache inside to vanish forever. The fight between her and Tobias had been wretched, and their days apart only reinforced how unsuited they were for each other. Except…she missed the dratted man, and was irrevocably in love with him.

Despite enduring such tempestuous passion for him, she would not seek him out in Town. He had left her…after everything they had shared. And it had occurred to her how silly she had been in trusting that he would always be there. How silly she had been to easily abandon her hopes for independence, and her dreams to be a painter. Only a day after his departure, she had launched into motion, refusing to pine away for a man who did not accept her completely.

Oh…what I wouldn't give for him to accept me…for me.

"Livvie?"

She glanced at the duchess. "Forgive me, I was lost in thought."

"I do not think you are enjoying yourself much. Would you like to leave?"

She grabbed a glass of champagne from a passing footman and took a sip. "I admit it, I am bored. I have never found balls entertaining."

"But at least you have secured several clients for your fabulous paintings. Are you at all worried about what Lord Blade will say when he discovers you have sold several pieces?"

Perhaps, but she would never admit it. "I do not give a fig what he thinks."

Adel chuckled, her eyes dancing with merriment and a good bit of mischief. "I hope not, for your work has become the rage and the entire ballroom is atwitter with the piece you did for Lady Branson, and now Lady Livingston is demanding you clear your schedule for her."

Livvie glanced at the painting hung above the fireplace at the far left at the ballroom. "Lady Branson is quite pleased with it, isn't she?"

"Hmm, and your earl has just entered, quite discreetly I might add."

Livvie froze.

Tobias is here?

Her gaze eagerly sought him, and when their eyes collided, she audibly gasped. He was shockingly handsome in black trousers and jacket, with a dark green waistcoat that she knew perfectly complimented his eyes. What was he doing here? Was it because he was aware she would be in attendance? Her heart thudded alarmingly, and she tried her very best to act blasé. What would he say when he realized her paintings were taking the *ton* by storm, as the duchess had claimed? Surely he would banish her then, for bringing the Blade name to more notoriety.

She tilted her chin in defiance, and acting on instinct, lifted her flute of champagne in his direction. He arched a brow, but the dratted man's face remained inscrutable. She wanted to rush over and kiss him, and then slap him for causing her anguish. The two desires melded in her so strongly, she forced herself to turn away to gather her composure.

"Oh," slipped softly from Adel.

Unable to restrain her curiosity, Livvie turned. A fist closed itself over her heart. The lady she had spied at Grangeville Park in the hallway of Tobias's room was practically draped over him. *Lady Arabella.* His head was dipped low as he conversed with her. The picture was intimate, and Livvie's heart broke. Had he taken back up with his mistress?

"I am sure it is quite innocent," Adel murmured sympathetically.

Livvie's throat worked but no sound issued forth. She silently urged her husband to look her way. Instead, he walked through the ballroom with his former—or his current—mistress strolling beside him. Arabella was smiling and nodding to varied ladies and gentleman while Tobias had his usual air of insouciance about him.

Unexpectedly, he glanced up toward her. For a moment, hunger flashed in his emerald depths and her heart seemed to stop. Then he lowered his eyes and bent his head to hear whatever Lady Arabella chose to lightly tip on her toes to whisper in that moment.

"I daresay, from the scandalously heated look your husband just gave you...Lady Arabella's presence is a mere annoyance and nothing more," the duchess said after touching Livvie's arm gently.

Her throat tightened. "I must leave."

"Surely—"

"I cannot stay. Do you see how everyone is staring at us?"

And they were. Some ogled discreetly behind their artful fans, while others stared blatantly. She hurriedly bid the duchess adieu, and with her head lifted high, she made her way to the entrance and ordered her carriage. Livvie waited in the foyer, her heart a beating mess. Should she have gone to Tobias? And what would she say if she did? Should she tell him her father had collapsed when he learned of William's behavior, and that her stepbrother had been sent away to Scotland to revive a flagging estate there? Should she ask him when the tension between them would be solved, and when would they have a reasonable conversation? The most pressing question...should she ask him if he had taken back up with his mistress?

The questions burning through her, she turned, and with determined steps, reentered the ballroom. She scanned the crowd and spied her husband exiting the room, Lady Arabella following at a discreet distance. Livvie's knees went weak and a blast of anger tore through her, leaving her hands trembling.

How dare he break his promises. A footman passed and she grabbed a glass of champagne from his tray and emptied it in one swallow. She took another, and followed the path her earl had taken. She went through the terrace door and allowed their voices to guide her steps.

She turned left at a column and froze. Lady Arabella was

kissing her husband. The pain that tore through Livvie's heart was like a poison-tipped knife.

Tobias pushed his mistress from him, a derisive smile tipping his lips, but Livvie was not mollified.

"How dare you," she breathed out.

The lady spun, her eyes widening in genuine shock. So this was not staged as how Lady Wimple had done.

"Why am I always coming upon you with a trollop twined around you, my lord?" Livvie asked cuttingly.

A muscle jumped in Tobias's jaw. "You will mind your tongue, countess, and we will have this discussion in private." Keeping his gaze firmly on her, he spoke. "You will excuse us, Lady Arabella."

"Darling, I—"

"Now." His voice vibrated with cold warning, and Arabella flushed.

She hurried away, and when she passed by Livvie she murmured, "He was mine first and I will have him again, you upstart."

Livvie swiveled and stepped in her path. "What did you say to me?"

Arabella faltered, no doubt not expecting Livvie to act with such bold impropriety. She was simply too out of sorts to be pretentious.

"I said nothing, Lady Blade," she said demurely, but her eyes fired with spite and there was a mockingly cruel slant to her lips. Then she mouthed the word *upstart*.

Livvie did not pause to think, she simply lifted her hand and delivered a sound slap to Arabella's cheek. The lady stumbled back and promptly burst into horrified tears.

"If the earl and I ever separate, you are welcome to him. Until then, if you dare try to disrespect me and dishonor my marriage, I will call you out and put a bullet in you," Livvie snapped low and hard.

Lady Arabella whitened, shock glazing her eyes.

There was a gasp behind Livvie, and in her periphery, she spied two ladies. They hurried from the terrace back to the ballroom, surely to spread what they had just witnessed.

"Countess!"

She glared at her husband and her hands trembled in reaction. Within two strides, he was in front of her, staring down, his mien wintry. "We will leave this instant," he said flatly. "Are you staying at your father's town house?"

"Yes."

"I will escort—"

"I am not going anywhere with you, my lord."

"Do you understand the magnitude of the scandal you just caused with your reckless—"

She stepped close to him so her breast was flushed against his chest. "You, my lord, have no cause to berate me. You came here with your mistress!"

A flush worked itself along his cheekbones. "I did nothing of the sort. I encountered her in the hallway and we only spoke of business. Now, we will leave, and I will escort you home where we will have a calm and reasonable discussion."

"No," she said. "I will stay at the ball and dance the night away." She was very aware of the crowd gathering on the terrace and the loud murmurings filtering through.

"She challenged Lady Arabella to a duel!"

"How shocking and scandalous."

The tick in her husband's cheek grew more pronounced. Embarrassment and hurt vacillated through her in equal measure. He would never forgive her now for the scandal erupting. The reconciliation she had been hoping for would never come. Tears pricked behind her lids, and she stood frozen. Livvie almost fainted when her husband grabbed her and threw her over his shoulder and calmly walked through the throng, as if such a spectacle was an everyday occurrence.

Chapter Twenty

The carriage traveled with speed through London, jostling Livvie uncomfortably. No doubt her father's coachman was responding to the veiled anger in Tobias's tone. She was still in a daze from being carted off from Lady Branson's ball. It was too overwhelming to even think of the scandal they would face tomorrow. He'd said nothing after he had none too gently stuffed her inside the carriage and taken a seat opposite her.

"You threw me over your shoulder," she finally said, still unable to reconcile his actions.

"It seemed the most efficient way at the time to get you to leave. I could see you were preparing to be stubborn."

"The scandal…it…"

"It will roar through the *ton* and linger for weeks, months, years," he said flatly. "No doubt they will all recall the way my father acted in the past and celebrate my behavior in a similar manner. Bevies of callers will descend on the town house and the papers will sensationalize everything and a great deal of lurid speculation will be attached to our names."

Her throat tightened. He appeared so dispassionate. "What were you thinking?"

"That is the problem, wife. I never seem to think or act sensibly around you."

There was an intolerable ache of tears burning in the back of her throat. She knew how much he despised the scrutiny of society and she had done nothing to temper the rage and pain she had felt. She had acted on pure emotions, a state in which he despised. "You must resent me," she said softly. "Since I've entered your life I have done nothing but cause you heartache."

The silence thickened and her heart broke a bit more. She gripped the edges of the cushioned seat, a strange sort of desperation worming through her heart. Was her mother truly correct in her insight? For their marriage to work, would she have to bury all sense of herself?

"Tobias—"

"I would never dishonor you by taking a mistress."

That blunt but earnest statement unnerved her. "Her lips were pressed to yours and her body contoured perfectly onto yours. I daresay you welcomed her advances."

Tobias sighed in evident disgust. "She flung herself at me. I was about to throw her off the balcony when you arrived."

"How convenient, but that is not what I witnessed."

He gave her a steely smile. "You will trust me, wife."

"My father—"

"I am *not* your father, nor am I like many men who take a mistress, dishonoring the vows they've made before God and their wives. I've made promises to you and I'll be damned before I break any of them. You frustrate me with your willful and reckless ways, but you also hold my desire unlike any other woman I've ever met."

Her heart lurched, and sweet hope bubbled inside her. Might their marriage truly work?

"You will return to the country," he continued dispassionately.

Her heart calcified in her chest. "Tobias—"

"You will return tomorrow, countess."

"And where will you be?"

"I will remain in Town."

More separation. She stared at him mutely. "Will you ever approve of me as I am...love me as I love you?" she managed to ask, her heartbeat in her throat.

He jerked and then stilled. Though she ached for him to say yes, she knew it would not be so. The very fact that he wanted her away from him spoke volumes. He fished a handkerchief from his pocket and held it to her. "Dry your tears," he said gruffly.

It was then that Livvie realized tears were streaming unchecked down her cheeks and her throat felt raw. She swiped at them furiously. The last time she had cried so piteously was when her father abandoned her. It infuriated her that Tobias would reduce her to a similar state of hopelessness. Her heart felt like it was being ripped from her chest and there was nothing she could do to stop the unrelenting ache.

He leaned over and cupped her cheeks, startling her. "Your crying has the power to gut me." His thumb brushed away one of the tears on her cheek.

Though she very much wanted to lean into him, climb into his lap, even, she pulled away. "Do you have any affections for me, Tobias? For our marriage to work...we need more than passion. Mutual regard is highly welcomed."

His eyes went dark. "I do not know. You make me feel... confused...desperate, feelings I am at loss with what to do with, feelings I do not welcome."

She swallowed. "Would you love me if I was the docile sort? If I did not ride and fence as well as you do? Was my mother correct, do I need to change everything about me, for you to admire me as ardently as I do you? If that is the case, my lord, we will never have a happy situation. I am deeply regretful for my impulsive behavior in the ballroom, I never meant to embarrass you or tempt you to act in a scandalous manner."

A severe frown split his brow. "I do not blame you for my actions. I was well aware when I lifted you what the reaction of the *ton* would be."

She nodded mutely, painfully aware he did not acknowledge the fact that she loved him or that more was needed for them to be happy together. It pained her to admit it, but she could not endure such a union.

• • •

Tobias stood beneath the low-burning gas lamp on the street in Mayfair and watched his wife enter her father's town house. His heart was a dull aching thud inside his chest. Not once had she glanced back as she alighted from the carriage and marched away with her head lifted high and proud.

Do you love me, Tobias?

Will you ever approve of me?

His town house in Grosvenor Square was only a short distance away and he started to walk home. He'd acted without thought when he lifted his countess in his arms and escorted her from the ball. The murmurings that had rippled through the crowd had unfazed him. The only thing he had cared about was that his wife's eyes had been shadowed by hurt and betrayal. He knew her willful ways and understood instinctively she would have forced herself to stay and endure unpleasantness because of pride. Instead of arguing with her, he had simply acted…much like the way his wife was— reckless and improper. He grimaced, hardly caring if the *ton* assigned such epithets to him.

What did he care about?

Do you love me, Tobias?

He faltered. Such a simple question yet so intricate. He commanded his feet to move and several minutes later he belatedly realized he was standing in front of his town house. He walked up the steps almost woodenly. His butler opened the door.

"Welcome home, my lord."

"Evening, Collins," he murmured, shrugging from his jacket and rolling his shirt to his elbow. Entering his library, he tugged at his cravat, loosening it. He strolled over to the windows overlooking the small gardens at the side of the house, lingering deep in his thoughts.

Do you love me, Tobias?

He had no notion of how long he stood at the windows looking out into the dark. He only knew his thoughts were filled with his wife and the fact that he needed to return to her father's town house and see her. The dawn broke as he stood there, bleak and dreary, so very different from the previous summer days, possibly a reflection of his mood.

His eyes were gritty and he was in need of sleep, but he could not delay. He must visit his countess. What he would speak of when he saw her, he was unsure, but the devastation her eyes had spoken of could no longer be endured. The volatile feelings she roused could no longer be withstood. A decision had to be made, and it was one they needed to do jointly. With rapid strides, he exited the library and went upstairs. He called for a bath, and his valet selected his clothes with welcomed efficiency.

An hour later, freshly shaved, trimmed, and dressed in buff-color breeches with a dark blue jacket and matching waistcoat, Tobias approached Lord Bathurst's town house. Instead of calling for the carriage, he elected to walk, desiring the cold, crisp air to help him clear his thoughts. After a sharp rap on the front door, the butler allowed him entrance after perusing his calling card. A few minutes later he was situated in an elegantly appointed drawing room, waiting on his countess to descend, anticipation and surprisingly nerves, had him tugging at his cravat.

Instead of his countess making an appearance, a woman who introduced herself as the housekeeper, Mrs. Andrews, handed him a letter.

"My lord, I was instructed by her ladyship for this letter to be delivered to you this afternoon."

Foreboding slithered through him. "Where is my wife?"

Mrs. Andrews fidgeted. "Her ladyship departed at the crack of dawn with her maid and a small valise."

"Thank you, Mrs. Andrews."

He stuffed the letter into his pocket and departed. On the walk home, unable to suppress the desire until he was in the privacy of his library, he halted on the side street and tore into the letter.

Dear Tobias,

I can see now the marriage I had desired is not to be realized—one of mutual regard and the deepest of admiration. It would be quite easy to render all blame to you, but I cannot. I contributed to the distaste you currently feel for me and may forever endure. I've brought unwanted scrutiny and scandal to our family's name with my bold and inappropriate behavior, despite knowing how much you abhor public scrutiny and aspersions. I hope you will eventually forgive me. I dearly wish I could change and conform to the expectations of society, those of the dowager countess, and even the ones you have. But I cannot bear the notion of living in a union so permanent and not acting as my true self but as a shadow of who I am.

I love you, most ardently, a state I am unsure will ever dissipate. It was clear to me that my sentiments were not returned and that you in fact wished me very far from your presence. The contempt I espied in your demeanor broke my heart, and I must leave until I no longer care that you see me as your inferior. Even if you cannot love me, I would wish for you to respect me as I am, admire me as I am, and enjoy me as I am. I do vow I will do all in my power, if the situation arises, to act with the proper deportment of a countess and never bring shame to our family name again. I fear I am acting the coward in fleeing before you banish me to either Scotland or your estate in Jamaica to only return upon your goodwill.

Perhaps in time there will be civility between us and we can live in relative friendship like in most marriages of the ton. Until that time I will leave you be and explore the world, the rolling hills of the countryside, the great sights of Paris and Vienna, and perhaps even the Rose Cottage again. I will return to England eventually, for I've been told every lord is in desperate need of an heir and I know my duty. I cannot bear living with a man who dislikes the heart of me. I know I must return… but for now I need the space to stop loving you.

I can only hope when I do return, whether it is weeks or years from now, that we will have a pleasant and amicable marriage.

Your wife,

Livvie

A swell of emptiness rose inside of him, expanded and filled every crevice of his being. His wife had left him. *God's blood.*

He forced himself onward at the sound of several footsteps behind him. The words of her letter replayed in his mind until cold, blessed numbness replaced the hollow, empty feeling.

• • •

Five days later, Tobias wondered if he should make a report to the runners of his countess's disappearance. He'd sent grooms and messengers to his various estates across England and Scotland and she was not in residence at any of his properties. She had vanished with no report as to when and how.

Where would his wife have gone? With what money? Was she safe? No one was missing save her maid, along with one of his swordsticks and a pistol, and her packet of books. The fear he had been suppressing reared its head viciously.

God, please...let her be safe. Where are you, Olivia?

He spent the days writing and the nights prowling the house, hoping she would reappear. It tormented him that his wife was out there, alone, hurting, and with no knowledge of how much he truly admired her.

A fist slammed into his side, and he hardly flinched from the pain, instead he danced away on light feet from the jab aimed at his eyes.

His brother halted on the mat, panting. "You are distracted."

Tobias inhaled, stripping the thin leather straps from his hands. "Is it safe to say our sparring is done for today?"

"I give up," Grayson snapped, throwing his hand in the air. "I have held my silence, but in good conscience I can no longer do so. What in God's name is going on?"

Tobias rotated his shoulders and went over to the table and grabbed a towel and raked it over his sweating skin. He and Grayson had been sparring for some time now. Tobias's muscles ached and sweat ran in rivulets down his forehead, but he still wanted a more strenuous activity. Peace seemed to elude him. All he could think about was Olivia. It infuriated him that he was so weak. Were these the emotions his father felt for Mother, the ones that led him down his path of ruin?

"Why do you believe something to be amiss?" he demanded, as he and Grayson left the room and headed to the library, where he entered and sank into the high winged-back chair near the window, uncaring of his sweaty body.

With a scowl, Grayson dropped into the seat opposite Tobias. "You have been in Town now for three full weeks without your countess. Every effort I have made to enquire about Olivia has been thwarted. And now all I have been hearing of in the clubs is 'the Quarrel.' Bets have been placed in the books at White's as to how long it will last for. Good God, man, I would never have imagined you to be embroiled in a scandal of such magnitude and seem so…so…unperturbed."

His brother sounded flabbergasted, a state Tobias would admit he had been in since his wife left him. He felt hollowed even admitting it to himself. Tobias considered his brother. "My countess is not your concern."

"Something is bloody well my concern. Do you think I have not noticed that you have hardly slept for the last few days? You've holed yourself up in the library, writing for hours on end. Dozens of callers are turned away every day. Does 'the Quarrel' have anything to do with the fact that Lady Blade challenged your former mistress to a duel? Olivia has been declared an original for her boldness and has become the rage. All the ladies of quality are banding together to form a society, a women's club of sorts to protect their husbands from the harlots in society. It's anarchy. The other lords are blaming you for not having a firm hand on your countess and all the ladies are celebrating her actions."

A tight feeling twisted in his chest. "The *ton* is simply looking for fodder for the gossip mill."

"This is more, brother. As a countess, Livvie has the potential to be a powerful force in society if they accept her. It is quite shocking to admit Livvie is more of a celebrity admired by women of all walks of society. There was a piece in the *Gazette*, which reported on the designs she wore her hair in weeks ago and the fashionable styles and bold colors she wore. It was humorously remarked that her eccentricity should have warned your mistress of your wife's temperament." Grayson frowned. "And the rampant rumors that you lifted her from the ballroom last Friday night and vanished with her?"

"It happened."

Grayson's eyes widened, and he gaped. "Where is my brother and what have you done with him?"

Tobias smiled, though he was not amused. "I find I am perplexingly unconcerned about our societal images."

His brother appeared dazed. "Then what *are* you concerned with?"

"My wife's tears."

The fact that she left me, the truth that I ache to see her dazzling smile. The very memory of her tear-filled eyes gutted him, made him want to find her and hold her until she wept out every pain and frustration against him and then make love to her for an entire night. God, he missed her.

"And you've been holed up writing?" Grayson demanded, his gaze flicking to the pile of paper spread out on the oak desk. "I daresay the rumors hinting of a separation are more important than whatever you're scribbling."

At Tobias's icy glare, Grayson snapped, "I've heard of a

possible separation directly from Viscountess Wimple, who heard it from her lady's maid, who heard it from her cousin, who is a footman at your estate!"

Tobias glanced down at the sheets on his desk, wondering what his brother would say if he knew every word Tobias had written was inspired by Olivia. He could do nothing without images of her dominating his mind. At night, he smelled her on the sheets even though she had never been in their town house. He heard her laughter in the hallway and like a madman dashed outside searching for her. Several days ago, his butler had looked at him as if he were afflicted. And maybe he was, because Tobias was damn well craving her, even knowing the danger she presented to his control. But did it truly matter?

"I almost beat a man to death."

Grayson inhaled sharply. "What? And when did this happen?"

Tobias allowed himself to slouch down in the chair and sprawled his legs wide. "Olivia's stepbrother attacked her. Instead of coming to me, she sought to defend her own honor. When I realized what was happening, I went to his estate and was almost too late. I lost control, Grayson. For the first time I can remember, I cared not a jot about scandal and its repercussion. I wanted to call him out and put a bullet through his heart. I am just like Father and all the other Blade men before him. Reckless and dangerous. My actions have haunted me, for I had the full intention of ensuring his demise, but the men I had watching him reported of his departure to Scotland."

There was a pulse of silence.

"But you did not kill him, you stopped."

"I wanted to. He hurt her," he said softly.

"Any reasonable man would have lost their temper, Tobias. Hell, if someone attacked the woman I love, I would kill the bastard."

His gut tightened. Did he love Olivia? Tobias scrubbed a hand over his face. The unrelenting ache he had for her inside, was it love, or reckless obsession like his father had possessed for his mother? "It's dangerous how she makes me feel."

"Dangerous to whom? To Livvie? You would cut your arms off before you would ever think to hurt her. You forget that you have something that Father and I doubt even grandfather had."

He considered his brother. "What?"

"Honor," Grayson said, his regard piercing. "You have *honor*, Tobias, and I do not speak of this lightly. Father abused his wife, mistrusted her, fought duels with many men because they simply stared at her. He gambled, partook in reckless racing. Your temper may rival his, but never would you act with such wanton disregard for another. I know you could never hurt Livvie, so exactly what are you afraid of?"

Everything. She made him feel lost and as if he belonged in the same breath. "With her...I am different." With his countess, he felt carefree, not so rigid and infinitely more in tune with his passions. It hit him then like a fist to his gut. What he was most afraid of was losing Olivia. He was afraid of the raw intensity of emotions he felt for her. The lust, the tenderness, the way she made his heart stir. Never had he felt such riotous feelings before. He'd been worried they were precursors to the obsession his father had showed toward his mother and the scandalous tales of the Blade men before him.

"I would never hurt Olivia."

And what do you think you are doing now? an inner voice taunted. Tobias surged to his feet and stalked to the windows. Hell, he had hurt her. In her eyes, he had seen the devastation when he walked away, and the damn fool that he was, he'd done nothing. Why had he even been surprised she was bold enough to leave him?

"Though I know I would never lift a hand to her…I would crush anyone who hurts her. Does that not make me reckless?"

Grayson stood, walked over to him, and clasped his shoulder. "No, it makes you human. Will you go to her?"

"If the men I have scouring England find her, thrice in a heartbeat."

"Does this mean you have some affections for your wife?"

The silence throbbed.

"Bloody hell, Tobias, do you love your wife?"

Desperately…

Christ, so desperately he was afraid of the emotions she roused. He missed everything about her—her smile, her kisses, and possibly her reckless nature. He lost his senses from the moment he met her and it seemed he would never reclaim them if he could long for any of her hoydenish ways. But he did. He was caught off guard by the tender emotions filling him. He rubbed the spot on his chest where he swore it physically ached.

Olivia was cheerfully stubborn, unconventional, but so full of life and dreams.

"Everything I have been writing is for her. It is the only way I know how to express what she means to me, through words."

His brother nodded. "Do not wait too long to find her," he murmured and then left.

Tobias glanced at the sheet of papers on his desk waiting for him to finish the story. He thrust his hands in his pocket, wondering what to do about his countess. Not that there was much to be done, other than for him to pull his head from his ass. His lips twitched. She was his wife…and would always be his wife. He needed to get control of his feelings for her…or embrace them in their entirety.

With her, Tobias admitted, he felt completed, a state

that had been missing from the first time he spied his father slapping his mother at the age of nine.

Never have I felt such inferiority. You will never accept me for the person I am.

He swallowed. He had left her alone with such doubt and pain to fester. Scrubbing a hand over his face, he moved to his desk and sat down. He would have to show her with words how much he desired and wanted her. Maybe if he revealed the bit of himself he kept closeted from the world, even from himself sometimes, she might find it in her heart to forgive him. To love him as he adored her.

• • •

Tobias admitted defeat. His wife did not want to be located. He'd hired a private team of dozens of investigators to find his countess and several days later, she was still not to be found. His gut clenched in hard knots as he glanced down at the letter that never left his person.

I cannot bear living with a man who dislikes the heart of me. I know I must return…but for now I need the space to stop loving you.

He wanted to roar his anguish, but he was aware of Westfall and Grayson's presence.

"Have you read today's scandal sheets?" Grayson asked him, his eyes dark with concern. "They are getting more ridiculous as the days go by. When will they move on to another story?"

"I have no interest in tattle." Yet Tobias took the paper when it was handed to him.

The Quarrel of the Season rages on! Mrs. Darwhimple has it on highest authority that the Countess of Blade has left her earl. This was after the earl himself was seen by the beau monde carrying his very daring and original wife over his shoulder from Lady Bronson's ball a few weeks ago. London's coldest earl has caused many hearts to flutter over his actions, but it seems his wife has no such similar sentiments. Lady Blade—

Unable to read anymore, he dropped the paper on his desk.

"Even the countryside is agog with the news of 'the Quarrel.' You and Olivia...you are notorious," his brother said with a grimace. "I know how much you despise—"

"I do not give a damn about the *ton* or what the gossip sheets report. I do not give a damn how long the scandal lasts, the only thing I care about is that my wife believes I despise her."

He pressed a hand to his forehead, battling back the surge of emotions.

"*Despise.* I've brought her low when I should have brought her to the highest peak of happiness life has to offer. I admire everything about her and there is nothing...*nothing* I would change of her character, but I do not know where she is, dozens of investigators have no clue, and my wife is brilliant enough that she could hide herself for years and not be found."

Westfall's golden eyes glinted with deep cynicism. "I never thought you, my friend, would fall prey to the vexing emotion of love. I do wish for you to locate your countess. There are dark whispers in the seedier parts of London being heard by lords who frequent those places and it would be better if she were found before they take root and flower among the rest of society."

Grayson frowned. "What whispers?"

"The ones that say Lord Blade was so disgusted with his wife's actions that he has done away with her and it is expected her body will be eventually found floating in the Thames.

That like his father, he may have beaten her so severely she perished from that brutality."

Wearily, Tobias leaned his head against the back of his chair and closed his eyes.

God's blood.

It was all his fault, because of a fear that seemed so pointless now. It had been three weeks since she left and he had no notion when she would return. Christ, her letter had said years. Worse, she'd resolved to kill the love she had for him. A thought blasted through him and he froze.

"What is it?" Westfall murmured. "I can see the cogs turning."

Tobias glanced at the neat pile of papers on his desk. "I know how to find her," he muttered, his heart doubling its beat.

"How?"

"The only things she departed with of her own were her books, several volumes of *In the Service of the Crown*."

Grayson blinked. "Books?"

"Yes. Not her jewels or her clothes, but her beloved books."

"And how does that help you?"

"Simple. I will use the latest volume to let her know how I feel."

"And how in God's name do you plan to achieve that? Do you know the author?"

"I know enough," Tobias said and walked from the library, ignoring the rare sight of his friend and brother speechless.

Chapter Twenty-One

Livvie strolled down the grassy knoll of the hillside. Pausing, she tilted her face to the sun, allowing the rays to warm her chilled cheeks. She had been walking for almost thirty minutes and she was quite happy to see the small village in the distance. It had been six weeks since she departed London, her husband, the scandals, condemnation, the keen contrition at her recklessness, and had buried herself in a sleepy and idyllic little village just outside of Bromsgrove, in Worcestershire. Without the support of the Duchess of Wolverton Livvie would never have been successful in fleeing. Not even her dearest Francie or her parents knew her whereabouts. The duchess had arranged for letters to be delivered from Livvie to her family and friends reassuring them she was indeed safe. She'd needed space to think, to heal her broken heart, and to reflect on her marriage and how she had contributed to their separation.

Her earl was not filled with vanity of his person and situation, he simply wanted order and peace, and her support to achieve it. How she regretted bringing scandal to their title. She sorely regretted slapping Lady Arabella and not trusting her husband. Livvie had promised herself, if they should ever reconcile, she would govern her emotions with the good sense and decorum of a countess. It had been painful to acknowledge she was no longer an irreverent girl, running wild over the lawns of Riverhill, uttering whatever came to her thoughts. She was now a wife, a countess, and with God's blessing, a mother to at least three children.

She was headed to the bakery as she had developed an awful craving for strawberry and bilberry jam tarts. The village was fortunate to have a doctor and after her third fainting spell, she had visited him yesterday where he had confirmed she was with child.

Livvie rested one of her hands on her still-flat stomach. *We are going to have a child, my love.* She had been shocked, petrified, and happy. Her feelings had vacillated for most of the day and had almost rendered her insensible. Her plans to leave England and travel to Paris as soon as she had saved some more money had been halted. But she had not felt in her heart she could rush home to Grangeville Park immediately. The doctor had assured her a stress-free environment, daily walks, and adequate rests were critical.

Though she desperately missed Tobias, and had long recognized her hope of lessening her love for him was a failing plan, she could not return to him just yet. Not when her heart ached every morning and each night as she laid her head against the pillows on her bed in the small cottage she had rented. On many days she had been tempted to write to him, but instead, she had concentrated on her painting and had produced several pieces that the local Squire's wife had been in raptures over. As the wealthiest landowner for several miles, they had bought several pieces and had recently commissioned her to make a landscape of their pleasantly situated estate, with the manor house detailed in the background.

"Good day to you, Mrs. Walters."

Livvie smiled, Walters was a name she had always admired and so she had taken it as her pseudonym. And to avoid aspersions to her character, she also had a husband who was currently working abroad.

"Vicar Primrose, how pleasant to see you."

She had found solace in his company several times and had found him to be amiable from the minute she had made his acquaintance. He had been the one to recommend her housekeeper and cook whom she currently employed to tend to her humble two-bedroom cottage where she and her lady's maid, Sarah, lived. And most enjoyably, she and the vicar shared a love of reading.

"My congregation is all a flutter."

"Oh, of what news?" she asked as he walked alongside her companionably. A stiff wind swept down the hill, doing its best to tug the bonnet from her head.

"A crate has arrived at Mrs. Well's bookshop, with at least one hundred books I am told."

"I think such news should hardly inspire an uproar?"

His brown eyes sparkled, and his kind face softened into a smile. "But it is the books the crate holds, my dear. That is why I hurried down the path to your cottage. I was very lucky indeed to see you meandering along, so I would not have to make the journey."

She was now beyond curious.

"It is the latest volume of *In the Service of the Crown*."

"Oh! I'd not thought another volume to be released until next year. I am certain that is the news I read in the *Times* a few weeks aback."

He grinned. "Gossip says there is some special message buried in this volume that hints at Aikens's secret identity."

Livvie gasped, a good deal of shock and excitement

rushing through her. "He has revealed himself? You must tell me quickly. Who is it?"

The vicar chuckled. "I've not grabbed a copy as yet, my dear. As you know, Mrs. Wells's bookshop is very modest and she is quite overwhelmed by the crowd."

They had arrived in the heart of the small village, which housed the bakery, a general store, a bookshop, and a haberdasher's shop. Livvie gaped at the line that led to the entrance of Mrs. Wells's store. "Upon my word, I never imagined there were so many readers here. Never in my visits have I seen more than one other person in the bookshop."

The vicar himself appeared bemused by the small crush. "Maybe one or two read seriously in the village. But it is the only bookshop for a thirty-mile radius, so many may have come from farther away. It is the curiosity and penchant for gossip and any unusual news that has them in the lines. I spy Mrs. Thackeray and she is just learning her letters, I doubt she will procure a copy, but she is still in the line."

Livvie laughed, delighted. "I must certainly grab my copy today, but I am uncertain I can outwait the line." She did a quick count—at least fourteen people seemed determined to get themselves a copy as well.

After bidding the vicar good day and promising to visit him and his wife for tea tomorrow, she went into the bakery and bought several pastries. Her stomach made a mortified rumble and she could not help sneaking one of the tarts into her mouth. She was quite relieved to see several minutes later that the line had been reduced by half. Walking over, she joined the line, eager anticipation churning inside of her.

"Good day, Mrs. Walters, I am so excited, they say he is married and it is for her that he wrote it," Mrs. Bennett, the seamstress, said with a dreamy mien. "I always said he was a romantic and passionate soul."

"Good day to you, too, Mrs. Bennet. But perhaps it is a

woman and she wrote a message for her husband. I'd always hoped Theodore Aikens revealed himself to be a young lady."

"How scandalous," the seamstress tittered. "I came from London a few days ago and the message is all everyone speaks of. They said he bought a printing press, and thousands of copies are all over the world, just so he could deliver a message to his lady love."

All over the world? Livvie doubted such assertions but she was much relieved to hear no mention of the ballroom scandal of the earl and countess of Blade. They spent the next few minutes in pleasant conversation, then it was Livvie's turn to purchase her copy. She handed over several shillings to Mrs. Wells, and took her book with a smile and thanks. Though Livvie knew the series was well loved and widely popular, she had never witnessed such enthusiasm for a new volume before.

An hour later saw Livvie snuggled comfortably on the sofa in the small living room of her cottage, a blanket drawn over her lap. She'd had tea and two tarts, and was now determined to read her book before nightfall. She welcomed the escape from her tortuous thoughts about returning to Tobias before she was ready.

She opened the cover and the dedication leaped out at her.

For my wife, my friend, my lover, and my most beloved countess. I love thee with every breath in my body and with every emotion in my soul. I admire you, respect you, and I will endeavor to make you the happiest woman in all of England once you have forgiven me for being an unmitigated arse.

Her heart jerked, and Livvie laughed. Oh, how wonderful it would be to be loved so passionately and ardently. She started reading and it was in the third chapter she paused, a frown creasing her forehead and her heartbeat increasing. The wordings were familiar. How could that be? She glanced at the outer cover to reaffirm she read the latest volume. Her eyes sought the passage that had confused her.

"An Insufferable fool, am I?"

"Most assuredly, Wrotham, I would have given you the papers I found without you putting your neck to such risk," Lady O snapped, her green eyes firing with anger and something deeper. Concern?

"You were being reckless! You missed the second pistol he had and if not for my quick thinking, you could have been shot!"

"I saved you," she growled, her breath heaving. *"I saw this…this…I have no clue what he is, creeping in the direction of where you headed and I decided to warn you."*

There! Were those not the words she had used with Tobias when the boy had tried to rob them on the way to Scotland? She read the passage for a third time. Then she glanced at the heroine's name, Lady O. As in O for Olivia? Her hands trembled in reaction and she skipped to the beginning and reread the dedication. She was mad to even contemplate with such meager indicators that Aikens was Tobias. Pushing the ridiculous notion aside, she continued reading. A couple hours later, Livvie was furiously thumbing through the pages, seeking the hints.

It was too fantastic for her to credit but could there be any other possibility? Lady O reminded her of, well…herself. While Wrotham was not fashioned like Tobias, his word usage and the places he had Lady O and his hero making love or even arguing was strangely and wonderfully familiar.

He felt lighter, more carefree, the vexing beauty needed him as desperately as he needed her. What was he to do with such knowledge? Kiss her, seduce her? Or punish her in the most wickedly sensual way for defying his order?

"Do you no longer wish to wring my neck?" Lady O murmured huskily.

"No, but I think it is time that I seduce you in a bed."

Livvie closed her eyes tightly, her hands trembling even more. Theodore Aikens was her husband. She groaned as she remembered the name printed in the marriage register she had signed. Tobias Theodore Walcott. And the papers that he kept locked away in his desk drawer. Her heart raced with a mixture of hope and remembered pain of their last encounter. She glanced at the dedication once more, still refusing to credit what her heart was telling her.

I love thee with every breath in my body and with every emotion in my soul.

She forced herself to read to the very last page. It was at the very end her world collided.

For my countess, Lady Blade.

For precious seconds, she had no notion what to do with herself. Her heart burst inside her chest and tears pricked behind her lids. To think her husband would make such a sacrifice for her. The scandal would not be contained for everyone in the *ton* knew the Earl of Blade. Jumping from the sofa, she hurried to the small kitchen where the cook was preparing a light meal for luncheon. "Mrs. Bradley I would like to hire your son for an urgent errand." The cook's eight-year-old son traveled with her most days to the cottage, and Livvie prayed he had accompanied her.

"He is outside in the gardens with Ms. Sarah, milady, would you like me to fetch him?"

"Please. I desire to hire the local coachman to take me to London. Inform Sarah that we are to depart immediately."

"London! You'll not reach there for four days milady."

She nodded vigorously. The journey would be as similar as the one when she'd just arrived, travelling for six hours daily with overnight stops at inns. "I know, but I have not a minute to lose, I must return." Then she turned and hurried from the room to her chamber to dress, and leave the village.

Chapter Twenty-Two

A few days later, Livvie arrived in Town to meet a cold downpour. The carriage she traveled in was surprisingly well padded and despite the anxiety in her heart, she'd actually slept for most of the journey — at least whenever she was not rereading over the passages, trying to convince herself she was not making a fool of herself or chatting dispiritedly with Sarah.

Livvie would ask Tobias if he was Aikens, and if he was not, she would rest and return to her hideaway until she was ready to inform him of their child. Dear Lord, she was being silly. He'd said, "*For my countess, Lady Blade.*" How could she feel so uncertain still? She prayed she would have the willpower to let him speak without dissolving into an emotional blubber. Deep in her heart, she feared she would succumb and kiss him thoroughly, and then proceed to give him a tongue lashing on his stubbornness. She grinned at the thought of provoking him to such an extent. For good measure, she would probably dissolve into tears, too.

The carriage came to a halt on Grosvenor Street and the

coachman opened the door.

"Right sorry, milady, I have nothing to cover you with."

She waved away his apology. "Thank you for coming to my aid at such short notice."

"I will send a footman to you, milady." Sarah made to get up. But Livvie was bursting with anticipation and could not wait another minute to discover the truth of the situation.

"That's quite fine, Sarah, I have no issue facing the deluge, you may wait here for the footmen to come and assist you and collect our luggage." Livvie rose and exited the carriage with the coachman's assistance.

Rain drizzled in her eyes, and the cold bit into her bones. Tugging her coat closer, she carefully hurried to the door and sounded the knocker. A stern looking man opened the door and looked down his bony nose at her.

"I am Lady Blade, is my husband home?"

The door was flung opened with such exuberance she almost giggled. She scampered inside and shrugged from her coat.

"His lordship is in his library, my lady," the butler said curiously, a heavy dollop of relief in his tone.

"Please send a footman outside to assist my maid with our luggage. She will also need a parasol."

"Did I hear the knocker, Collins, who—?"

Tobias faltered and scrubbed a hand over his face.

When he started moving closer, a tentative smile stretched her lips, and he stumbled.

Livvie rushed forward. "Are you well?"

"Yes...you smiled," he muttered, appearing dazed. He turned away from her and started down the hallway. He paused and glanced back. "Are you a hallucination?"

She blinked, noting he looked leaner and his eyes were red. Alarm skittered through her. "Have you been drinking?"

"No, but I have not been sleeping well. In fact, I have

been awake for two days now and my thoughts are decidedly muddled."

"Tobias, I—"

Her heart skittered wildly when her husband came toward her with clipped strides. "I'm sorry." He cupped her face between his palms and smoothed the stray hairs from her face and kissed her cheek. "I'm so damn sorry."

The butler cleared his throat and Tobias glanced up with a distracted frown.

A blush heated her cheeks; she had forgotten their audience. "My lady maid awaits assistance from the coach outside, and my luggage—"

Before she could complete her sentence, Tobias started clipping commands. "Carry her ladyship's cases upstairs to her rooms and send her maid to the kitchen to have a hot drink and supper."

"Very well, my lord," the butler answered.

"Let us retire to the parlor," she said, hope beating in her chest with such vigor she felt faint.

He grabbed her hand, and he fairly ran down the hallway as she hurried her steps to keep pace. Tobias opened the door and ushered her inside. She turned around and he was leaning against the closed door, torment in his eyes, before he wiped all expression from his face.

"You've returned," he said mildly.

"Yes."

"You've been missing for several weeks," he said hoarsely. "I am most relieved to see you are well."

"I anticipated that you might send me away, so I ran, for I could not endure my heart to break again." She got right to the heart of the matter before she lost her will and launched herself at him. "You wrote these?" She held up the several slim leather volumes carefully tied together.

The dratted man's inscrutable expression became even

more closed. "Do not shy away from me."

An eyebrow arched in outrage. "I am not shy, countess."

"Then—"

"I wrote them."

Though the evidence had been overwhelming, delight and disbelief filled her. She tugged out one of the book from the small pile and held it forward with hands that trembled. "You wrote these. You, the Earl of Blade, are *Theodore Aikens*?"

"Yes."

Livvie's heart started to jerk an erratic rhythm. "Aikens… writes romance—passion and secret trysts and dueling," she whispered.

"Yes."

"But…but you would never do anything like that in reality. Your hero, Wrotham, is brilliant, wild, and unpredictable. He revels in his temper…"

"Wrotham is everything that I am that is not possible to show to society, that I cannot allow myself to feel," he said, his voice rough with unnamed emotions.

The silence throbbed between them with intensity. The awareness of how much he would have worked to ensure his book found her ahead of his schedule bloomed. It would have taken such dedication and an atrocious amount of money. The knowledge filled her with tenderness. "The rumors said you bought a printing shop."

He smiled. "Two. I wanted thousands of copies to flood the bookstores in London, Scotland, Paris, and Vienna. I'd hoped the fascination of the *ton* and readers of the series would spread across borders and countries to find you wherever you were."

Oh!

"Writing has always been an escape for whenever life seemed turbulent. It has been most private and I want to share everything about me with you, as you have showed me without restraint who you are."

In that moment, she realized her aloof earl was sharing a part of him he had never revealed to anyone else. It humbled her. She grabbed the latest copy and thumbed through the pages. "Lady O…that is truly me?" The idea seemed so farfetched, but Lady O and Wrotham's courtship and romance was so similar to Livvie and Tobias's, so fiery and passionate, so everything she wanted them to be and more.

"Yes."

Her heart went wild. He had modeled the lady who his hero had fallen in love with on *her*, and she was not shy, demur, or the very picture of female respectability and correctness. In fact, his Lady O was fierce, bold, a delight to read and learn, and the passages showed how much the hero had fallen in love with his Lady O. Livvie's throat tightened and she could only stare at Tobias in mute delight. He willingly went through such lengths to have her back at his side, sacrificing their reputation to scandal and scrutiny. "You truly love me," she breathed in sheer shock.

Before he could respond, she thumbed the pages furiously and started to read, "'*Death had almost claimed his mysterious Lady O. Never had Wrotham felt such passion for a woman and such need. He loved her and it petrified him, for he could not lose her. She was an elite assassin who had dedicated her life to the order after the terrible way in which society had abandoned her. Could he truly risk his heart by asking her to flee this life with him, to abandon intrigue and danger, for love and happiness?*'"

A smile tugged his lips and he slowly pushed from the door. "Is there a reason you are reading my words to me, countess?"

Her throat worked. "I…I was going to read the part when he confessed his love to Lady O."

"Hmmm," he said, prowling even closer, his eyes intent.

"I already know what they say, I wrote it, but if you will recall, that volume ended without his intriguing Lady O answering his declaration."

Livvie nodded happily. "So you love me?"

"You ensnared me from the moment I met you...intrigued me, inspired me, and I cannot bear life without you, Lady O. I have no future without you. I love you most ardently."

At her silence, he lowered his lashes, hiding his emotions, but she was not mistaken in the flash of doubt she had seen in his eyes. How could he not realize she was passionately in love with everything he was?

"Come, Olivia, end my misery, I must have some new material for my next release."

She laughed, launching herself at him, and with a groan of relief, he crushed her to him. "Good God, woman, you took too long to respond."

"I love you, Tobias," she whispered achingly. "More than my words or actions will ever express."

His arms tightened around her. "Never leave me again, countess."

"Never," she promised.

"And you can cry all over me whenever you wish," he said gruffly.

She grinned against his chest. "And swoon now and then?"

He grunted.

"I will never act with a willfulness that will taint our name," she murmured. "I will indulge in all my passions and emotions in private. You have given up so much for me, the *ton* will be rabid with speculations about you, us."

He pressed a tender, reverent kiss atop her forehead. "I do not give a fig about the *ton*, or anyone's opinion but yours. All I need is your adoration and I am certain of it. I never want you to change, but my heart would appreciate the restraint."

She laughed softly, nodding her head. "I'm with child," she said into the soft of his neck.

He froze, and then he shifted one of his hands between them and placed it above her stomach. Emotions darkened his eyes to jade. "Are you well?"

She smiled tenderly. "Yes."

"We will argue again. I daresay we will both have cause to find each other frustrating. But I will do all in my power to never hurt you again. I may not succeed, and I give you leave then to swoon."

Livvie chuckled.

He smiled with tender amusement. "I swear I will endeavor to make you the happiest woman in all of England."

"And I will make you the proudest man in all of England."

He arched a brow. "Only in England?"

Tobias did not wait for an answer, nor could Livvie give him one. For he claimed her lips in a hungry kiss, which said more than even his words had done. Livvie's fingers were already unraveling his cravat as she gloried in her husband's love.

Epilogue

Four months later…

Livvie lay on her side with Tobias curved behind her, his hands resting on the swell of her stomach, and her head nestled in the crook of his shoulder. Their baby kicked with exuberance and she felt his smile against her hair. They had been so blissfully happy despite their notoriety. The scandal that roared through the *ton* after Tobias's revelations had been unquenchable. They had been flocked with so many callers, reporters, and friends, they had departed London to Grangeville Park less than a week later. The scandal sheets had even compared her and Tobias's scandal to the duke and duchess of Wolverton's infamy over a year ago.

Livvie had been pleasantly surprised they were admired for their daring and originality. In fact, their new fame had done wonders with the support Tobias needed in helping those suffering in England. Many now wanted to be associated with them, and had lent their support to his and Westfall's cause. Monies poured in and several charities were established. The demand for Tobias's books had seen thousands of copies being reprinted, with the royalties earned donated toward his, Wolverton, and Westfall's goal of alleviating England's suffering.

Livvie was also in the process of launching her art gallery in London with the full support of her husband. She had done several pieces to highlight the plight of England's children, and the art critics Tobias had gotten to view them had praised her work. Pride and anticipation of opening her gallery once again welled within her.

Tobias kissed the delicate pulse just beneath her ear. "Good morning, wife."

"Husband," she murmured with contentment bursting in her heart.

"I have sent word for our town house to be prepared. With Parliament opening, we must return to London, then travel to the country when it is close to your lying-in."

He tugged her even closer to him, nestling her head under his chin.

"Do you think the scandal has abated?" she asked with an indelicate yawn.

"Most assuredly."

"You sound confident."

"That is because I've had cause to read a scandal sheet, specially delivered to our doorstep this morning. My curiosity got the better of me as to why Wolverton would believe I read such claptrap. I could not wait for you to rise, wife, though the duke's note was addressed to both of us."

With a gasp, Livvie wiggled and shifted so that she faced her husband. His eyes were glowing with amusement.

"There is another scandal!"

"Yes."

"Oh do not keep me in suspense any longer. It is quite nice to think the scrutiny around us will be abated."

Tobias dipped his head and brushed a kiss across her lips. "It seems our friend the Marquess of Westfall was caught with Lady Evelyn, the earl of Gladstone's daughter."

She stared at him in shock. "Caught doing what?"

"The sheets report they were alone together on the outskirts of London, after midnight."

Oh dear. "We must lend our support to Lady Evelyn when we travel to Town. Society may be unforgiving."

"We will," Tobias reassured.

Livvie thought of Westfall and winced. He did not present as a man inclined to bow to society's expectations. "Do you think he will marry her?"

"I could never deduce what Westfall is thinking. He despises high society, but he's always possessed a particular weakness for Lady Evelyn."

Livvie's eyes rounded. "He does?"

"Hmm," her husband muttered distractedly, and it was then she realized he had been inching her night rail from her shoulders.

"I will talk no more of Westfall when I am trying to ravish my wife."

Her giggle turned into a husky moan of desire as he gently drew her up and flicked his tongue over her sensitive nipple. *Oh!* The pleasure was electrifying. He trailed kisses up, over to her collarbone, her flickering pulse to her lips. His mouth was sweet and sultry, flavored with a hint of coffee he must have drank while she was sleeping.

He loved her gently, passionately, and nothing else intruded in Livvie's thoughts as she reveled in being wicked in her husband's arms.

Acknowledgments

I thank God every day for loving me with such depth and breadth nothing can take his love from me.

To my husband, Dusean, you are so damn wonderful. You've read all my drafts for *Wicked in His Arms* and without your input I would never have found the strength to continue in the face of being ill. You reminded me that I am a kick-ass ninja and I love you for it!

Thank you to my wonderful friend and critique partner Gina Fisovera. Without you I would be lost. Thank you for all the messages asking "Have you finished the damn book?" I have! Thank you for the amazing feedback, and I promise to sort out my plurals. LOL. I love you, and I thank you for your continued encouragement and kindness.

Thank you to my amazing editor, Alycia Tornetta, for being so patient when I miss my deadlines and overall a kick-ass, amazing, wonderful, and stupendous editor.

To my wonderful readers, thank you for picking up my book and giving me a chance! Thank you.

Special THANK YOU to everyone who leaves a review—

bloggers, fans, friends. I have always said reviews to authors are like a pot of gold to leprechauns. Thank you all for adding to my rainbow one review at a time.

About the Author

I am an avid reader of novels with a deep passion for writing. I especially love romance and enjoy writing about people falling in love. I live a lot in the worlds I create and I actively speak to my characters (out loud). I have a warrior way "Never give up on my dream." When I am not writing, I spend a copious amount of time drooling over Rick Grimes from *The Walking Dead*, Lucas Hood from *Banshee*, watching Japanese Anime, and playing video games with my love — Dusean. I also have a horrible weakness for ice cream.

I am always happy to hear from readers and would love for you to connect with me via Website | Facebook | Twitter

To be the first to hear about my new releases, get cover reveals and excerpts you won't find anywhere else, sign up for my newsletter.

Happy reading!
Stacy

Get Scandalous with these historical reads...

HIS LORDSHIP'S WILD HIGHLAND BRIDE
a *Those Magnificent Malverns* novel by Kathleen Bittner Roth

Ridley Malvern, Lord Caulfield, desperate for a dowry, agrees to marry a wealthy Scot's daughter sight unseen. All Lainie MacGregor desires is to return to her clan. Attempting to make things right, Caulfield takes Lainie back to the Highlands only to discover that his wife is wanted for murder. For her safekeeping, they must remain in England. Now Ridley needs to win her affections and prove that a wild Highland lass and an English lord, can find a love match, after all.

SEDUCING THE MARQUESS
a *Lords and Ladies in Love* novel by Callie Hutton

Richard, the Marquess of Devon is satisfied with his ton marriage. His wife of five months, Lady Eugenia Devon wants her very proper husband to fall in love with her. After finding a naughty book, she begins a campaign to change the rules. Her much changed and decidedly wicked behavior drives her husband to wonder if his perfect Lady has taken a lover. But the only man Eugenia wants is her husband. The book can bring sizzling desire to the marriage or cause an explosion.

Confessions of Love
a novel by Melissa Blue

London, 1817

Lieutenant Jonathan Rycroft is intoxicating. His hands know just where to touch her, his lips know just how to trip her pulse, and his body knows just how to bring about every forbidden desire Lindsay Dunsfield has ever felt. He's the one man that's owned her heart…and he shattered it two years ago. When one scorching kiss reignites the flames of their passion, Jonathan inadvertently drags Lindsay into a mire of murder and deception. In a world where Lindsay can trust no one, will she find renewed faith in the last place she expected to look?

The Love Match
a *Sisters of Scandal* novella by Lily Maxton

Olivia Middleton prefers gothic novels to hunting for a husband. Only the charming and infuriating Mr. William Cross (a rake in the making, and certainly not a suitable husband) holds the slightest fascination for her. After watching his father die of a broken heart, William has sworn never to wed for a love match. Yet he's intrigued by the bookish Olivia. And though he tries, staying away from her turns out to be impossible.